The Churchill Diamonds

Other Walker Adventures by Bob Langley

Falklands Gambit
Autumn Tiger
East of Everest (forthcoming, July 1987)

The Churchill
Diamonds

Bob Langley

Walker and Company
New York

First published in the United States of America in 1986 by the Walker
Publishing Company, Inc.

Published simultaneously in Canada by John Wiley & Sons Canada, Limited,
Rexdale, Ontario.

Library of Congress Cataloging-in-Publication Data

Langley, Bob.
  The Churchill diamonds.

  I. Title.
PR6062.A5328C5   1987b   823'.914   86-24674
ISBN 0-8027-0934-6

Printed in the United States of America

10 9 8 7 6 5 4 3 2 1

FOR MY WIFE

PROLOGUE

Sergeant MacAngus lay where he had fallen, blood from his hip oozing into the coarse desert sand. He was flanked on one side by a narrow defile, a long bow-shaped scar in the earth where streams would flow when the rains came, and on the other by the flat pebble-strewn plain of the empty *reg*. Several feet away, its sorrowful face grinning incongruously, sprawled Sergeant MacAngus's camel. It was an ugly brute with a series of ancient knife wounds on its neck, and for eight days MacAngus had driven it to the point of exhaustion until, with its last vestiges of strength now depleted, it lay in the dust, spittle oozing in long shiny strands from its blubbery grey lips.

MacAngus knew there was water in the leather-skinned *guerba* strapped to the camel's saddlehorn, but he doubted seriously if he could reach it because, several minutes earlier, at half-past two on the afternoon of 19 July 1898, in the region known as the Jesira Desert of the central Sudan, a Dervish bullet had entered the front of MacAngus's abdomen and emerged through the *erector spinae* muscles on his lower back.

He felt no pain, which surprised him, only a strange numbness which dulled the feeling in his legs and feet and crept in a slow insidious wave to the lower tip of his diaphragm. His lips were cracked and raw in the sun and his cheeks, baked red and covered with bristly beard stubble, looked hollow and ravaged beneath the bony protuberances of his skull.

He was not wearing the khaki uniform of his regiment, the 10th Westmorland Lancers, but the blue *gandoura* and *chech* of the Kel Ahaggar Tuareg, a tribal people who inhabited the Hoggar Mountains of the Sahara nearly a thousand miles to

1

the east. His loose-fitting robes were ragged and sweat-stained, and at the point where the bullet had entered his body there was a rapidly widening circle of scarlet coated with a thin film of orange dust from the desert floor. His right hand clutched the ribbed handle of a heavy Navy Colt revolver. His left, the fist tightly clenched, lay pressed against the side of his chest.

Several yards away, where the defile blended into the pebbled hardness of the empty *reg*, the body of a man clad in metal armour and chainmail lay huddled on its side, his knees drawn up foetus-like as if, at the moment of dying, he had experienced an instinctive yearning for the comfort of the womb. His helmet had come off with the impact of falling and his dark face, ear-ringed and bearded and frozen into the glassy rigidity of death, contrasted strangely with the protective shell of his medieval apparel. Nearby lay two more corpses, both clad similarly in armour and chainmail, both clutching shields and lances from which pennants fluttered gaily on the dry desert wind.

Vultures hovered among the camel scrub. They did not approach the corpses, for they sensed the sergeant was still alive and therefore waited with the timeless patience of their species for death to take its natural course.

Sergeant MacAngus did not notice the scavengers, for his eyes were turned inward, seeing only himself. He did not hear the soft clinking of accoutrements, or the shuffle of approaching hooves as a reconnaissance patrol of British and Egyptian cavalry picked its way though the clumps of mimosa and spindly acacia trees. They moved slowly, riding in almost perfect formation, their brown jerseys, sand-coloured trousers and dark blue puttees etched sharply against the sky, their rifles glinting in the sunlight. Far to the right and left trotted their outriders, four blacks mounted on camels, squinting at the trail ahead.

The troop was led by a young British subaltern whose nose had skinned in the heat and whose hair was bleached white by the sun. Accompanying him was an Egyptian sergeant, the illegitimate offspring of a Sudanese soldier from the 14th infantry battalion.

2

'Look, *bimbashi*,' the sergeant said, spotting MacAngus and the corpses lying in the defile.

The young British officer was not a *bimbashi*, he was only a lieutenant, but in the Egyptian army there were no British officers below the rank of major and it pleased the sergeant to flatter the subaltern placed temporarily in command of his daily patrol. The Englishman himself gave no sign that he had noticed this undeserved promotion, but reined in his mount, peering curiously across the sand.

'Tell your men to wait here,' he ordered in a crisp voice, and, kicking his horse into a trot, rode through the mimosa clumps to where the first of the bodies lay sprawled in the dust.

'Good Lord,' he exclaimed, as he realised for the first time that the carcasses were dressed, not in robes and sandals, but in breastplates, chainmail and metal helmets. 'What have we here, the Knights of the Round Table?'

The sergeant followed him, and drawing his horse to a halt, spat on the ground. 'They are from Agaiga,' he said. 'They ride under the green flag of the Sheik-ed-Din and Ali Wad Helu.'

'But that armour they're wearing, it must be centuries old.'

'Oh yes, *bimbashi*. Their Saracen ancestors took it from the Crusaders in the thirteenth century. They, and their fathers before them, have worn it in battle ever since.'

'Incredible,' the officer said, dismounting.

He moved forward, pistol drawn, studying each of the corpses in turn. When he reached MacAngus he said: 'This one's different. A regular Dervish from the look of him. I think he's still alive.'

The sergeant frowned as he slid from his saddle and joined the young officer at the defile. 'This man is not a Dervish,' he said. 'The clothes he is wearing are the clothes of the Kel Ahaggar, the people of the Hoggar.'

'Tuareg?'

The sergeant nodded. 'I have never seen a Targui warrrior so far east,' he admitted. 'You see this cross?' He indicated a silver ornament dangling from MacAngus's throat. 'That is the cross of the Kel Ahaggar. It has been fashioned by the Inadan, the artisans of the Tuareg society.'

'Is he dying?' the officer asked.

The sergeant knelt down and examined MacAngus carefully, turning him on to his side. 'He is losing blood,' he announced, 'but the bullet has not lodged in his body. If we take him back to camp, he may yet survive.'

The sound of voices made MacAngus stir. He turned his head, crusted with dust, and squinted up at the figures crouching above him. Though his vision was clouded, he was able to discern, framed against the sun, the pale outline of the officer's face, and he realised that he was not, as he had first assumed, in the hands of Dervish savages, but by some unaccountable miracle had been discovered by members of his own race.

'Wha's the time?' he whispered hoarsely.

The sound of MacAngus's voice speaking words of English made the young officer start. He leaned back on his haunches, frowning curiously. 'Who are you?' he demanded. 'What are you doing dressed like this?'

MacAngus coughed. It was a painful racklng cough that lodged stubbornly in his throat. Turning his head on one side he spat into the dust.

'The diamonds,' he whispered.

'Diamonds?' The officer frowned. 'What diamonds?'

'Ye must tell Coffey about the diamonds.'

'Who on earth is Coffey?'

'He's at the river. Hurry. Mebbe ye'll still be in time to save him.'

'What are you talking about, man?'

MacAngus struggled to speak again, but his eyes were glazing; his features slackened, then his head lolled back, and spittle traced an uneven line to the corner of his chin.

'He has fainted, *bimbashi*,' the sergeant said.

The young officer nodded, still frowning. Leaning back, he noticed for the first time a small stone caught in MacAngus's belt. He bent down and prised it loose with his thumb. It was roughly the size of a walnut, its corners jagged, its surface greasy to the touch. An uncut diamond.

'Now look at this,' the officer breathed, whistling as he held it to the light. 'Why, it must be worth a fortune.'

He glanced again at MacAngus's camel, his eyes narrowing

as he studied the bulging saddlebags. 'Strap those pouches to my pony's bridle,' he ordered, 'then call your troop and get this man mounted. God knows who Coffey is, but if we don't want this poor beggar to bleed to death we'd better get him to the MO as quickly as possible.'

Several minutes later, with MacAngus lashed to the hump of a baggage camel, the patrol rode back the way it had come, the young officer keeping a wary eye on MacAngus's wound for any sign of haemorrhaging. It was not a significant episode in the young officer's life, nor one he was particularly disposed to remember, but four hours later he delivered MacAngus and his possessions to the British forces on the River Nile. The officer's name was Winston Spencer Churchill, future prime minister of Britain, knight of the British realm and winner of the Nobel Prize for Literature. Though he mentioned the incident in a letter to his mother postmarked Khartoum and dated 11 September 1898, he did not include it in his published dispatches of the Sudanese campaign, nor did he ever refer to it publicly again.

ONE

A light rain was falling as the TV crew, three men, young, casually dressed, sober-faced, carried their equipment across the white-pillared lobby of the Coffey Foundation headquarters in London's West End, registered at the reception desk and took the elevator to the building's basement. They were met, as the doors opened, by a man in a dark grey uniform. 'BBC?' he asked.

They nodded silently.

'My name is Johnson, chief security officer. You do understand that all visitors to the basement must go through our special screening procedure?'

'That's already been explained,' the TV director told him gently.

'Then will you please use these cubicles and remove your clothing. Just leave your equipment on the floor. It will be quite safe until you are ready to proceed.'

The three men showed no surprise; without a word they swiftly undressed and, naked, submitted themselves to a stringent examination. They were photographed from three different angles, their fingerprints recorded on sensitised tape and their biological statistics, including scars and birthmarks, fed into a computer. Thirty seconds later, the computer clicked out a clearance order.

Their equipment was then placed on a moving conveyor belt which carried it through an electronic X-ray machine. Only when the officer tried to include their can of unexposed film did the director object. 'You'll ruin our stock,' he complained.

Smiling apologetically, the officer returned the can untouched and the director tucked it defensively under his left arm. When the examination was over the three men put on their clothes and sat waiting for someone to collect them. After a few moments a new man appeared. He was middle-aged and athletic-looking with a trimmed moustache and hair that was just beginning to grey above the temples. 'I'm Webster,' he smiled, sticking out his hand. 'Welcome to the Coffey Foundation. Mr Cray is waiting for you at the vault. Will you please follow me?'

Carrying their equipment, they walked through a series of corridors in which the dull throb of the air-conditioner hung hypnotically on their senses. At three different checkpoints, guards in security uniforms scrutinised Webster's ID card before waving them on. The guards were completely enclosed in metal cages protected by wire grills. It was clear no one could pass the checkpoints undetected.

Webster stopped at a door marked: 'Maximum Security. No entry under any circumstances without authority of Foundation Director.'

He slipped his ID card into a slot in the wall and the door slid open with a muffled click. The TV crew stepped into a room which looked at first glance like a computer centre. Around the walls a myriad of dials and instrument panels hummed softly. The air was hot, almost overpowering.

A second man came towards them, smiling.

'This is Mr Cray,' Webster explained, 'our Class One manager.'

Cray was short and slender. His hair was grey and combed upward from the parting to hide a conspicuous bald patch in the centre of his skull. There were dark blotches on his face which looked like the result of some ancient skin complaint.

'It was good of you to admit us, Mr Cray,' the TV director said as they shook hands.

Cray chuckled. 'You don't realise how privileged you are. This is the first time in the Foundation's history that outsiders have been allowed to set foot on the basement floor.'

'I gathered that. It's a bit like penetrating Fort Knox.'

8

Cray indicated a heavy steel door set into the adjacent wall. Fixed on its surface was a clock-dial with a single hour hand. 'This is the vault,' he said. 'It's on a time-lock, so we'll have to wait for it to open.'

'How long?'

'A few seconds, no more. We estimated your time of arrival and set it accordingly.'

The TV director studied the dial with interest. 'Supposing you tried to open it early?'

'Then the entrance chamber would seal itself off and we'd have hell's own job getting out of here. These walls are built of reinforced concrete, fifteen feet thick. You'd need an atomic warhead to blast your way through.'

He paused as a click sounded deep inside the vault's mechanism.

'Spot on,' he grinned, with a note of satisfaction in his voice. Stepping forward, he pulled hard on the metal wheel and with a gentle creak, the massive door swung slowly open.

The interior of the vault reminded the TV director of a primeval cave. It was dim and claustrophic, the walls lined with padded upholstery. In the centre of the floor stood a metal dais supporting a heavy steel container. Cray beckoned to Webster who hurried in to join them.

'The container can only be opened by Mr Webster and myself inserting separate keys at precisely the same instant,' Cray explained. 'If anyone attempted to force the lock, the doors would automatically shut and the alarm would sound at the security desks outside.'

'You've thought of everything,' the director muttered.

'That's our job,' Cray said.

The two men slipped their individual keys into openings at opposite sides of the dais and the lid of the container slid back with a gentle buzzing sound. Lying on a shallow tray in the container's bottom the director was able to discern, dimly, a cluster of precious stones, each roughly the size of a small plum. They were cut and polished into a variety of different shapes, and as their textures caught the refracted striplights, they glittered fiercely under his gaze.

9

'Beautiful,' he breathed at last, studying them intently.

Cray nodded in agreement. 'Apart from the cutting and polishing, they are exactly as Sir Stephen Coffey discovered them during the reconquest of the Sudan in 1898.'

'How many are there altogether?'

'182. There were originally 183, but the most extravagant stone now forms part of the British Crown Jewels. This is the first time they've ever been filmed for television, by the way. Company policy has always been to resist unnecessary public attention whenever it can. I can only assume someone at your office has a very persuasive tongue.'

The director glanced quickly around the vault. 'We'll have to rig up some lights in here. Got any plugs in the immediate vicinity?'

'You'll find some in the corridor outside.'

'Excellent. We'll run in leads through the outer room. See to it, will you, Andy?'

The director's bearded assistant nodded wordlessly and moved into the exterior chamber.

'In the meantime,' the director added, grinning apologetically, 'I think I'll have to go to the washroom.'

Cray laughed shortly. 'I know how you feel. The first time I saw those diamonds they had the same effect on me too. You'll find it at the end of the corridor, on the right.'

Still clutching his film canister, the director squeezed past his crew and walked casually along the passageway until he reached the lavatory door. Once inside, his air of composure vanished completely. A series of small shudders ran through his body and beads of moisture glistened on his temples and pallid cheeks. For a long moment he stood with his forehead pressed against the wall mirror, savouring its coolness. Then with trembling fingers he groped inside his pocket and took out a small phial of yellow tablets. Thrusting two into his mouth, he scooped a palmful of water from the washbasin tap and tipped it between his lips. He felt better as the effects of the drug infiltrated his bloodstream.

Locking himself in the lavatory booth, he took the can of unexposed film from under his arm and carefully prised open the lid. Taped to the tin bottom was a Walther 9 mm P.38

automatic pistol with a heavy metal silencer. The director tugged the weapon loose and screwed the silencer to the metal barrel, his movements deft, even and unhurried.

Rising to his feet, he shook his head to clear it. He stepped from the booth, moistened his handkerchief at the washbasin and gently mopped his face and neck. Then with the gun in his hand, he walked back to the vault where his TV crew were busy laying in cable from the wall-sockets in the corridor. Cray and Webster were standing just as he had left them, laughing at some joke or other. When they saw the Walther, their laughter froze.

'Let's have no trouble,' the director said, his voice like ice. 'There is no need for trouble, and there is no need for anyone to get hurt. Do exactly as I say and you will both come out of this unhurt. Try to resist, or refuse to co-operate in any way and you will both be killed immediately, is that understood?'

The two men did not answer. They were looking at the Walther as if they believed the director was only semi-serious. His voice, cold and deadly, convinced them otherwise. 'Is that understood?' he repeated.

The two men nodded slowly.

Turning, the director gestured to his film crew and one of the men stepped into the tiny vault carrying a leather satchel which had previously contained pieces of sound equipment. He handed the satchel to Cray.

'Place the diamonds inside,' the director ordered.

Cray stared at him, his face ghastly. He was not a cowardly man, but faced with a threat from such an unexpected quarter, his body seemed incapable of response. 'You're mad,' he whispered.

'Just do as I say.'

'If I touch those diamonds, it will trigger the sensor devices. You know what that means? The alarm will sound at the security checkpoints along the corridor, and the outer door will automatically seal itself shut.'

'I am aware of that,' the director answered evenly. 'Please follow my instructions.'

Glancing at his companion, Cray leaned forward and began to scoop the diamonds into the leather satchel. Dimly, along

11

the corridor, they heard the furious clatter of the alarm bell. With a gentle buzzing sound the door to the outer chamber began to slide forward, but to Cray's surprise it suddenly stopped short with a little jerk, leaving a space nearly a foot wide still unclosed. With a small tremor of shock, he realised what had happened. The heavy T V cable which the raiders had so carefully and cleverly run in from the outside corridor had jammed the door's progress, holding it firmly ajar. The cunning bastards, he thought.

He finished gathering up the diamonds and looked at the director questioningly. The director nodded to his assistant who took the satchel and fastened the metal clasps.

'Now,' the director said, 'in a moment the guards from the security desks will come along the corridor to investigate. You will persuade them that in setting up our lights we disturbed the diamonds accidentally. It will be up to you, Mr Cray, to put their minds at rest. Act sensibly and both you and Mr Webster will be able to return to your families this evening unhurt. Attempt to be heroic, and it will be the last act you ever perform.'

They heard footsteps clattering along the passageway outside. The director slipped the Walther into his jacket pocket and jerked his head toward the vault entrance. Without a word Cray stepped past him and raised his hands in a placatory gesture as the three uniformed guards burst into the room beyond.

'Sorry,' he declared, trying hard to smile, 'false alarm, I'm afraid. We were setting up the lighting gear and one of the leads fell into the diamond container. It must have triggered the sensor device.'

The guards looked at him inquiringly. 'Are you sure everything's all right here, Mr Cray?' one of them asked.

'Of course. Just a little slip on our part. Nothing for you to worry about.'

The guard frowned and glanced at his two companions. He was a tall man with a slightly brutish face, but there was an air of keen intelligence in his eyes. He studied Cray shrewdly, noting the tautness of the jawline, the sickly pallor in the narrow cheeks.

12

'I'll just check everything's in order,' the guard said, moving toward the vault door.

Deliberately, Cray blocked his way. 'That's hardly necessary. I've already explained what happened.'

'It'll set our minds at rest, Mr Cray.'

'Let him look,' the director ordered quietly, his hand still resting in his jacket pocket.

Without a word Cray moved aside. The guard strolled to the container and peered down at the metal tray. They saw a tremor ripple through his body as his brain registered the fact that the diamonds were missing. When he moved back to the vault doorway he found his two companions standing with their hands in the air. The director was covering them calmly with the Walther automatic.

'Step forward three paces,' the director ordered. 'Keep your hands where I can see them and do it slowly and easily.'

His cheeks flushed with anger and alarm, the guard joined his two companions and the director switched the gun to his other fist.

'Everyone into the corridor,' he instructed. 'You three . . .' He pointed his gun at the motionless security guards. 'Remain where you are.'

He moved back, dragging the heavy TV cable behind him, grunting with satisfaction as the door slid shut and the lock engaged with an audible click, then he turned to face the others, pushing the pistol back into his jacket pocket. 'Now we are going to walk out of here,' he said, 'the six of us together. We are going to go through the checkpoints and take the elevator to the roof. It will be your job, Mr Cray, to placate any security guards we might encounter en route. Should anything happen to prevent us reaching the roof, should either one of you attempt to attract the attention of the guards, or should the guards, with or without your help, become suspicious and decide to investigate, I will kill you both before turning this pistol on myself and my companions. Is that understood?'

The two men nodded, their features deathly pale.

'Then let's go.'

Down the softly humming corridor they strode, Cray and Webster walking side by side, the bogus TV crew following

13

half a pace behind. They went through the three check-points, empty now, and crossed the marbled landing toward the elevator shaft. A solitary guard stood by the line of call-buttons. He looked apologetic as he saw Cray approaching. 'I'm sorry, Mr Cray,' he said, 'but something's activated the security system. Probably a false alarm, but nobody's allowed to leave the floor until the police arrive.'

Cray did not answer. Now that the first shock was over, his brain was beginning to function again. He realised his only chance of stopping the raid was probably this moment. Calmly, and with the full realisation of what he was doing, he said: 'It's no false alarm, officer. These men are imposters. They have stolen the Churchill Diamonds which they are carrying in that leather satchel there. I estimate you have about one second to use your mini-radio and alert your companions upstairs. Good luck.'

Unfortunately for Cray, the guard's reactions were slow and confused. He froze, staring at Cray with a startled expression on his face. He was still staring when the director hit him hard in the pit of the stomach. It was a vicious blow and the man slammed back against the marble wall, his mouth opening in an inarticulate cry of protest. The director swung his pistol in a savage arc, and as the guard instinctively lifted his arm to protect his face, the second blow shattered his wrist. Screaming with pain, he staggered back against the elevator door and the director, following, hit him twice on the side of the skull. The man tumbled to the ground, tracing a smear of blood along the polished surface.

Livid, the director turned to face Cray, his lips writhing in anger. 'You stupid bastard,' he hissed, 'I told you not to do that and you went and did it, you stupid bastard.'

He brought the pistol round in a dizzy blur. Cray saw it coming and tried to jerk back but the barrel caught him across the front of the nostrils, breaking his nose with an audible crack. He howled and clutched both hands to his face, blood welling between his slender fingers. The director hit him again, aiming for the temple, swinging the pistol hammer-fashion, once, twice, three times. Cray crashed to the ground with a terrible thump, blood oozing through his light grey hair.

The director seized Webster by the throat, jamming the Walther muzzle against his lower ear. 'Do exactly as I tell you,' he snarled, 'or I blow the top of your bastard head off. Which one is the express elevator to the boardroom on the top floor?'

Weakly, Webster indicated a separate door with a red light gleaming above it. The director pushed him into the narrow cubicle and jabbed the button on the side wall. They clattered upwards and the doors slid open with a muffled click. They were on a plushly carpeted landing with a sign saying 'Boardroom' and an arrow pointing to the left. The director ignored it, and turning to the right, opened a door leading into a narrow passageway lined with empty buckets and rows of cleaning mops. Beyond lay a flight of concrete steps. Jostling Webster ahead of them, the raiders galloped up the stairway. Approaching the roof, Webster heard a roaring sound echoing in his eardrums and as they burst into the open he saw a helicopter hovering just above the building's summit, its giant rotor blades creating a vicious downdraught which tore at his hair and clothing. From the open hatchway, a cable dangled like a slender umbilical cord.

Without a word, the director's bearded assistant scurried across the rooftop and hooked his arms through a canvas harness fluttering at the cable's end. Webster watched drymouthed as, still clutching the leather satchel, the man was winched briskly into the aircraft's interior. One by one each member of the raiding team took his place on the cable and vanished into the gleaming fuselage. The director himself was the last to go. Webster stood trembling as, hair fluttering wildly, the young man was hauled up through the open doorway. For a moment the helicopter seemed to hover, its massive blades thrashing frenziedly at the air; then with a thunderous roar it banked sharply into the sky and sped off in the direction of the River Thames. Only when it had vanished from sight did Webster hear the mournful wailing of police cars in the street below.

We've just heard within the last few minutes that the legendary Churchill Diamonds, reputed to be the most valuable collection of its kind in the world, have been stolen in a daring daylight robbery by a gang posing as a television film crew. According to eye-witness reports, the raiders made their escape by helicopter from the roof of the Coffey Foundation building in London's West End after locking three security guards in the vault chamber. One guard and a company executive were slightly hurt. The diamonds, said to be worth approximately 140 million pounds, derive their name from Sir Winston Churchill who stumbled across them during the reconquest of the Sudan in 1898, but they were never owned by the Churchill family. It was the Foundation's creator, Sir Stephen Coffey, who successfully claimed them from the military authorities, using them to finance his multi-billion dollar business empire. The Coffey Foundation is famous for its charitable enterprises and extensive relief programmes in the underdeveloped countries of the world. Sir Stephen was knighted for his services to humanity in 1936. A Foundation spokesman described the diamonds as an integral part of Britain's heritage, and said the theft was a tragedy, not only for the owners, but for the entire nation.

We'll have a full report on our main bulletin at six o'clock.

The old lady sat in front of the fire, her face unnaturally tense. Her legs were wrapped by a heavy wool blanket, her grey hair coiled into a single braid bound tightly on top of her skull. Her skin was stretched taut across the bony prominences of her cheeks, and her eyes glittered feverishly beneath the cornice of her wrinkled brow. Though she was very old, and though time had imprinted its inevitable hallmark upon her features, her age seemed diminished in some strange way by the tenacious life and vitality burning within her.

Sounds drifted through the open window – rain pattering on the patio outside, the distant baying of sheepdogs, the murmur of a power saw as groundsmen cleared timber from the lower end of the estate.

She heard the room door click and glanced up to see Evans, her butler, standing there. The old lady's eyes detected the worried expression on his face and her brow puckered into a frown. 'Did I call you, Evans?' she demanded.

'You did not, ma'am,' Evans replied evenly.

'You know I like to sleep in the afternoons.'

'Indeed, ma'am, but in this instance, I felt the occasion warranted the intrusion. Mr Webster has been on the telephone.'

'Mr Webster? What on earth for?'

Evans coughed delicately, raising one hand to his lips. Every gesture he made was elegant and graceful, as if it had been rehearsed a thousand times over.

'It's the Churchill Diamonds, ma'am. Mr Webster says they've been stolen.'

For a long moment the old lady remained perfectly still. In the corner of the room the grandfather clock ticked monotonously, its sound strangely discordant in the heavy silence. No expression crossed the old lady's face, but a faint shudder ran through her small, frail body.

'All of them?' she inquired at last in a quiet voice.

'Yes, ma'am, I understand so. The gang posed as a television crew and smuggled a pistol past the security desks. They made their escape from the roof by helicopter. The police have put out a check on all airports and landing fields, but I gather that so far they've drawn a complete blank.'

The old lady did not reply. Instead she turned and peered into the flickering flames, her body hunched, her sharp eyes glowing with a curious luminous intensity. She was still sitting there long after Evans had tactfully withdrawn, closing the door gently behind him.

TWO

The limousine pulled into Baymont Avenue, slowing sharply as the driver drew alongside the kerb. Sitting in the rear, Thomas Kengle, fresh-faced, stockily built, forty-four years old, peered out at the rain sweeping the London streets and tried to think about nothing. He had a capacity, one he deliberately nurtured, for switching his brain into neutral at moments of great crisis; it gave him a clarity of vision which helped enormously in his decision-making, and making decisions was something Thomas Kengle was noted for. Six years earlier, at the remarkably youthful age of thirty-eight, he had taken over the presidency of the powerful and influential Coffey Foundation, running it with a flair and vision that had astonished his most virulent critics. Kengle's devotion to his job was legendary; he was an extraordinary man, brilliantly gifted, who lived his life constantly on the move, racing to factories and offices all over the world, exuding an air of strength and energy which galvanised the people around him.

In some respects the Coffey Foundation was too complex, too diverse for any one individual to embrace completely, spreading as it did across a vast network of interests ranging from oil and automobiles to pharmaceutical products and heavy engineering, but so infatuated was Kengle with his role that he regarded it as some kind of divine cause ordained on high, and no part of his empire was too intricate or too trivial to escape his assiduous attention. In the first place he was gratified that a group so prosperous, so aggressively successful, should channel billions from its profit margins into the field of international relief work (a fact which allowed him to

18

assume an almost priest-like purity in his own mind) and in the second, though he rarely admitted this to any but his closest colleagues, he was constantly amazed that someone like himself, a man of such unpromising beginnings, could have aspired to such elevated circumstances. Today, however, his customary confidence was unexpectedly dulled, and as the limousine slowed to a halt outside the chrome-and-glass façade of the Coffey Foundation headquarters, he groaned as he spotted a cluster of newspaper reporters waiting patiently beneath a canopy of umbrellas.

Beside him, Kengle's escort, Ben Crowley, cursed under his breath. 'Damned press.'

Crowley was a heavy-set Irishman in his early sixties who bore a striking resemblance to the late Spencer Tracy. He had worked for the Coffey Foundation for as long as anyone could remember and was now responsible, not only for the safety of its president, but for the security of its entire worldwide operation.

Kengle's aide, Norman Elkins, sitting beside the driver said: 'I'll get Pembroke to sneak us around the rear.'

'No,' Kengle said.

Ben Crowley looked at him with surprise. 'You want to talk to those bastards?'

'Somebody'll have to, sooner or later.'

The driver clambered out, opening the rear door for Kengle to alight, and seeing his arrival the reporters came clattering down the steps, droplets of water dancing from their umbrellas. Kengle held up his hand, stilling the barrage of questions before it could begin. 'Gentlemen,' he said, 'I must warn you I only have a couple of minutes. I've just returned from New York and I heard the news myself barely an hour ago.'

'Any word from the police yet, Mr Kengle?' a man inquired.

'I expect to talk to them later in the afternoon.'

'Is it true the entire collection was stolen?'

'That's my understanding, yes.'

'An inside job, Mr Kengle?'

'Sorry, I can't comment on that at this stage.'

Kengle felt at home with the press. In normal circumstances he enjoyed being put on the spot, enjoyed the cut and thrust of argument and debate; like a politician, he welcomed the chance to show off his paces.

'What is your personal reaction, as president?' a woman asked.

'Shock, naturally. We thought our security system was impenetrable.'

'How would you assess the importance of the Churchill Diamonds?'

Kengle considered for a moment, selecting his words with care. 'I would say that for the better part of a century they have symbolised the adventurous spirit upon which this Foundation has been based. To a certain extent they have also helped to maintain public confidence in the fluctuating money markets, though today of course the Coffey Foundation is too vast, too complex to be affected in any real financial sense.'

'Is it true the diamonds were discovered by Winston Churchill himself?'

'Not entirely,' Kengle declared, switching direction with the ease of a born diplomat. 'It's true Churchill figured prominently in their discovery, but the title "Churchill Diamonds" is a facetious one given to the collection in more recent years by the British press.'

'Will today's events have any bearing on your relief programmes in the Third World?' a reporter inquired.

'None whatsoever. The guidelines for the Foundation's charity work were laid down during the early years of the century. They remain an integral part of organisation policy.'

'Will there be a reward offered, Mr Kengle?'

'That is something I shall have to discuss with members of my board.'

'Is it true,' a man queried, 'that the Sudanese government has been trying to claim the diamonds back?'

Kengle looked at him sharply. The question was a sensitive one but he was practised enough to allow no sign of irritation to appear on his face.

'I understand so. However, their claim is tenuous to say the least. It's unlikely we would have agreed to give them up.'

'Have any of the Foundation's directors been questioned by the police?' another man asked.

20

At this point Ben Crowley, standing on the sidelines, stepped forward and took Kengle's arm, pulling him gently away. 'Sorry gentlemen,' he stated, raising one hand, 'we're already ten minutes late. We'll issue a full statement at the end of the afternoon.'

He hustled Kengle up the steps and through the glass swing-doors, Norman Elkins scurrying along in their wake. They took the elevator to the fifth floor and made their way to the corporation boardroom. A number of men were seated around the polished conference table, executives who had assembled when the news of the robbery had broken. They rose to their feet as Kengle entered.

'Gentlemen,' he said, 'I'm sorry we're late.'

As usual the proceedings were being conducted by the board chairman, Henry Silvers. 'Hello, Tom,' he smiled, then turning, indicated a good-looking man in his early fifties. 'You know Commander Webber who used to be with the Serious Crime Squad at Tintagel House?'

Kengle shook the detective's hand. 'It was good of you to come, commander.'

'Delighted to help in any way I can, Mr Kengle.'

As Kengle took his customary place at the table's head, the other executives settled back in their chairs. They watched him carefully, ready to adapt to any changes in his mood and behaviour. Though he was not a tall man, Kengle radiated an air of authority which dominated every gathering. 'Anything new?' he demanded.

Henry Silvers shook his head. 'Nothing concrete, Tom. It was a sound professional job, probably planned weeks – maybe even months – in advance. We'll have to give the police a little more time, I'm afraid. At the moment they've got the basement sealed off and they're pulling the place to bits. Nobody's allowed up there until they've finished.'

'Whose decision was it to let the TV people in?'

'Freddie Richardson's. He thought he was acting in our best interests. They said they were making a documentary on Britain's heritage.'

'For God's sake, we've always resisted publicity in that direction. Company policy insists on it.'

21

Silvers said soothingly: 'Tom, their credentials appeared above suspicion. The request came on headed notepaper, complete with photographs, fingerprints and identifying statistics. Freddie thought he was doing the right thing, giving the public a chance to see what the diamonds looked like.'

Kengle sighed. Leaning forward, he laced his fingers and bent the knuckles till their joints cracked. Somewhere a buzzer sounded, and they heard the clickety-click of high heels as a secretary hurried by in the corridor outside.

'Well, gentlemen,' Kengle demanded. 'Any ideas?'

A man with a sallow face said: 'It's not the end of the universe, Tom. With or without the diamonds the Foundation will still survive.'

'I appreciate that. But those diamonds have provided a financial bulwark for this organisation since the beginning of the century. Losing them is like losing our right arm. In financial terms it may mean very little but it puts a tremendous dent in our reputation. It weakens our credibility, for one thing; it shows the world the Coffey Foundation is vulnerable.'

'I think everyone appreciates that, Tom,' Silvers said.

'Good,' Kengle nodded, settling back in his chair. The light from the window fell across his cheeks, picking out the lines and furrows, spoiling to some degree the youthfulness of his features. 'Then everyone will appreciate why we've got to get them back.'

There was a ripple of surprise among the gathered executives.

'How?' a man asked. 'Surely that's up to the police?'

'I don't know how. But I have no intention of leaving this entirely in the hands of other people. That's why I invited Commander Webber to join us today. He retired from the Serious Crime Squad two years ago and he knows how criminals act, how they think. He will be our guide and counsellor.'

Sitting at Kengle's side, Commander Webber looked slightly discomforted. He cleared his throat in a self-conscious way and, leaning forward, filled a glass from one of the water jugs placed at strategic intervals along the table's centre.

'Let me point out from the beginning that I'm here in a private capacity only,' he insisted. 'However, I'm happy to offer whatever advice I can. My first instinct is that the job was a commissioned one. In other words, it's unlikely the thieves who carried it out intended keeping the diamonds for themselves.'

'Why?' Kengle asked.

'Several reasons. Their professionalism suggests they're probably men with extensive criminal records, yet they were quite happy to leave their fingerprints and photographs on your company computer. That could suggest someone's promised them a new identity, a new beginning, possibly in a different part of the world.'

'Who?' Kengle persisted.

'Well, the gems themselves might offer a clue to that. Unlike gold and silver, diamonds have no standard measure of value. Each stone depends upon its individual characteristics, making the market a jungle for anyone approaching it with a less than practised eye. Now, according to my research, the Churchill Diamonds are extraordinary first of all because of their size. Even the smallest is reputed to be as large as a pigeon's egg. The stone are greenish in colour, especially when held to the light. Since diamonds are cut along the grain, it will not be possible to re-cut them without destroying their intrinsic value. Therefore, bearing in mind the fact that their peculiarities would be instantly recognised by a professional *diamantaire*, the stones cannot be resold on the open market.'

'So in other words, whoever stole them is now stuck with them?'

'Correct. Now the raiders used a helicopter for their getaway and that kind of transport costs money, lots of money. Also, they had cast-iron credentials and they knew the security system inside out. So the raid was risky and it was expensive. Which means it had to be bankrolled by somebody with capital to burn.'

Kengle hesitated. 'It could have been the Sudanese,' he said. 'They've been asking for the diamonds back for years.'

Commander Webber looked at him. 'You mean the Sudanese government?'

'It's possible, isn't it?'

'Hardly. If they had the diamonds they'd want to put them

on public display, and that would be an admission of guilt. No, I think they were taken by somebody else, someone who didn't give a damn about their monetary value. I think our culprit had some other motive. Revenge maybe. Some kind of personal grudge. Who knows? Maybe he hated Sir Stephen Coffey himself. A man like Coffey must have made lots of enemies during his lifetime.'

'Commander, Sir Stephen has been dead for more than thirty years.'

'I realise that. But is it possible, just possible there's somebody still alive who considers they have a better claim to those diamonds than he did?'

'I don't see how,' Kengle admitted.

'Well, let's consider it for a moment. What were the precise circumstances of the diamonds' discovery?'

'Commander, it happened back in 1898.'

'So?'

'So everyone involved will be long dead by now.'

'What about their descendants? Sometimes these things get passed from generation to generation.'

'You mean like a vendetta?'

'It's worth checking out, Mr Kengle.'

Kengle looked unconvinced, but settling back in his chair he looked round at the assembled executives who were staring back at him placidly. 'Very well,' he said, 'what *were* the circumstances?'

For a long moment there was total silence, then Ben Crowley, looking vaguely uncomfortable said: 'Nobody knows, Tom.'

Kengle blinked. 'That's impossible.'

'It's the truth. I ran an investigation on the story myself to mark the Foundation's bi-centenary celebrations. We thought we might get a little press coverage, that kind of thing. I came up with a big fat zero.'

'A diamond discovery that size? Somebody must have written something, for God's sake.'

'Just the broadest outlines. No details.'

'Did you check Sir Stephen's memoirs?'

'He skims over the whole event.'

'What about Winston Churchill?'

24

'He wrote a letter to his mother after the fall of Khartoum, but all he mentioned was finding a wounded soldier in the Sudan. The man later died from his injuries in a British field hospital.'

'And the military authorities?'

'Another blank. Their records were either lost or destroyed.'

Kengle shook his head in disbelief. In all his years with the corporation he had never bothered to investigate the precise details of the diamonds' discovery. Like the Grand Canyon they had always been there, part of history, part of his heritage.

'Did your try the newspapers?'

'All the major publications. Plenty of stories about the diamonds, but nothing concrete, nothing specific.'

'This is incredible.'

Commander Webber interrupted. 'What was Sir Stephen Coffey doing in the Sudan in the first place?'

'He was serving in the British army,' Crowley explained.

'I see.' Commander Webber toyed with the glass at his fingertips. 'And while he was there he came across a diamond hoard that turned him into one of the richest men in the world. Yet for some reason none of us can explain, no record of how that hoard was found still exists. Does that not strike you as strange?'

Kengle stared at him in silence for a moment. The sound of a radio reached them from the room below, sending vibrations along the boardroom floor. Kengle took out a small notebook and opened it on the table, smoothing back the pages. He unclipped a pen from his inside pocket and carefully unscrewed the top.

'The commander is right,' he said crisply, 'I think we'd better start at the beginning, don't you?'

The rain pounding the window-panes had slackened to a thin drizzle by the time the executives finally departed, leaving Kengle and Ben Crowley alone in the boardroom. Kengle took off his jacket and slipped it over the back of a chair, then he leaned forward, pressing his palms against the base of his spine. Crowley studied him, his quick eyes noting the signs of strain in his employer's face. 'You look a little groggy,' he observed.

Kengle ran his fingers through his hair. 'I feel awful, Ben, and that's the truth.'

Crowley was silent for a moment then he rose to his feet, opened the drinks cabinet and poured Kengle a stiff whisky. 'Take this,' he said.

'No thanks.'

'Get it down,' Crowley pushed the glass into Kengle's hand, 'it'll do you good.'

Kengle chuckled dryly. 'What are you trying to do, nurse-maid me?'

But he took the drink nevertheless, sipping gently as the fiery liquid sent a flush of warmth through his stomach and abdomen. Though he would never admit the fact even to himself, Kengle secretly enjoyed being pampered by Ben Crowley. He found Crowley's creased face, square chin, and above all his air of calmness and strength deeply reassuring.

'What do you think, Ben?' Kengle asked. 'Was the commander fantasising?'

'Who knows, Tom?'

'1898, for Christ's sake. That was practically the Dark Ages.'

He swirled the drink around in his glass, pursing his lips speculatively.

'It *is* strange though, the way there's no information to be found. Almost as if somebody'd tried a cover-up.'

'I was thinking the same thing myself.'

'I'm worried, Ben. What if Commander Webber talks out of turn?'

'He won't.'

'But just *supposing*. He could damage Sir Stephen's reputation, drag it through the gutter.'

Crowley sighed. 'Tom,' he said, 'Sir Stephen Coffey's been dead since 1954.'

'Not to me, he hasn't,' Kengle told him bluntly. 'To me he's still here, right here in this building. I can feel him like a palpable presence in the corridors, in the offices.'

Crowley compressed his lips till the flesh showed white through the skin. He had worked for Kengle for a good many years, liked him, respected him, regarded him a close personal friend. But in one area, Kengle exasperated him beyond reason – his adulation and devotion to the corporation's founder.

He said: 'Tom, you always talk about that old character as if he was some kind of god.'

'Coffey *was* a god,' Kengle declared, smiling, 'I tell you, Ben, we'll never see his like again. He went into the wilderness and came out with a fortune beyond men's wildest dreams. He created an empire that turned the business world on its head. And not content with that, he used his billions to help the weak, the poor, the destitute. If that's not godlike, I'd like to know what is.'

Kengle peered up at the massive portrait hanging on the boardroom wall. The painting, commissioned in 1936, showed the organisation's founder sitting with his wife in the garden of their Dorset home. Coffey was a striking man with a handsome hawklike face. His eyes were clear and penetratingly blue, and his jagged cheekbones displayed an air of strength and purpose which had never failed to impress itself upon Kengle. Coffey's wife, Victoria, seemed by contrast beautiful and aloof, but even there, Kengle detected a hint of wilful defiance. She looked like a woman who would make her own decisions, who would never be led, never be dominated.

Kengle had studied the painting so often the two figures on it had become almost an integral part of his consciousness; he knew their features as well as he knew his own, every line, every brush stroke, every shadow.

'You know,' he murmured reflectively, 'when they first asked me to take over the Coffey Foundation I was barely thirty-eight years old. I couldn't believe it. It was as if the heavens had opened and somebody'd shone a celestial light in my face. Little Tommy Kengle from Toxteth, Liverpool, head of one of the biggest financial corporations in the world. It was like waking up one morning and finding I'd suddenly been blessed with immortality. I used to stand for hours looking at this picture. I used to try and visualise the kind of man Coffey must have been.'

27

'An ordinary man,' Crowley said patiently, 'with the same strengths and weaknesses as any other ordinary man. Don't build him into something he never was, Tom.'

'Ordinary?' Kengle laughed, 'I idolised Coffey, Ben. Whenever I had a decision to make, I used to ask myself: what would Stephen Coffey do? Damn it, now I feel I've let the old boy down.'

Absently, almost without realising, Crowley tapped the watch in his waistcoat pocket; it was a habit he had, one he reverted to at moments of deep reflection. The watch was a cheap old-fashioned one which had once belonged to his grandfather. Years before, when Crowley had been a youthful detective in the CID, the watch had saved his life, stopping a .22 bullet fired from the gun of a young bank robber. Crowley had worn it ever since.

'One of these days, Tom,' he said, 'I'm going to tell you the truth about Sir Stephen Coffey.'

Kengle frowned. He looked at Crowley blankly. 'What are you talking about?'

'There was something odd about that man, something that never quite sat right.'

'Like what, for God's sake?'

Crowley sighed, shaking his head. 'Tom, this mystery over the diamonds, it's not the only strange thing going on around here. There've been weird things happening for years. I've never mentioned them before because . . . well, there didn't seem any point. But now . . .' Crowley shrugged.

Kengle studied him in silence; there was something in Crowley's expression that disturbed him. As a rule, Crowley was open and direct. Deference had never been his strong point and Kengle had always admired him for that, but this Ben Crowley was different. For a man who carried an air of such rocklike dependability, he seemed agitated, unsettled, unusually tense.

'You'd better explain that, chief,' Kengle said.

Crowley reached up and loosened his necktie, using his fingers to massage the muscles of his throat. 'Ever hear of a group called the Driscoll Dozen?'

Kengle shook his head.

'It's a committee. It exists right here in the Foundation.'

'That's ridiculous. How could it exist without me knowing?'

'It's secret, Tom. Sort of a secret society. Coffey and his wife were founder members. Their daughter, Lady Catherine, too, the whole time she was running the organisation. The others I was never able to identify, but I do know they met on the first Monday of every month.'

'To do what?'

'Your guess is as good as mine. There were no minutes kept, no written records. No one ever referred to them and there was no explanation for their existence.'

Kengle felt puzzled. There was an intensity in Ben Crowley he had never seen before. He found it vaguely disquietening.

'Years ago,' Crowley went on, 'I discovered something I've never shown to a living soul. I'd like to show it to you now.'

He hesitated, studying Kengle shrewdly. 'Would you want to see, even if it hurt?'

Kengle nodded.

'Then come down to my office.'

Wonderingly, Kengle followed his bodyguard along the corridor. Inside his own room Crowley bolted the door then moved to the window and carefully drew the shutters. Switching on the desklamp, he knelt down and unlocked his bottom drawer while Kengle stood baffled, watching him in silence. Crowley drew out a cardboard file and placed it on the desktop. He peered at Kengle, his face strangely greenish in the glow of the lampshade. 'When I first joined the Coffey Foundation,' he said, 'I came fresh from the CID. I'd only been with the company a month or two before Sir Stephen Coffey died. Part of my job was cleaning out his personal effects. I found these among his belongings.'

He opened the file, took out a letter and handed it to Kengle. 'This is a copy of a cable from Sir Stephen Coffey to a certain Garry Kurtzman. Read it.'

Curiously, Kengle held the paper under the circle of light. His eyes scanned the typewritten sentences. 'Dear G,' it said, 'Good luck with the Los Angeles project. If Barney brings off his end of the deal, I will attempt to join you at the beginning

29

of next week. Sorry can't speculate on how many expected for dinner. Phone, soonest. S.'

Kengle read the paper through several times before handing it back. 'It's meaningless,' he grunted.

'It could be innocent, of course. On the other hand, it could also be a word code, a cryptogram. I found nearly a dozen like it.'

'So?'

'So nothing. I was never able to get them unscrambled. But I also found these.'

He took out a faded photograph and pushed it into Kengle's hand. 'That was taken in Miami, Florida, 1934. The man with Sir Stephen Coffey is the same man those cables were addressed to, Garry Kurtzman. Here's another. This one was taken in Washington, 1942. It shows Kurtzman with Sir Stephen and Lady Victoria. Here they are again in London, 1946.'

Kengle frowned, studying the photographs intently. 'What are you getting at, Ben?'

'Kurtzman was a notorious American gangster,' Crowley told him evenly. 'A close friend of Lucky Luciano. After the war, when organised crime in the United States went "legit", he acted as the mob's personal launderer, taking the money from a thousand dirty rackets and processing it through respectable business concerns into clean untraceable capital.'

Kengle said nothing, but he felt his throat contract.

'Look at this,' Crowley continued, handing him another photograph, 'Las Vegas, 1947. Sir Stephen and Lady Victoria were somewhat elderly then, but just cast an eye at their entourage. There's Kurtzman again. And at his side, Bobby Diapoulas, Hank Manera, and the *capo di tuttu capi* of the Mazoni family, Aldo Barello. Quite a gathering, eh? Strange bedfellows for people of the Coffeys' reputation.'

Kengle felt the colour drain from his cheeks. He studied the figures on the photograph, a series of small shudders running through his body.

'What are you trying to say, Ben?'

'Tom, even with those diamonds behind him, have you ever wondered how a man like Sir Stephen Coffey could build up such a fortune completely from scratch?'

'He was a genius, that's how.'

Crowley nodded. 'It's possible. I will admit it's possible. But for someone with no business experience at all, I wouldn't call it genius, Tom, I'd call it a bloody miracle.'

Kengle breathed hard, angry and tense. It was always the same when someone cast aspersions on the Foundation's creator. 'Spit it out, Ben. What are you implying?'

'Tom, is it possible – just remotely possible – that Sir Stephen Coffey built up his fortune, not through personal enterprise, but through an association with the American underworld? That he used his bewildering array of front companies, the dozens of charitable ventures the Foundation set up, to cream off fat profits laundering money for the American mob?'

'You're crazy,' Kengle choked.

'Organised crime isn't a new thing, Tom. Gangs were running the city of New York right back into the last century.'

'Are you seriously trying to tell me that this empire – an empire I am personally controlling – has been built on things like narcotics, extortion, prostitution, and I don't know a thing about it? Are you asking me to believe that this godlike figure I've looked up to for years, this world-famous humanitarian whom most people regard as some kind of saint for Christ's sake was nothing more than a cheap vicious crook?'

'The Foundation itself is legitimate, Tom,' Crowley explained reasonably, 'I'm suggesting it's the Driscoll Dozen which launders the money supplied by organised crime.'

Kengle leaned against the table, supporting himself with his knuckles. He was breathing heavily like a man who had just undertaken a hard bout of physical exertion. Beads of sweat glistened on his face.

'There's a basic flaw in your argument, sport,' he said softly.

'What's that?'

'Why would a man who was already richer than Croesus turn his hand to crime? It doesn't make sense.'

Crowley sighed. 'Tom, Coffey wasn't as rich as you think he was. He was serving with the British army when he discovered those diamonds. Strictly speaking, they came under the category of the spoils of war. When Coffey claimed them for himself he had to reach a compromise with the military authorities. The largest and most valuable stone was presented to the British nation and became part of the Crown Jewels, the others he was allowed to keep on condition that he never disposed of them separately or outside the boundaries of the British Isles.'

'I know all that,' Kengle snapped.

'Then can't you see? Without splitting the collection or taking it out of the country, Coffey could never find a buyer. The Crown had been wickedly clever. They'd kept the diamonds on British soil and ensured that Coffey would be little more than their custodian. That collection must have seemed like a millstone around his neck.'

For a long moment Kengle stood in silence, his brain desperately trying to reject the images invading it. Throughout his career he had accepted without question the sanctity of the organisation for which he worked, had regarded his role within it as some kind of holy mission. Now he felt the very cornerstones of his life beginning to crack.

'Ben,' he said hoarsely, 'I've got to know if what you're telling me is the truth.'

Crowley nodded. 'I understand. But there's only one person alive who can answer that. Coffey's daughter, Lady Catherine herself.'

Kengle stared at him, his face stricken. He looked like a man in the first stages of a stroke. Leaning forward, he stabbed the button of the intercom. 'Myriam,' he said, 'tell my driver to pick me up in front of the entrance lobby. If anybody wants me, I've gone to Dorset.'

THREE

The house stood on a broad promontory of land surrounded on three sides by deep grassy combes where the ground rippled and undulated toward the grey sheen of the distant ocean. It was a large house with granite walls and soaring watchtowers which always reminded Kengle of a Bavarian castle rather than an English country mansion. He studied it moodily as his driver turned in at the gate, following the narrow lane between trimmed lawns and clumps of flowery rhododendrons. The London rain had given way to the gentle sunshine of an English summer evening, and seldom had Kengle seen the countryside look so beautiful. The rolling fields and leafy woodlands presented a lushness he found reassuring, despite the fraught condition of his mind. He had stopped only once during the long drive south – at the local library to pick up a book on the 1898 Sudanese campaign. But though he had tried hard to read he had found concentrating difficult as his brain worried at Ben Crowley's disclosures like a terrier tearing at a bone. Kengle was a confident man as a rule, secure in the knowledge of his own place in the order of things, secure in his awareness of the Foundation's strength behind him. But Ben Crowley had menaced that strength in the most direct and unexpected way, and Kengle, though he could not even now believe it, found his customary composure extremely difficult to maintain.

It just wasn't possible, he thought, not if you looked at it in the cold light of reason. He couldn't have run an organisation for six whole years, six years in which he had become closely and personally involved in every facet of its operation, without being aware that something didn't sit right. It had to be a mistake. The Coffey Foundation was not simply a business empire pursuing its own selfish ends. It was humane, compassionate. It had saved the lives of millions of people all over the world. How could it be guilty of the kind of duplicity Crowley was accusing it of? The idea was preposterous.

The car swung to a halt in front of the huge grey-stoned mansion and Kengle, after telling his driver to wait, knocked loudly on the heavy oak door. It was opened a moment later by Evans the butler. His eyebrows lifted as he recognised Kengle. 'Why, Mr Kengle sir. Lady Catherine is in the rose garden. I'll tell her you're here.'

'Don't bother,' Kengle answered, 'I'll tell her myself.'

Still clutching his briefcase, he followed the footpath around the side of the house. Here, the lawns gave way to an elaborately designed flower and vegetable garden bordered by a high Victorian wall which protected the plants from the full blast of the spring and autumn winds. A line of greenhouses lay gleaming in the sunlight, and beyond them rows of green shoots sprang from the soil in a breathless profusion of new life.

Lady Catherine was pruning the rose bushes which bordered the stone patio. She was dressed in denim dungarees and her grey hair was covered by a bright silk scarf. Kengle's lips twisted into a wry grin when he saw her. For nearly thirty years Lady Catherine had run the Foundation single-handed after her parents had died. Only when age and ill-health had begun to take its toll had she agreed to step down, allowing Kengle, at the board's invitation, to assume the presidency. But he was only too painfully aware the old lady had vehemently opposed the move. She had disapproved of him from the beginning, insisting that he was too young, too inexperienced to take over the Coffey Foundation. Though he admired her strength, her single-mindedness, he could never rid himself of the thought that the old lady was his enemy, and their relationship had always been a difficult one.

Lady Catherine did not look up as Kengle approached. She was crouching over a particularly extravagant bloom, snipping at extraneous stalks with a pair of secateurs, and when

34

Kengle's shadow fell across her she said: 'I named this after my mother, Victoria. It's a new species. Like it?'

'Very pretty,' Kengle murmured.

'Took me fourteen years to get it right. Sometimes the leaves fall off before it blossoms, but I'm expecting an excellent crop this year.'

She straightened, peering directly into his face, her small eyes shrewd and hard. 'I had a feeling you'd turn up sooner or later,' she grunted.

'How's that?'

'You always do when trouble arises.'

Kengle shifted the briefcase to his other arm. The old lady always made him feel uneasy. Partly, he supposed, because she was Sir Stephen Coffey's daughter, but there was something else, something he could never quite put his finger on, a kind of elusive haughtiness as if Lady Catherine could never rid herself of the conviction that she was in the presence of an inferior being.

'I have to talk to you,' he said.

'Do you indeed? I hope you're suitably ashamed of yourself, young man.'

Kengle was surprised. 'Of what?'

'Letting my diamonds go, that's what.'

Kengle sighed. 'Lady Catherine, it's not the diamonds I've come about. At least not directly.'

'What then?'

'I have some papers I'd like to show you.'

'What kind of papers?'

'Personal things. Photographs, letters, a few legal documents. They belonged to your father.'

She frowned. 'My father's been dead for more than three decades. What possible significance could such articles have today?'

He hesitated. There was no easy way to do it, he realised. He couldn't soften the blow any more than Ben Crowley could. He said gently: 'Lady Catherine, it's about the Driscoll Dozen.'

Not a flicker of expression crossed her face, he had to admire her for that, but her features seemed to settle into a

35

frigid mask, the muscles tightening around the framework of her skull. Her eyes, sunk deeply beneath her protruding brow, glittered in the morning sunlight. For a long moment she stared at him in silence then, peeling off her gloves, she said: 'I think you'd better come inside.'

She dropped the secateurs on to a nearby deckchair and Kengle followed her silently across the patio and through the rear entrance into the massive stone mansion. The corridors were panelled with oak, their walls lined with elegant oil-paintings. The butler met them in the hallway and Lady Catherine, without pausing in her stride said: 'Evans, I don't want to be disturbed before dinner, is that understood?'

'Yes, ma'am,' he replied dutifully.

She led the way into the library, carefully closing the door behind them. Though it was early June and the evening warm and sunny, a small fire flickered in the metal grate. The windows were open and Kengle could hear birds singing in the trees outside.

Lady Catherine indicated an armchair. 'Sit down,' she ordered. 'You must forgive the fire. When one gets to my age, the damp has a habit of seeping into one's bones, even on the warmest day.'

Clutching the briefcase on his knee, Kengle sat. The old lady settled herself opposite him. There was no sign of strain on her face, no sign of anything at all except perhaps an air of businesslike precision; she looked like a magistrate about to pass judgement. 'Now,' she said, 'tell me what this is all about.'

Kengle opened his briefcase and took out the cardboard folder. For some reason he could not explain, he felt as if he were the guilty party, not Coffey.

'This file,' he said, 'was compiled by my chief security officer, Ben Crowley, from personal papers he found amongst your father's things. Some of them are messages, possibly in code. They are addressed to a certain Garry Kurtzman, a notorious member of the American crime syndicates. You will admit, ma'am, he makes a rather strange associate for people of your parents' reputation unless – and I hesitate to say this – unless Ben Crowley's suspicions contain an element of truth.'

'What *are* Ben Crowley's suspicions, Mr Kengle?'

Kengle took a deep breath. 'He believes that for many years now the Foundation has been used to launder money for the American mob. He believes this operation has been conducted and controlled by a secret society within the Foundation called the Driscoll Dozen.'

She sniffed and held out her hand for the file. Carefully she sifted through the papers inside, studying the photographs intently. From time to time she made little gutteral noises deep inside her throat, or taking out a sheet, held it to the light, her thin lips moulding the syllables as she scrutinised each word.

At length she said: 'Ben Crowley is a damn fool. We should have retired him years ago.'

'But Lady Catherine, can you explain the existence of this material?'

'There's nothing to explain. It's perfectly innocent.'

'Innocent, ma'am? I would hardly call it that.'

Her eyes studied him, shrewd and speculative; they were elderly eyes, but they still had the glint of insight in them – a hint of fire and passion, faded now, but not about to be dismissed lightly. 'How much do you know about my father?' she demanded.

'Until today I thought I knew everything. Now I'm just not sure any more.'

'He was a remarkable man, Mr Kengle, a remarkable man.'

'I don't think anyone disputes that, ma'am. The question is – and it's a question I'm almost afraid to hear the answer to – was he also a crook?'

Her eyes hardened. 'You're such a fool. Stephen Coffey was a giant, a great visionary.'

Kengle shifted uncomfortably in his chair. 'Lady Catherine, I have a question to ask you and it is very important that you tell me the truth. Was there something in Sir Stephen's early life you've deliberately kept secret?'

She peered at him sharply. 'Like what?'

'I don't know. Something unsavoury perhaps? Something you wouldn't want other people to know?'

Reaching back, she drew a shawl from the armchair rim, gathering it around her shoulders. The gesture was a reflective rather than a conscious one, as if she was somehow playing for time.

In a moment of impulse, Kengle said: 'Something to do with the Churchill Diamonds?'

'I don't know what you're talking about,' she snapped.

But it was already too late. Kengle had seen the glimmer of alarm flash across her eyes and knew he had touched a sensitive nerve. He was filled with a strange intuition, as if suddenly he could engage her very senses. He leaned forward. 'Lady Catherine, I know this sounds incredible, but did Sir Stephen Coffey do something in the summer of 1898 which resulted in some strange way in the jewel robbery which took place this morning? Was that robbery part of some ancient vendetta? An act of vengeance, perhaps, of retribution?'

'You're quite mad, Mr Kengle.'

'You know why those jewels were stolen, don't you, ma'am? And you know who took them. It had nothing to do with monetary gain. It was something else, something that has been passed down from generation to generation. Am I right?'

The old lady's eyes left his face, dropping in a self-conscious way to the Georgian card-table in front of her and finally to the fire itself. She stared at it hungrily as if she found some solace, some trace of strength in its flickering embers. Then she nodded.

Kengle felt triumph gathering in his chest. 'Lady Catherine,' he whispered, 'if I'm to carry on as head of this organisation, I have to know.'

'That's impossible. It's too dangerous.'

'Why?'

'Please don't ask. I can tell you nothing.'

Kengle was silent for a moment, thinking hard. He knew he had to judge this carefully. If he pushed too hard she would close up like a clam.

He decided to try a different approach. Rummaging inside his briefcase, he took out the book he had borrowed from the library. 'I did a bit of reading on my way here this evening. This is an account of the British reconquest of the Sudan in 1898. Perhaps you've read it?'

The old lady shook her head.

'Fascinating tale,' Kengle said, 'I must confess it was a revelation to me. Did you know the Anglo-Egyptian army assembled for the task was the finest in our history? It numbered nineteen battallions of infantry, ten squadrons of cavalry, four field batteries and a camel corps of eight companies.'

'I've heard the story a thousand times,' the old lady admitted.

'The officer in command of the expedition was Herbert Horatio Kitchener. Quite a character, it seems. Noted for his patience and attention to detail. He could have dashed downriver to engage the Dervish forces at Khartoum, but instead he opted for a more cautious advance, reinforcing his supply route all the way.'

Lady Catherine hesitated. She realised she was being drawn deliberately into this new field of discussion. 'That's quite true,' she declared in a cautious voice. 'He laid a railroad track from Wadi Halfa to Fort Atbara, a distance of 250 miles across some of the most uncompromising country in the world.'

'And he used it, Lady Catherine, to ferry carloads of men and equipment southward. Am I right in thinking, ma'am, that among those men was your father, Sir Stephen Coffey?'

She nodded wearily in agreement. 'Yes,' she whispered, 'among them was my father.'

Kengle leaned forward. 'Begin there, Lady Catherine. Tell me what happened after your father arrived in the Sudan.'

She looked at him, her expression calm, composed, dignified. 'Mr Kengle, knowledge can be a dangerous thing. Let me prevail upon you one last time. Forget Stephen Coffey. Forget the past. Continue to run the Foundation as you have for the past half-dozen years and in a month or two this entire episode will have been forgotten.'

'Supposing I refuse?'

She paused for a moment, then she said: 'I know your temperament, Mr Kengle. You have chosen to idolise my father. If I tell you the things you wish to know, it could have the most disastrous consequences, not only for the Foundation itself but for you as an individual.'

Kengle felt his throat tighten. 'Lady Catherine,' he murmured, 'I must have the truth.'

She laughed shortly. 'The truth? What makes you think you could accept the truth? What makes you think you could believe the truth? You would have to know my parents as I knew them, their secret thoughts, their secret desires. You would have to know the emotions which governed them, the instincts which motivated them. Then maybe, just maybe, you might begin to understand.'

Kengle settle back in the armchair, resting his head against its padded upholstery. He felt his body trembling, and a curious sense of dread seemed to lodge in his chest as he studied her in the pale light of the early evening. 'Tell me about it,' he said.

THE SUDAN, 1898

The camel tracks looked blurred in the fading sunlight, forming a ragged trail which meandered diagonally eastwards away from the railroad line. They were flanked on one side by a series of jagged outcrops and on the other by rolling sanddunes, some nearly fifty feet high, their crests cluttered with acacia trees and clumps of twisted camel thorn.

Lieutenant Stephen Coffey of the 10th Westmorland Lancers, dark-haired, slimly built, raised his arm to bring his troop to a halt, and after glancing briefly at the ground motioned to Sergeant MacAngus to examine the tracks more closely.

Coffey's eyes were startlingly blue, forming the focal point of his entire face, and across his cheeks the sun had burned a livid weal beneath the shade of his pith helmet.

MacAngus, by contrast, was a rawboned, heavy-shouldered man with skin the colour of burnished copper. He moved lazily as he dismounted, his long body peeling itself away from the saddle, and with the same inherent grace he strolled toward the camel tracks and began to scrutinise them carefully.

Coffey sat in silence, watching his sergeant pick up the tiny balls of camel dung and crumble them in his palm. He knew MacAngus was a thousand times better than the Arab trackers the army employed, most of whom were spies for the Khalifa anyhow. He watched the sergeant hold one of the dung balls to his nose, breaking it into pieces between his fingers. 'Droppings're still warm,' MacAngus said. 'They canna be far in front of us, sir. Ten, twenty minutes mebbe.'

'Dervishes?' Coffey asked.

'Looks like. Probably eight. No more'n ten, I'd say.'

Coffey thought for a moment. He had nineteen men in his own troop. Counting himself and MacAngus, that made a total of twenty-one. But his orders had been clear. Patrol the railroad, report sightings of Dervish movements but under no circumstances engage the enemy.

Lieutenant Coffey was bored. He had been in the Sudan for more than four months now and most of his days had been spent guarding the train installations, combating the heat, the flies, the monotony and discomfort. He was eager for action, eager for excitement, but he knew that if he attacked and lost, he would face an immediate court martial.

Rising, Sergeant MacAngus looked at him shrewdly, his hard eyes noting the expression on Coffey's features. He added in a soft voice: 'There's something else, sir.'

MacAngus indicated a series of dark stains on the ground, almost indiscernible among the balls of camel dung. They looked like small patches of dirty sand, their colour drained by the orange hue of the earth itself.

'Blood,' MacAngus said simply. 'Somebody's hurt. Man or animal.'

He indicated a separate line of tracks with his foot. 'This one's a wee bit older than the rest. Not much, two or three minutes mebbe. See how the rear tracks look smudged as if the creature was dragging its hind leg. My guess is, whoever's riding it is on the run.'

Coffey was about to speak when suddenly, like a twig snapping in the dry thin air, they heard the crack of a rifle shot. Coffey froze in his saddle, listening hard. Another shot rang out, sharp and discordant in the pink glow of evening. Coffey glanced at Sergeant MacAngus. 'Close,' he whispered.

MacAngus nodded. 'Aye. Just over yon ridge, I reckon.'

'Remount, sergeant,' Coffey snapped.

He ordered the troop to remain where it was, and with the

sergeant following, trotted up the trail to a narrow finger of rock which descended steeply into a gully on the other side. Below him the earth sloped into a steep 'V' formed by a dried-up riverbed. At the very tip of this 'V' a man lay crouched among the rocks, an Arab in soiled robes and dirty headcloth who was firing spasmodically with an ancient Remington.

Crack – crack – crack, the shots seemed flat and spiritless on the oven-hot air, and as Coffey watched, another man, his naked body blue-black in the flushed light of evening, rose from the spot where he had been hiding and scuttled across a stretch of open ground, dropping to a crouch behind a cluster of camel thorn. Coffey spotted eight more figures, all naked like the first and clutching shields and spears, scattered among the rocks and scrub.

'Fuzzies,' Coffey whispered to MacAngus, using the nickname given by the British troops to the Beja hill tribesmen. The Bejas were a primitive people poorly armed and badly led, but they fought with a ferocity and courage which had wrought a grudging respect from their British and Egyptian adversaries.

Coffey watched the small group of naked men slowly working their way toward the solitary Arab who, trapped in his arid cul-de-sac, could only fire futilely each time he spotted a flash of naked skin. All his shots went wild, for the tribesmen, with the inherent cunning of wild animals, moved only one at a time and then always from a different direction, making it impossible for the beleaguered man to switch his aim effectively.

Coffey could see the sprawled figure of the man's camel which, wounded, had finally collapsed, leaving its rider to the mercy of his pursuers. The Bejas' own mounts stood in a group on the gully rim.

'Now here's an interesting situation,' Coffey said, chuckling under his breath. 'A Dervish under attack from his own people. What do you make of that, Sergeant MacAngus?'

MacAngus didn't trouble to answer. Instead, he moved his head slightly and spat on the ground. Coffey had long grown used to the fact that MacAngus seldom spoke unless he had reason to, and even then kept his words to a minimum.

'The question is,' Coffey went on thoughtfully, 'do we sit here and watch the fun, or invite ourselves down to the party?'

He leaned forward in the saddle, resting one hand against his thigh, his body throbbing with excitement. Some instinct, some inner sense of caution made him pause. More than likely the Arab was an enemy, a deserter from the Khalifa's army, or possibly a thief who had rebelled at the thought of the traditional Dervish punishment – the cutting off of the culprit's hands – and had decided to make a bolt for freedom. Risking the lives of British cavalrymen for such an unsavoury creature would hardly be justified in the eyes of the British high command. On the other hand, the Bejas were indisputably the enemy, and those tribesmen down there offered a tempting target, spread out as they were, unsuspecting and exposed.

Coffey came to a decision. 'Sergeant,' he snapped crisply, 'order the men to right wheel into combat formation. Let's find out what our hairy little friends are made of.'

The troopers moved into position along the gully rim, their lances poised in the evening glow. Beneath the helmets, their faces looked pale at the prospect of action. Amazingly, although they were clearly outlined against the sky, the tribesmen below, totally absorbed with the business of wearing down their quarry, failed to observe the danger threatening them from above.

Sweating hard, Coffey drew his sword. The sound of the blade sliding from its scabbard made a soft metallic rattle on the still evening air. A horse snickered somewhere at the end of the line and leaning forward, its rider, squeezed its nostrils to prevent it snickering again. Sergeant MacAngus sat with the reins gripped tightly between his teeth. He had left his sword still sheathed, and instead gripped a revolver in each fist; the first was his service pistol, a Browning, which he carried in a wooden holster attached to his webbing belt, the second was a long-barrelled Navy Colt, MacAngus's own private possession which he kept tucked in the mapcase flapping against the saddle at his thigh.

Slowly Coffey raised his sword high in the air, and almost in

43

slow motion the lances lowered, their tips slanting downward, pointing along the line of the horses' necks. Coffey took a deep breath, then, with one swift motion, he brought the blade down and the line of cavalry broke into the charge.

The ground sloped so steeply there was no room to go through the customary procedure of fast walk, canter and gallop. Coffey found most of his attention taken in steering his Arab pony down the twisting treacherous hillside. The gallant horse, feeling the earth sliding away beneath its hooves, picked its way desperately to and fro between the hollows and fissures. But not all his men were as lucky to have mounts so sure-footed, Coffey saw, as on the periphery of his vision he glimpsed a trooper pitch from his saddle and go tumbling downwards in a great cloud of billowing dust.

The ground swayed, the rocks blurring into a grey contourless smudge, and then, among the mass of undulating earth, he glimpsed figures moving about and realised the tribesmen had spotted them at last. The Bejas were not running, Coffey noted with surprise. Instead they were coming forward to meet the British attack, their dark bodies flitting among the clumps of camel scrub, their long spears poised for action as they prepared to take the full impact of the cavalry charge. In spite of himself Coffey felt a tremor of admiration. The stories of the Dervishes were absolutely true. Savage and cruel they might well be, but there was no disputing their courage.

Coffey's pony steadied as they reached the gully floor. His vision cleared and he became icy calm as he glimpsed ahead the little cluster of sandy rocks and blue-black bodies flitting between them. From out of the ground a man rose suddenly, seeming almost to materialise from thin air, his sinewy skin gleaming in the flush of the dying sun, his wild hair wafting in the breeze. His arm was drawn back, the spear poised and aimed as he crouched in Coffey's path motionless and unafraid. Coffey felt his stomach lurch as the man moved, bringing the spear forward in an effortless blur, and with a sudden spasm of panic Coffey swung his sword blade to the left, clipping and deflecting the spear tip as its shaft left the thrower's hand and swished past his face.

Unsettled for a moment, Coffey barely had time to swing his sword in a backhanded curve before the tribesman blocked his blow with his shield, and, drawing a wicked-looking twelve-inch knife, dived directly under the heels of Coffey's pony.

Coffey hauled on the reins, wheeling hard. He knew what the Beja was up to. British cavalrymen had learned to their cost the effectiveness of the Dervish on foot. Agile as a monkey, he could roll under the very hooves of a cavalry charge and hamstring the horses from behind. Coffey twisted madly. He saw the Beja slashing out at his pony's legs, and by sheer physical strength hauled his mount around just in time. Leaning sideways out of the saddle he slashed viciously downwards, feeling a jolt run along his arm as his blade connected with the tribesman's wrist, amputating the hand from the forearm. Blood spurted from the man's severed limb but he stared up at Coffey, showing no sign of fear or pain, and tried to direct the gushing fountain into the Englishman's eyes as he scrambled in the dust for his fallen knife. Coffey didn't give him a chance to use it again. Leaning forward, he drove the point of his blade into the warrior's throat, pinning the man back against the desert floor, his muscles thrashing in the last spasms of approaching death.

Coffey felt sick as he wheeled away. He could see the rest of the tribesmen retreating, scrambling for their camels along the gully's rim. The attack had been short, sharp and effective. Coffey waved his sword arm in the air. 'Let them go,' he yelled.

He was already ashamed of his eagerness to fight, and the savage little engagement had left his body weak and trembling.

He glanced around the gully bottom. Four tribesmen lay dead in the dust, but he noted with a sense of relief there were no British casualties. The man who had fallen from his horse during the initial scramble down the hillside was limping badly as he struggled to remount, but apart from a few scratches the rest of the troop appeared untouched. They were laughing breathlessly, surprised at the success of their assault – and relieved too, Coffey imagined, that they had come through unscathed. It would be something to tell their companions when they got back to camp that evening.

Sergeant MacAngus looked as calm as ever. His expressionless face seemed curiously remote as he sat reloading his revolvers. Coffey saw the Arab they had rescued coming toward them, holding his Remington loosely at his side. He was a big man with a dark bearded face and wild flashing eyes. For a moment Coffey thought he was smiling, then he saw the impression was a false one created by a jagged scar which sliced through the left cheek and twisted the side of the mouth into a manic grin.

'Our friend doesn't look too happy to see us,' Coffey murmured softly. 'You wouldn't think we'd just saved the beggar's life.'

MacAngus grunted, and, slipping his service pistol into its holster, rested the Colt across the front of his saddle, his fingers lightly touching its grip.

'Ye'd better stay out of my line of fire, sir. If the bastard tries to use that Remington, I'll blow the top of his bastard head off.'

Coffey spurred his mount forward and brought it to a halt, swinging the beast sideways as he studied the Arab's approach. The man seemed caught in the grip of some feverish excitement.

'That's far enough,' Coffey ordered.

The Arab halted and stared at him wildly. Then he said in unmistakable English: 'God Almighty, you came down that hillside like the hounds of hell. I thought it was the devil himself coming to carry me off.'

Coffey's eyes widened with surprise. He glanced back at MacAngus, then turned to examine the man again. 'Who are you?' he demanded.

The man saluted casually. 'Lieutenant Walter J. Driscoll, Military Intelligence under the command of Major Reginald Wingate.'

Coffey whistled under his breath. Wingate's reputation was almost legendary. Using dubious information and little financial backing, he had set up a sophisticated network of agents operating behind the enemy lines.

'You've been living with the Dervishes?'

'On and off, for the past eight weeks,' Driscoll grinned.

Coffey studied him with a new respect. 'What are you doing here?'

'Well, I was trying to reach the railhead when those Beja bastards picked up my trail. They'll have a go at anybody if they think there's an ounce of profit in it. Bandits, the lot of them. How far off are we?'

'About an hour's ride, no more.'

'Who's in command there?'

'Colonel Philip Guthrie.'

'I have to speak to him right away.'

Coffey nodded. He knew if the Beja tribesmen had reinforcements in the vicinity he would be well advised to get his men back to camp as quickly as possible.

'I say,' Driscoll whispered, moving closer, 'you don't happen to have a smoke by any chance? Those Dervish bastards don't approve of tobacco, and eight weeks without a cigarette is more than any man can stand, even for Queen and Country.'

Coffey chuckled and glanced back at MacAngus who by now had slipped his pistol into its customary slot inside the mapcase. 'Sergeant?' he commanded.

MacAngus fumbled inside his tunic and brought out a thin cheroot. Leaning from the saddle, he passed it down to Lieutenant Driscoll. The lieutenant looked at it dubiously.

'What on earth's this?' he demanded in an affronted voice.

'That's the sergeant's secret weapon,' Coffey explained. 'When he runs out of ammunition, he simply lights up one of those things and chokes the Dervishes to death.'

Lieutenant Driscoll watched suspiciously as MacAngus struck a match and carefully lit the cheroot's tip. 'Christ,' he exclaimed, coughing, 'this thing's bloody lethal.'

Coffey glanced at Driscoll's camel sprawled in the dust. 'Is your mount dead?' he asked.

The lieutenant nodded. 'One of those blighters got him with a spear thrust early this morning. It's a wonder the poor beast managed to survive so long.'

'Well, we'll just have to ride double. Think you can clamber up behind me? It'll be a tight squeeze, I'm afraid. These things

47

weren't built for comfort.'

Driscoll gave a wary suck at his cheroot, letting the smoke curl from his lips and nostrils. 'Lieutenant,' he said, 'if you can stand the stench of this thing, I think I can stand a sore backside for a while.'

FOUR

The camp stood on a bend of the river, bordered on one side by the desert scrub and on the other by the muddy Nile. It was nearly a mile across, secured by lines of thorn bushes staked down to form a *zariba* or palisade. Inside the central gate rose the grass huts and blanket shelters which marked the bivouacs of the Egyptian and Sudanese brigades. Toward the centre fluttered the white tents of the British division. At the railhead, a solitary locomotive stood motionless on the tracks, hissing steam between its massive wheels. Beyond it, a clump of palm trees indicated the location of the officers' mess.

Coffey rode in, his pony picking its way carefully through the clumps of coarse grass swaying eerily in the darkness. No sound rose from the men behind him beyond the clinking of their accoutrements. As the flush of victory faded, so too had their exhilaration. The patrol had been long and arduous. They had ridden far and tasted blood. Now they were weary and ready for bed.

Coffey could hear Lieutenant Driscoll grunting behind him in the saddle. He knew how uncomfortable the journey must have been for Driscoll, perched on the edge of the leather rim, but Driscoll had never complained, even for an instant.

'Feel good to be back?' Coffey asked.

Driscoll muttered something unintelligible. It might have been assent, or even, Coffey thought, an exclamation of derision. Curiosity filled Coffey as he thought of the Englishman living, sleeping, breathing in the very heart of the Dervish stronghold.

'It's a miracle you've managed to survive living with those bastards for eight weeks,' he grunted.

Driscoll eased himself more comfortably in the saddle. 'That's no miracle, lieutenant,' he muttered, 'just common sense. I've learned to think the way they think. Most of the time I'm a Dervish myself.'

Coffey shook his head in wonder. 'I don't know how you stand it.'

Driscoll grinned wolfishly. 'I like the bastards, that's how. The Dervish may be a savage, but he has a simplicity of nature that appeals to my basic instincts.'

'How can you talk like that when he keeps seven-eighths of his countrymen enslaved?'

'Well, the Dervish doesn't look at things the way we do. He sees slavery as a natural part of life. The more slaves a man owns, the more important that man is. And they're not treated badly, by European standards. Would you mishandle a good stallion, for instance? A slave is the Dervish's property so why should he damage his own property? Other people, now, he can be utterly ruthless with. You heard what happened to the Batahin? They made the mistake of refusing to send any more men for the Khalifa's army. The Khalifa rounded up seventy-seven of their finest warriors and mutilated them in front of their wives and children. By our culture the man's a monster, but it's a savage land he has to control and he achieves it by being just as savage himself.'

Coffey grunted as he drew to a halt at the camp commander's tent. The red flag of Egypt fluttered from its roof and two sentries in brown jerseys and blue puttees guarded its entrance flap. With a murmur of relief, Driscoll slid to the ground. He stood looking up at Coffey for a moment, the scar on his cheek twisting his lips into a savage grin. 'In case I haven't done so already,' he said, 'I'd like to thank you for saving my life.'

'A pleasure, lieutenant,' Coffey told him as he shook the officer's proferred hand. 'You can do the same for me sometime.'

'It's a promise,' Driscoll answered.

Coffey watched him duck beneath the tentflap, then, handing his pony to the ostler's assistants, he ordered MacAngus to dismiss the troop and made his way to his quarters through the crowded campsite. It had been a long day and he was feeling desperately tired. Saving Driscoll's life had been an unexpected bonus; it would look good on his report, might even save him a reprimand for disobeying orders, but he had to admit it had been a stroke of unbelievable luck. If he had got it wrong, if instead of Driscoll the rescued Arab had turned out to be nothing more than a wayward Dervish, Coffey's position would have been a lot more untenable, he had to admit. He had taken a chance back there. Had been hasty, impetuous. He would have to watch that in future.

His nostrils picked up the odour of engine oil, blancoed webbing, horse sweat, tobacco smoke. The blur of tartan kilts showed through the darkness as soldiers from the Seaforth Highlanders gathered around a cooking fire, their cigarettes glowing like fireflies in the soft desert night. Arab orderlies polished equipment, laid out bedding, scrambled for water along the network of camp roads, their pale robes gleaming in the eerie starlight.

Coffey loved the army. From the beginning he had felt at home here. The sad thing was - and he could think of no way to reverse this fact - the army did not love Coffey. He was an interloper. An intruder. Someone who did not know his place. A man of his social background clearly belonged in the ranks, and the fact that he had aspired to higher things made him, in many ways, something of an untouchable among his fellow officers. His father, a poor farmer who scratched out a living from the harsh hill country of the Cumbrian fells, had sent Coffey to officer school with what savings he'd managed to scrape together in the belief that he was giving his son a reasonable start in life, but Coffey had quickly discovered that in the British army of the 1890s a subaltern's pay was simply not enough to keep a young man in sound wind and limb; mess bills, uniforms, dining-in nights, soldiers' charities, even the simple cost of providing and looking after one's horse ran far above the meagre remittance offered by the Crown, and while Coffey's associates supplemented their incomes with regular allowances from their families, he had been reduced to the

51

dubious expediency of gambling in an effort to make ends meet. In the snobbish privilege-ridden establishment of the Victorian army, gambling, though a respectable pursuit for officers with money to burn, was an unthinkable social disgrace when a man did it in order to survive, and Coffey's constant battle against financial disintegration made him a figure most ambitious young subalterns preferred not to know too well. He was tolerated, in some respects even patronised, but the fact remained that Coffey, despite his unarguable assets – intelligence, flair, ability, imagination – was a social outcast simply because of his poor beginnings. And yet, though he could not have known it as he strode to his tent on that summer evening in 1898, he was about to embark on the greatest adventure of his life, an adventure which would turn him ultimately into one of the wealthiest and most powerful men in the world.

Sergeant MacAngus lit a cheroot, peering contentedly at the stars. It was the time of day he liked best, when night brought a blessed respite from the heat of the sun, and the harsh metallic earth smell which came drifting in from the desert floor conjured up memories of his early youth. MacAngus felt at home in the desert. He had spent many years with the British army in India, had served on the Khyber and in the desolate hill country of Afghanistan. He did not hate wild places as some of the others did, and he did not fear them either. Instead he welcomed their harshness like an old familiar friend.

He drew hard on the cheroot, spotting Private Higgins crouching by the cooking fire, filling his mug from the coffee-pot on the grill. MacAngus moved toward him and Higgins looked up as he approached.

'Coffee, sarge?' Higgins asked, his voice an octave higher than usual.

MacAngus took the cheroot from his mouth and carefully nipped its end. He slipped it inside his tunic and squatted down at Higgins's side. Picking up a spare mug, he filled it from the coffee-pot and cradled it gently between his palms. Higgins, he noted, looked tense and distraught. He carried the haunted air of a man who had discovered an unsuspected truth about himself and had not yet come to terms with it.

Sipping gently, MacAngus felt a warm glow spread through his stomach.

'Are ye no ready for bed?' he said. 'That was a long ride today.'

'Couldn't sleep,' Higgins muttered, rubbing his cheek with his fingertips.

His skin looked sweaty in the flickering firelight.

'Still thinking about this afternoon?'

'No, no,' Higgins assured him hastily. 'What we done was our duty out there. I mean, they's heathens, ain't they, them fuzzy-wuzzies? Sellin' people into slavery an' the like. That ain't Christian, sergeant. No Christian man can rightly stand by an' watch that happen. We're British soldiers an' a British soldier's more'n a match for any Dervish what ever lived. It's just that . . .' He hesitated. 'Well, there was only nine of them today. There's sixty thousand of the bastards waiting for us at Khartoum.'

MacAngus studied him shrewdly. He was just a wee bit of a lad, fuzz on the cheekbones, pimples around the shirt collar. 'You'll be all right, Higgins,' he murmured.

Higgins looked at him. 'I'm not scared, don't think that.'

'Wouldn't be human if ye weren't.'

'What I mean is . . . I'm not afraid of dyin'. It's the thought of pain what worries me most. I don't mind dyin' if it's quick an' clean an' smart, like. I don't want to be lingering on afterwards, that's all.'

A tiny nerve flickered high on Higgins's cheek and MacAngus watched it as he sipped at his coffee. He understood how Higgins felt. He had felt the same way himself once. You never got over that, not truly. The knowledge of consequences, the awareness of pain, death, obliteration.

'How old are you, laddie?' MacAngus asked.

'Seventeen,' Higgins said.

MacAngus could not remember being seventeen. It was as if a veil had been drawn across his life. Expediency had expunged his youth from his mind, like the cauterising of an old wound.

Fumbling inside his tunic, he selected one of the cartridges he kept for his Navy Colt. They were .44s, not service issue. He held it to the light, rolling it between his fingertips. 'See this?' he grunted.

Higgins blinked. 'What is it, sarge?'

'Magic bullet. Got it from an old holy man in the Himalayan mountains. He told me the bullet was blessed. Whoever carries it is protected by the *prana*, the life force. I've hauled it around in ma pocket ever since.'

Higgins's eyes widened and he stared down at the cartridge with awe.

'Does it work?' he whispered.

'Och, soldier, ye'll no find any holes in me, 'cepting the ones twas meant to be there.'

'Jesus, sergeant,' Higgins breathed, peering down at the tiny canister which carried such remarkable powers. MacAngus flipped it into the air, caught it neatly and handed it to the young soldier. Higgins hesitated, staring at MacAngus with disbelief. Lightly, he moistened his thin lips.

'I . . . I can't take this,' he muttered.

'Of course ye can. I've been carrying it around for damn near twenty years. High time I got along without it for a bit. Man can't spend his entire life relying on magic charms.'

Higgins accepted the bullet eagerly, rolling it in the palm of his hand. MacAngus smiled as he watched the tension drain from the boy's eyes. It was something a man got used to, that sense of his own mortality. He learned to live with it, and recognised it freely in other people. And yet, when you came right down to it, acknowledging its existence solved nothing. Better to turn the eyes inward where a man couldn't see the truth.

He finished his coffee and pushed the mug in the sand alongside the others.

'Reckon I'll turn in,' he said. 'It's been a long day and ma bones are no as young as they used to be.'

Higgins smiled up at him as MacAngus rose to his feet. 'Thanks, sarge,' he whispered softly, and MacAngus nodded. 'You hold on to that bullet till I ask for it back,' he said. 'Nothing can harm you as long as you're carrying it in your britches.'

He felt tired as he strolled back to his tent, his body moving lethargically as if the hard day's ride had loosened the joints inside their sockets. He was thinking about Higgins, wondering if in the fullness of time the boy would overcome his fear, when he glimpsed, waiting outside his bivouac door, Sergeant Blakey of C Troop. Blakey was a big man with a permanent shine to his cheeks. He was not a particular friend of MacAngus's, and though they were on amicable terms, their relationship was principally a working one. MacAngus was surprised to find him there.

'Blakey,' he grunted, 'I thought ye were up in Cairo.'

'Came in on the evening train,' Blakey told him with a faint smile.

MacAngus picked up a tin dish, walked to the line of water *guerbas* and filled it to the brim. The cool night air bathed his face and throat, and he felt the little droplets of moisture splashing across his wrists. 'How did your leave go?' he asked over his shoulder.

'Vigorous, as usual,' Blakey said. 'Madame Hortense sends her love.'

'My God, she still in business?'

MacAngus placed the dish on a camp table and wearily stripped off his shirt. Blakey had brought trouble, he could tell. The man was hesitant, wary, wondering how to phrase what was on his mind.

'There's something I want to talk to you about, Mac,' Blakey muttered.

'Aye?'

'There was someone else in Cairo, waiting for that train. Man named Lewis.'

MacAngus leaned forward and splashed water over his face and neck. The name meant nothing to him, but then names seldom did.

'Said he worked for Scotland Yard.'

MacAngus's great head swung upward, peering at Blakey through the darkness. Water dripped from his nose and chin.

'He was looking for you, Mac. Had a photograph, warrant, everything.'

MacAngus stood rigid for a moment, then without a word he turned, still dripping, and plucked a towel from the guy-rope.

He pummelled himself vigorously, rubbing the coarse cloth over his short cropped hair.

'He said the charge was murder,' Blakey added gently.

MacAngus went on towelling, the muscles on his arms rippling in the firelight, and watching him, Blakey looked uncertain. 'Just thought I'd let you know,' he said, 'I told him nothing and he'll get nothing from the army either. But it might be a good idea to make yourself scarce for a few days. Keep out of the way until the bastard quits snooping around. A word to the wise, you understand.'

MacAngus stared at Blakey calmly, no expression on his face. 'Thanks, Walt,' he said, 'I appreciate that.'

Blakey nodded, and still looking uneasy shuffled away through the darkness. For a long time after he had gone, MacAngus stood looking after him. Only when the cool night air chilled his naked flesh did he pick up his shirt and move inside the tent.

'At ease,' Colonel Guthrie ordered.

Coffey relaxed.

'I suppose you're wondering why I sent for you?'

'Yes, sir.'

The colonel was sitting at his desk, sipping a mug of steaming tea. Beside him stood Lieutenant Driscoll, still wearing his Arab robes. Guthrie was a barrel-chested man with heavy jowls, greying hair and brown blotches on his cheeks formed by constant exposure to the wind and sun. He had joined the Egyptian army in 1887 after serving with the British in the Afghan war, and had commanded the 11th Sudanese at Gemaizeh, Toski and Afafit. His rare gift for handling troops of different nationalities, and his reputation for coolness under fire had made him a celebrity in Kitchener's army.

'Dined yet?' he asked.

'No, sir,' Coffey said.

Guthrie took a spare mug from the tray and, filling it to the brim, pushed it toward Coffey across the desk top. 'This damned heat wears a man down,' Guthrie complained. 'At least in India you could escape into the mountains. Here, it's like a hot barber's towel, night and morning. Leave this wilderness to the savages, I say. They don't know any better.'

He reached up and undid the collar of his tunic, breathing gratefully as he massaged his throat with his fingertips. Then he indicated the man standing beside him. 'I believe you've already met Lieutenant Driscoll?'

Coffey nodded to Driscoll who grinned back, his eyes glittering fiercely above the hooked Arab nose.

'I've heard about your little escapade tonight,' the colonel said.

'Yes, sir.'

'Impetuous,' Guthrie continued tonelessly, as if disobeying orders was an irritation he had come to expect from his junior officers. 'As far as you were concerned, Lieutenant Driscoll was an enemy Dervish who'd fallen out with his own people. You had absolutely no right to interfere, no right at all.'

'No, sir.'

The colonel rose to his feet and crossed the tent to where a jug of water stood on a table by the door. He pulled down a towel which was hanging from a roof rail, soaked it thoroughly in the liquid, then laid it across the back of his neck. His eyes closed as the cool moisture trickled down his spine.

'God Almighty,' he hissed, 'I'll never get used to this climate.'

Coffey watched him in silence. He scarely knew the colonel, beyond the occasional exchange during dining-in nights at the mess, but he'd heard stories about the man, numerous stories; Guthrie's blandness was by all accounts a front – he could be ruthless when he wanted to, cold, resolute, even cruel – but as if it were an essential part of the ethics, he never allowed his feelings to show.

Guthrie ran the towel over his face then tossed it into a corner and strolled back to his desk. 'Under normal circumstances,' he admitted, 'I'd have your hide for what you did tonight, but as it happens I'm both relieved and grateful. You did us a considerable service. Lieutenant Driscoll is not a man we'd care to lose.'

Tiny blobs of moisture trickled down the colonel's face, gathering on the end of his nose; he flicked them absently away.

57

'You were a farmer in civilian life, weren't you, Lieutenant Coffey?'

'Yes, sir.'

The English Lake District. Wordsworth's country. I knew it well. Spent my honeymoon there. My wife is a great walker, you know. We did them all, the three-thousand footers, Scafell, Gable, Skiddaw. I remember those mountain streams, how green and cool they were.'

Coffey didn't answer. He had been in the middle of scribbling out his daily report when the sentry had appeared, summoning him to the colonel's presence. He wasn't used to being called to the camp comander's quarters at such a late hour, particularly at the end of a long patrol, and the order had unsettled him.

Colonel Guthrie examined his desktop, brushing flies from his blotting pad.

'Lieutenant Driscoll has brought me a piece of disquieting information,' he said, 'disquieting because I am unable to act upon it in an official sense. At the same time, in the name of humanity I feel equally unable to ignore it.'

Coffey listened to the roaring of the hurricane lamps and waited for the colonel to continue. A slight breeze ruffled the tentwalls. He heard the sound of soldiers marching by outside; their sergeant's voice rose on the air, harsh and discordant.

'Come over here,' Guthrie grunted, 'I want you to look at something.'

Coffey followed the colonel to the back of the tent where he took out a large wall map and hung it from one of the ridge poles. 'Recognise this?' he asked.

'Looks like an outline of the Nile.'

'Correct. But with one small difference. This isn't the Nile as it stands today, but as it appeared thirteen years ago, before the fall of Khartoum. When the Dervish armies laid siege to the city, they swept across the Nubian Desert occupying all the towns and villages along the riverbank. One of those towns was El Serir, situated just below Khegga.' Guthrie's finger stabbed at the chart.

'Most of the inhabitants were slaughtered in the initial holocaust,' he said. 'The lucky ones were sold into slavery.'

58

'I know what happened at El Serir, colonel,' Coffey said. 'The events were well documented at the time.'

'Indeed they were, lieutenant, but the full story was never told in the British press. A number of Europeans were taken prisoner, for example, but to avoid distress to their relatives, they were listed as having been killed. Sometimes it's necessary to bend the truth a little for compassion's sake.'

'What happened to them, sir?'

'Dead, happily. Their sufferings are over. They were taken to Hamira, to the prison fortress there. I don't know what you've heard about Hamira, lieutenant, but it's understood to be a Dervish hellhole. The captives were kept in a small communal cell with the barest sanitary arrangements. Their clothes swarmed with vermin. They seldom saw the light of day. According to reliable witnesses, the heat and stench of perspiring bodies was so intense that someone died every night. It's hardly surprising that most of the Europeans succumbed during their first year of captivity.'

Coffey caught the inference. 'Most?' he echoed softly. 'Not "all"?'

'Not quite all. Among them was a British missionary, Charlton Routledge, and his daughter Victoria. According to Lieutenant Driscoll here, they appear to be very much alive.'

Driscoll peered at Coffey with his crazy grin. 'I talked to a Dervish who saw them at Hamira only last month,' he said. 'The old man was released from the prison eight years ago. Now he spends his time helping the local craftsmen at the carpentry store.'

'And the girl?'

'Slave, naturally. That's the Dervish way.'

'Can you imagine it?' the colonel growled softly. 'The girl was little more than a child when she was taken. Today she's a grown woman. She's spent thirteen years of her life in the hands of barbaric savages.'

Horses snickered in the night, and far off, like the distant wail of a stricken animal, Coffey heard the whistle of a train. The colonel sat down at his desk and, leaning forward, rubbed his eyes with his fingertips. 'I have a daughter Miss

59

Routledge's age,' he explained. 'It gives me a feeling of personal commitment.'

'Commitment, sir?' Coffey whispered, feeling his senses quicken.

The colonel studied him thoughtfully. 'Strictly speaking, I have no right to interfere at all. Hamira lies to the west, 140 miles across the desert. The British advance must continue south down the Nile to Omdurman and Khartoum. There is no hope of the Routledges being rescued for some considerable time, unless . . .'

His voice trailed away. The clinking of rifles reached them from the tentflap as the sentries changed guard.

'Unless we send in a flying column with the specific intention of bringing them out,' Coffey said.

Guthrie nodded. 'It would be a mission of mercy, lieutenant. Dangerous in the extreme. It would mean not only crossing the Baiyuda Desert, but moving through country crawling with the enemy. I've no doubt you've heard lurid stories of what happens to men who are taken prisoner by the Dervishes.'

Coffey felt tension rising inside him. 'With respect, sir, I understand clearly your concern for both the lady and her father, but it's one thing to send a reconnaissance patrol along the area covered by our railroad, and quite another to venture through hostile territory without support troops. We wouldn't survive a day.'

'I agree,' Colonel Guthrie admitted, 'if we attempted to send a column across that desert, it would be cut to pieces. But Lieutenant Driscoll here has suggested an interesting alternative.'

Driscoll moved in front of the hurricane lamps, the outline of his chest and hips plainly visible through his coarse, loose-fitting robes.

'Instead of taking an entire troop, we go ourselves,' he explained, smiling. 'Three men, four at the outside, dressed as Tuareg tribesmen. The Tuareg belong to the Kel Ahaggar, more than a thousand miles across the Sahara. They have a tradition of covering their faces, so if we run into Dervish cavalry we'll be nicely disguised. Also, the Tuareg speak a

60

language virtually unknown in the Sudan, which means that if we get questioned by Dervish patrols, their suspicions won't be aroused if we fail to understand.'

There was an air of madness in Driscoll, it surrounded the man like a living force. Partly, it came from the wolfish grin, but there was something else, an element of wildness, of reckless irresponsibility, that filled Coffey with a feeling of deep unease. He sensed the colonel's eyes upon him.

'I know what you're thinking, lieutenant. It's a harebrained scheme, with little chance of success at the end of it. Even if you did manage to run the gauntlet across the desert, you'd still be faced with the problem of springing Miss Routledge and her father from under the Dervish noses and spiriting them back to safety. I couldn't blame you if you decided to refuse.'

He hesitated and looked down at his hands. 'I also know the problems you've been facing since your arrival here,' he added softly.

'Problems, sir?'

'Your finances. You can't imagine you've kept them secret, surely?'

Coffey swallowed, feeling the colour mounting in his cheeks. 'I've always paid my debts, sir,' he answered stiffly.

'Of course you have. That's not what I'm getting at. The point is, I've always regarded you as one of the most promising officers in the regiment. Unfortunately, because of the curious structure of the military world, it has not been possible to acknowledge that fact. The truth is, Lieutenant Coffey, you are considered by your superiors as a rather dubious prospect. It has nothing to do with your ability. It is simply the feeling they have, rightly or wrongly, that you belong to an inferior species. In other words, you are not a gentleman.'

Coffey's cheeks were scarlet now, but mingled with the embarrassment was an element of anger. Guthrie sighed. 'I didn't make the rules, lieutenant. The British army has existed for more than a thousand years on a foundation of privilege and inequality. I want to help you in every way I can, but you must understand that I am bound by the system too. On the other hand, should you become involved in, shall we say, an

61

undertaking of an audacious nature, one which may save the lives of innocent civilians and perhaps even attract the attention of the world press, then any shortcomings you may suffer in the financial sense would, I am sure, appear unimportant by comparison.'

Guthrie paused, pursing his lips as he studied Coffey coolly in the lamplight. A fly settled on his cheek but he ignored it stoically as if its presence was too trifling to be acknowledged at such a critical moment.

'What I am saying, Lieutenant Coffey,' he added softly, 'is that some kind of personal success . . . a spectacular success . . . would make it much easier for me to recognise your true value in this regiment.'

Coffey struggled to keep his face impassive. He was being manipulated and he knew it. But he could see no way of withdrawing gracefully.

The colonel looked down at his desk and then at the ground. 'Lieutenant Driscoll has proposed a strike force of three of four mounted men to bring the Routledges back,' he announced. 'He's asked for you to take command. You appear to have made quite an impression on him after that little affair with the fuzzy-wuzzies. Naturally I can't order such a thing. It's above and beyond your role as an oficer with the Westmorlands. All I can say is, please consider the plight of this unfortunate young woman and her father. The final decision of course is up to you.'

Coffey swallowed. Almost in a dream he heard his voice whisper: 'I . . . I'd like to give it a try, sir.'

Colonel Guthrie nodded. 'Thank you, lieutenant. I never doubted it for a moment. The intention is to depart tomorrow evening on the gunboat *Zafir*. It will transport you upriver behind the enemy lines. From there you will cross the desert to Hamira and effect the rescue of the Routledges by whatever means are necessary. Lieutenant Driscoll here will ride as guide and interpreter. Let him do the talking. He knows the enemy and the way they think. If you're intercepted, he'll explain that you're Tuareg warriors travelling home from Mecca and ask the Khalifa, son of God the Prophet, messenger of the religious and scourge of the Infidel, to grant you safe passage across his lands. In addition I'm giving you Sergeant MacAngus and Second Lieutenant Benson.'

Coffey felt something jolt in his chest. 'Benson?' he echoed thinly.

Benson was a young officer who had arrived at the railhead fresh from Sandhurst barely six weeks earlier. He represented everything Coffey hated about the military class-system: privilege, snobbery, arrogance, disdain. He had been quick to sense Coffey's lowly beginnings and quicker still to take advantage of them, taunting Coffey mercilessly until at last Coffey had taken him to the back of the railhead and thrashed him to a standstill, splitting his cheek with a vicious right hook that had laid Benson cold. Since then, Benson had stopped his sneering, but there was no mistaking his dislike or his hostility.

'With respect, sir,' Coffey declared in a clear voice, 'I'd prefer someone else if it's at all possible.'

Guthrie frowned. 'I can't afford anyone else, lieutenant. Benson is expendable because of his lack of experience. It's a question of economics, as simple as that.'

'You don't understand, colonel. Lieutenant Benson and I have certain . . . differences.'

Guthrie pursed his lips. He belonged to the old school. Duty was everything. A man played his part, whatever the circumstances.

'I can't adapt strategies to fit the rivalries of my junior officers, lieutenant,' he declared coldly. 'It's a war we're fighting. You'll make a point of getting on together for as long as it's necessary. That's what you're here for.'

'Yes, sir,' Coffey whispered.

'Our advance forces are expected to reach Ashidi by noon tomorrow. When that happens, I shall dispatch two troops of Sudanese cavalry to wait for you at the old ruined fortress of Malawa, eighty miles south-west of Atbara. They'll have fresh horses, water and supplies. If once you're clear of Hamira you can reach Fort Malawa, your troubles will be over. Any questions?'

Coffey shook his head and the colonel, as if he knew the madness of what he was asking, looked relieved. 'Good,' he said.

Leaning down, he opened a drawer, took out a whisky bottle and three glasses, and placed them side by side on the desktop. 'Since we're officers serving in the field, I realise this is against regulations,' he said, 'but in the circumstances, I think it's high time we all had a drink.'

They set out on the evening of 11 July on board the gunboat *Zafir,* one of the three sternwheelers which now formed the British and Egyptian war fleet. Three more, the *Malik, Sultan* and *Sheik*, were waiting upriver for their sections to be put together against the high Nile.

The gunboat crews were regarded as the swashbucklers of the British troops, for while the rest of the army made its slow tortuous advance southward, the river craft were already foraging more than a hundred miles behind enemy lines, steaming cheekily under the noses of the Dervish riflemen to blast their flimsy nuggar boats out of existence.

It was nearly midnight when the *Zafir* captain brought his craft alongside the western bank and the sailors waded ashore, tying her forward and aft to stunted acacia trees. The *Zafir* had been constructed in tiers, more like a building than a warship, and with its shallow draught (even fully loaded it drew only two feet of water) and lofty gun platforms, it could cover the highest banks even at the river's lowest level.

Standing on the bridge with the gunboat's captain, Commander Keppel, Coffey peered down at the shattered wreck of an Arab dahabeeyah which had run inelegantly aground. Its wooden hull was splintered and torn, and the remains of its crew lay lifeless and bloody across its battered deck. The bodies were still fresh, Coffey observed, and several had their insides taken out, either by shrapnel or desert scavengers. Coffey counted eight bodies on the craft itself and a ninth floating face-down in the water, entrails eddying with the current like the tendrils of a macabre sea anemone.

Commander Keppel followed Coffey's gaze. 'I see you've spotted our friends down there,' he said. 'Not a pleasant sight, are they? We had a little difference of opinion early this morning. A test of wills, you might say. They insisted on trying to blow us out of the water. I had to chastise them for such impertinence.'

Coffey studied the stricken dahabeeyah. In its stern he spotted an ancient cannon, so old its metal was smooth and scarred by centuries of handling. By its side stood a barrel caulked with tar. Gunpowder, Coffey thought wonderingly. It was like a relic from a different age.

'Against your Maxims, those poor bastards wouldn't stand a chance,' he whispered.

'Quite right, lieutenant. You've just witnessed one of the tragedies of this war. The enemy are fighting the way they fought against the Crusaders six centuries ago. They're using the same weapons, the same antiquated cannonry. We, on the other hand, have all the aids of modern science at our disposal. Hardly an equitable conflict, is it? Still, once you leave the safety of the *Zafir* you and the Dervishes will be more or less on equal terms. I have a sneaky feeling you'll be ready to sell your soul for an efficient Maxim then.'

Coffey stared at him. The commander's expression was bland, even benign, but Coffey noted the edge in the man's voice and knew he had touched on a sensitive nerve.

Like the others, Coffey was dressed in loose baggy trousers acquired from the local Greek merchants, a white gown, blue jelleba and black cotton headgear which covered almost his entire face. Only the eyes remained exposed. He felt ludicrously theatrical in such an unorthodox outfit as he stood watching the camels being unloaded, roaring in protest as the Egyptian troops dragged them down the flimsy gangplank and began to strap saddles to their unwieldy backs.

'Not exactly pretty brutes, are they?' Commander Keppel said, regarding the animals with an expression of distaste.

Lieutenant Driscoll, overhearing Keppel's remark, paused on the gangplank, chuckling. 'I had the troopers plaster them with mud,' he explained. 'Trouble with the Camel Corps is, they groom their mounts every day. Now a clean well-groomed camel is an immediate giveaway to shrewd-eyed Dervish. The natives like to keep their animals coated with dirt to prevent them getting colds at night.'

'Camels don't get colds,' Coffey echoed unbelievingly.

'Oh yes they do. They're a lot frailer than you realise. Try ill-using your beast and he'll lie down and die on you without warning. He can stand heat, drought, flies and duststorms, but he has to be cosseted in between.'

Coffey shook his head as he followed Driscoll gingerly down the gangplank to the shoreline. He was putting the finishing touches to his saddle equipment when Lieutenant Benson, dressed similarly in Tuareg costume, moved from the paddleboat to join them. Benson was a slim young man with a cold aristocratic face. His skin was pale, his eyes hard, and there was a livid scar on his cheek where Coffey's fist had opened up the flesh during their fight at the railhead.

Coffey studied him coolly. He felt uncomfortable having Lieutenant Benson along and regretted Colonel Guthrie's stubborn refusal to listen to reason. Benson for his part seemed equally dismayed at the prospect of Coffey's company, and the scar on his cheek flushed visibly as he stared through the darkness with undisguised distaste. His teeth, knocked crooked by a glancing blow from Coffey's elbow, now parted into a V-shaped aperture at the front.

'This your idea?' he demanded softly.

'What?'

'This whole crazy escapade?'

'As a matter of fact it's not. If you want somebody to blame, try Lieutenant Driscoll.'

Driscoll grinned at them wildly, his eyes flashing in the shadows. Benson's face remained cold. 'It wasn't Driscoll who asked for me,' he stated.

Coffey looked at him. 'No I suppose it wasn't.'

'You know damn well I'm a stranger here. I've no experience of the desert.'

Suddenly Coffey understood. It wasn't the thought of riding with Coffey that Benson objected to. It was the mission itself. Well, Coffey couldn't blame him for that. 'You'll learn,' he said gently.

'Do you take me for an imbecile? I know damned well what you're doing.'

Coffey frowned. 'What are you talking about, Benson?'

'You're dragging me into that emptiness so I'll be helpless and alone. You're trying to kill me.'

Coffey straightened from his camel. He stared at Benson

66

for a long moment, then reaching out, he grabbed the front of Benson's robes, pulling him close.

'Listen, you stupid bastard,' he said in a mild voice, 'I didn't ask for you to go on this jaunt. If you want to know the truth, I advised against it but the colonel overruled me. As a matter of fact, I didn't want to go myself. But since we have to, and since our survival for the next days will depend to a large degree upon each other, I suggest you put aside your feelings toward me and get your stupid backside into that camel saddle.'

Balefully, Benson glared at him, then jerking his camel into a crouch, he carefully mounted. The Southern Cross hung in a faultless sky as the four men set off away from the shoreline. Cicadas screamed from the grass-tufts and the air felt soft against their faces. They could see little beyond the few bare feet on which they rode, for the night had drained the density from the air so that hollows and fissures lay like simple patterns on a flat unending landscape.

Commander Keppel stood on the *Zafir*'s bridge, watching them fade into the darkness.

'Think they'll pull it off, sir?' his aide asked.

Keppel sighed and shook his head. 'Not a chance,' he said softly. 'Once beyond the river they'll be in a land as arid as the surface of the moon. They'll be alone and beyond the reach of military assistance, surrounded by sixty thousand hostiles. It's just a bloody sad waste of four good men.'

FIVE

The *reg* fell in a series of softly undulating slopes, bordered to the east by rolling foothills which looked almost blue in the afternoon haze. Coffey lay among the rocks, training his field glasses on the waterhole below. He could pick out only dimly the crude timbered pulley-structure that straddled the desert well, and by its side the rough outlines of two thorn *zarebas* – constructed, he supposed, for defensive purposes. Beyond them, he spotted the black hummocks of nomad tents, and the miniscule figures of men moving about.

He handed the field glasses to Lieutenant Driscoll who swivelled the lens into focus, studying the scene in silence for a moment. For three days they had moved steadily westward, encountering occasional straggling bands of Dervishes, avoiding them when they could, bluffing it out with Driscoll doing the talking when they couldn't. Now their water *guerbas* were running low and Coffey knew that if they didn't replenish them soon, they could run the risk of major dehydration. Six pints per day per man was the statutory rule. Without it he lost his wits, became disorientated. Deprive him long enough and he fell down and died. They had to get liquid. But the only source in more than fifty miles was now surrounded by at least thirty hostiles.

'Any idea who they might be?' he asked Driscoll.

The Englishman shrugged as he handed the field glasses to Lieutenant Benson.

'Far as I can tell, looks like a slave caravan on its way north from Central Africa.'

'Think they'll move on if we hang about long enough?'

'Hard to say. If they've come up from the bush country the men will be tired. They could decide to rest for several days.'

Coffey swore. He had been afraid of that. There was something disturbingly settled about the camp below. 'We must have water,' he declared.

Driscoll rubbed his nose. After thirty hours in the desert his veiled mask and *gandoura* were coated with orange dust, his eyes rimmed red from the sun.

'Why don't we ride in and take our chances?' he suggested.

'There must be thirty warriors around that waterhole.'

'True. But they have no reason to attack us. We're a party of Tuareg travelling west to our homeland. You're forgetting desert hospitality.'

Coffey was silent for a moment. Until now they had been lucky. The few enemy bands they had encountered had been easily won over by Driscoll's persuasive tongue. But Coffey wondered how much of that persuasion had depended on a glimpse of the Martini rifles he and his men were carrying. Down there, rifles or not, they would be hopelessly outnumbered.

'Look,' Driscoll said, 'no one's suggesting we take on the bastards in a stand-up fight. We'll bluff it out, the way we've been doing. If those tribesmen have slaves with them, they'll not run the risk of damaging valuable property by starting up a shooting match. Let me do the talking.'

Coffey nodded dubiously. The sight of the occupied waterhole depressed him for some reason and he felt his optimism fading into a sense of dark premonition. Nerves, he thought. He'd been in the desert too long. Long days, long nights. The constant worry of capture or discovery, they wore a man down. Still, they had to have water and Driscoll's suggestion seemed the only sensible one.

'We'll give it a try,' he agreed, 'but be ready to move like hell if those bastards turn unfriendly. We won't stand a chance down there once they've got us surrounded.'

They mounted and rode in slowly, making – Coffey knew – quite a sight against the skyline, their blue robes and heavy face cowls fluttering in the wind, their saddle ornaments reflecting the desert sunlight, their rifles resting casually across their thighs. Between the cluster of nomadic tents he could see the pale columns of smoke from the cooking fires; enamel pots dangled from wooden trestles and bundles of food hung in the branches of the few spindly trees out of reach of marauding scavengers. At the well, a group of young warriors were busy drawing water, pouring it into huge earthenware jars. In front of the tents, turbanned elders sat watching their approach through timeless implacable eyes.

Drawing closer, Coffey saw for the first time the reason for the thorn *zarebas*. They had been constructed not for defensive purposes, he realised, but to serve as makeshift prison stockades, for, crouched inside, strapped by their necks to heavy wood logs, were thirty or forty black men and women. Their hands and feet had been tied with leather thongs and their eyes displayed the hopeless air of livestock in a cattle pen. Because of the heavy trunks which linked them all together, it was impossible for one to move without causing pain and discomfort to the others, and Coffey would well imagine the agonised misery of squatting for long hours in the blistering sun. Until this moment he had thought little about the Sudanese practice of slavery; now, witnessing with his own eyes the bowed heads, the slack lips, the brown skins caked with dust - marked in places with scarlet weals where the slavers, in their hurry to move northward, had whipped the column to keep it moving - he felt a sudden surge of fury.

Beyond the waterhole the ground flattened into a pebbly plain and here, tied to a wooden stake sunk deep into the ground, Coffey spotted another negro, this one clearly a troublemaker, for a tall sapling had been bent over and its tip strapped to the offender's skull. Now, his muscles and sinews were desperately straining as he strove to withstand the ferocious pressure tearing at his neck. Sweat streamed down his massive body and his features screwed into a mask of agonised concentration.

Coffey felt his stomach quiver. It was clear that as soon as the victim's strength gave out, the remorseless tug of the sapling would steadily intensify until by morning, or noon tomorrow at the latest, it would spring upright, ripping his head from his shoulders.

70

Lieutenant Benson nudged his camel alongside. 'Look at that poor devil,' he whispered. 'My God, have you ever seen such barbarism?'

Coffey growled an assent. He jerked his camel to a crouch and warily dismounted, struggling to quell the anger bubbling inside him. The slavers were clearly men who placed little value on human life or human suffering, but he would have to check his feelings – the situation was delicate enough as it was, without any futile tantrums on his part.

'They'll probably offer us tea,' Driscoll explained. 'If they do, drink it quickly and lick your lips to show that it's appreciated. If they offer four rounds, that means it's not convenient for us to stay and we'll have to move on as soon as we've filled up the water skins. If, on the other hand, they offer us three rounds and no more, that means they'd like us to remain a while as their guests. It would be churlish to refuse.'

Coffey nodded and Driscoll, after tying his animal to a clump of camel thorn, crossed the compound toward the watching tribesmen. There was an air of peace and tranquillity in the scene that seemed strangely unreal. The warriors were affecting casual disinterest in their arrival as if desert meetings like this were commonplace, but Coffey noticed that none of them strayed far from their weapons.

Driscoll reached the elders and after a short consultation called Coffey and Benson over. Coffey felt nervous, aware that he was in the presence of men capable of the most appalling savagery, yet Driscoll seemed unperturbed as he squatted cross-legged on the palm-leaf mats, prattling away with the air of a man who liked nothing better than a chance to pass the time of day engaged in idle chit-chat.

The tea was served in tiny glasses, very sweet and minty. Coffey found it not to his taste, but, remembering Driscoll's instructions, he gulped it down appreciatively, struggling to keep his face cowl in place. The glasses were filled three times and no more. A good sign.

'We're in luck,' Driscoll whispered. 'These are people of Dawasir. They've been south, replenishing their slave complement. They're a bit out of touch, and anxious for news of the war against the Infidel. They've invited us to stay the night.

71

They say we can have the caravanserai – that's the stone shelter beyond the *zaribas*.'

Coffey glanced at the caravanserai, a flat-roofed pillbox of a building constructed as a shelter for travellers camping by the waterhole.

'You trust them?' he asked.

'Not entirely. But it would be an insult if we attempted to leave. Once inside those walls we should be reasonably secure. Get the *guerbas* filled and I'll keep them talking while you see to the defences.'

The groans of the negro tied beyond the waterhole rose on the air in a bizarre symphony.

'What about him?' Coffey asked.

Driscoll frowned behind his face mask. 'Sorry old boy, I don't quite follow.'

'We can't just sit here and let them torture the poor bastard to death.'

'Frankly, I can't see that it's any of our business. The man doesn't belong to us. He's the Dawasirs' property.'

'He's a human being, for Christ's sake.'

Driscoll glanced at the negro and gently scratched his beard. 'Well, that's true,' he admitted, 'but at the moment I'm afraid he's in imminent danger of losing his head.'

'Don't make futile jokes.'

Driscoll's eyes flickered. 'You're not seriously suggesting, lieutenant, that we interfere in this matter of Dawasir justice?'

'Can't we buy him?' Coffey asked.

'With what, old boy? We need every damned thing we've got. The camels, the rifles. We're not exactly overloaded.'

'Persuade them then.'

'I'm afraid that won't be easy.'

'You can try, dammit.'

Driscoll sighed. Shifting back on his haunches, he made a great show of dusting the front of his robes. 'Look here, squire,' he said reasonably, 'I seem to have convinced our hosts here that we are indeed who we say we are. But if I start arguing about the way they treat their slaves, they're bound to turn suspicious. After all, the Tuareg are noted slavers too.'

Coffey felt the resolution strengthening inside him; it was

ill-advised, he knew, reckless in the extreme, but he had to do something, for God's sake.

'We can't leave him, Driscoll. We can't just turn our backs and ride out of here, pretending it isn't happening. When we go, we're taking him with us.'

'Are you mad?' Lieutenant Benson hissed, his eyes bulging above the line of his face mask. 'The man is dying, can't you see that? By daylight his head will be ripped from his shoulders. It's ghoulish and it's cruel but it has nothing to do with us. We're here for one purpose only, to rescue Miss Routledge and her father. Bring that black along and you'll endanger not only our lives, but theirs as well.'

Coffey was silent. He knew Benson was right. His job was to replenish the *guerbas* and press on as swiftly as possible. But something inside him rebelled at the thought of leaving the black man to such a slow hideous death.

'Benson,' he said, 'we keep telling ourselves that the main purpose behind this war is to try and abolish slavery. How can we help the Routledges and ignore the sufferings of this poor devil.'

Benson turned away disgusted, making a hissing sound inside his face cowl. Coffey could sense his antagonism through the rigid set of his shoulders.

By contrast, Driscoll's wild eyes were glittering with amusement. 'This really is highly irregular, old fellow.'

'I'm aware of that,' Coffey grunted.

'You realise, of course, that we're hopelessly outnumbered?'

Coffey didn't answer. He felt his anger slowly strengthen. It was strange anger, directed more at himself than at the Dawasir, for he knew in his heart that what he was proposing was foolishness.

Driscoll chuckled. 'Not to worry,' he said. 'We do have one thing in our favour.'

'What's that?'

'Smell the air. Dust storm. I can sniff them ten miles away. It's heading in this direction.'

'You're sure?'

'No question, squire. It'll be here in an hour at the latest.'

73

Coffey felt hope surge in his chest. 'We'll wait then.'

Driscoll laughed softly, his mad eyes dancing. 'That's right,' he said, 'we'll sit tight till the storm breaks, then while the Dawasir shelter inside their tents, we'll cut loose your friend and bolt like buggery out of here.'

Night came swiftly to the desert. One minute the land was caught in the flush of the setting sun, the next the sky was dark and full of stars. Coffey sat in the caravanserai peering out through the narow window holes waiting for the dust storm to strike.

He felt tense and apprehensive. He had taken a decision he knew to be unwise. They were both right, Benson and Driscoll; he had deviated from his orders. If anything went wrong, if they failed to rescue the black man or if, for some reason, they ended up dead or as prisoners of the Dawasir, the responsibility would be totally his. It was an awesome prospect to consider, but it made little difference. There were other bonds, other claims which went beyond the realms of the British army. He had to live with himself when all this was over. There was no other way.

The winds came gently at first, stirring the palm trees, lifting the sand in circular spirals of spindrift which whirled across the ground like miniature tornadoes. There was a different feel to the air, a sense of change, of movement. He watched the tribesmen shading their eyes against the lifting dust, peering into the haze obsuring the skyline. Within twenty minutes the wind was stampeding across the desert like a living force, covering the entire campsite with a thick orange cloud. The Dawasir protected their heads with their jibbah hoods and crouched motionless on the ground, looking like lumps of inanimate stone.

Clutching his rifle, Coffey sat studying the men facing him. Outside, the storm whipped its dust clouds against the caravanserai wall. 'Everyone clear about what they're doing?' he demanded.

They nodded silently, their eyes expressionless behind the dark face masks.

'Lieutenants Benson and Driscoll will head straight for the

camels. Sergant MacAngus and I will take care of the prisoner. Avoid trouble if you can, deal with it swiftly if you can't. Above all, do not fire your rifles.'

He paused to see what effect his words had had. They stared back at him impassively, waiting for the order. He felt a fleeting tremor of anxiety but dismissed it at once. It was pointless delaying any longer. He had made his decision, he would have to see it through. 'Right, let's go,' he snapped.

Sergeant MacAngus moved first, ducking beneath the door rim, battling his way into the open. His robes whipped out behind him as he staggered momentarily, knocked off-balance by the incredible force of the blast. Then he recovered and stumbled headlong into the thick orange fog.

Coffey followed, his heart thumping. The power of the wind seemed almost beyond belief; he could feel it pounding, eating, tearing, gouging, knocking the air from his lungs by the sheer intensity of its attack, shrieking and roaring about his ears as it ricocheted wildly off the caravanserai roof. The sand came from everywhere, there was simply no defence against it. It whipped in savagely, blinding his vision as he stumbled on in MacAngus's wake, squinting through the billowing shroud for a glimpse of the sergeant's fluttering *gandoura*. At moments, the fury of the bombardment forced Coffey to duck his head behind the crook of his shoulder. Even his face cloth gave no protection against the dirt driving into his cheeks; the harsh grains battered their way inside his clothing and stung his skin. It took away initiative, that constant pummelling, drained a man of his senses, replaced every feeling with an overriding sensation of discomfort and pain.

There was no sign of the Dawasir, thank God; they were probably huddled within the flimsy protection of their voluminous robes, waiting with the eternal patience of all desert creatures for the storm to pass. Even Coffey's fear was lessened by the intensity of the wind's onslaught, for nothing was real beyond the battering he was receiving. Ahead, the storm seemed to solidify, taking on form and substance, and as Coffey approached he discerned the outline of the unfortunate black man, his head and body completely furred by dust. MacAngus was slicing with his long curved sword at the rope holding the negro's skull. Coffey saw the line snap and the sapling spring free. A low moan of relief issued from the victim's lips, to be lost instantly in the thunder of the howling gale.

MacAngus moved swiftly, sawing with his blade, severing the thongs which bound the prisoner one by one. Free, the negro tried to rise, but collapsed instantly on the ground. He had been tied too long, his limbs had lost all feeling.

Coffey hooked his wrist under one armpit, MacAngus took the other, and together they half carried, half dragged the man toward the waiting camels. Coffey gripped his rifle in his free hand, staggering slightly as the wind caught him off-balance, ducking his head against the monstrous fusillade of dust-granules, his right arm trembling under the weight of the negro's body. For a moment he thought they were going to make it. He saw the camels grouped together in the storm. He saw Benson and Driscoll mounted and waiting. Then, like ghostly shrouds materialising before his disbelieving eyes, dark figures suddenly reared in his path, their bodies moulded against their robes by the buffeting blustering gale. The Dawasir, he thought wildly.

A man seized him by the arm, his fingers digging deep into the flesh. Letting go of the negro, Coffey turned and swung his rifle butt, the hard wooden stock streaking out in a feathery blur. Even above the thunder of the storm he heard the snap of bone as his blow broke the attacker's wrist.

Wildly, through the waves of dust, he glimpsed a figure leaping in toward him, robes whipping to and fro like a schooner sail. In the clouded air, Coffey caught the glint of a long curved sword as it swung down in a vicious arc, its blade aimed directly at his skull. Coffey blocked the attack with his rifle barrel, feeling the force of the blow rippling along his forearms, then, without pausing, he jerked up his knee, stabbing it hard into the tribesman's crotch. The man's cry was lost in the howling of the wind, but Coffey glimpsed his face, bearded and crusted with dust, twisting into a grimace of anguish as he doubled over clutching his genitals.

Coffey leapt forward, swinging the rifle, scattering his assailants with the sheer fury of his onslaught. A face swayed into his vision and he lashed out at it, seeing the man pitch to the ground with blood spurting from his nostrils. Someone seized him from behind, and Coffey drove the Martini butt down on a sandalled instep, then, twisting sideways, swung his elbow savagely into the man's abdomen.

Startled by Coffey's aggressiveness, the attackers fell back, pausing to re-compose themselves. Without hesitating for an instant, Coffey slithered desperately across the shifting ground, seeing the camels looming through the storm ahead, seeing MacAngus, his limbs working furiously, strapping the helpless negro to the shaggy spine of their baggage animal.

Coffey mounted his own beast at the run and for a moment almost tumbled over the other side, but Driscoll's hand gripped his shoulder, holding him firm. He turned once to check that MacAngus was ready, then with their robes streaming behind them they pounded frenziedly into the dustbound night.

Morning brought a tranquillity that surprised them all. The wind dropped and the air was still as death. Yet so intense had been the storm that the desert, instead of clearing, seemed to shimmer with a strange misty light.

They rode in silence, their robes coated with orange dust. Behind, Coffey could see more dust churning skyward in an ominous swirling column, drifting across the *reg* like distant smoke. He knew what it was. The Dawasir, riding in close pursuit. The suddenness of their escape had gained them a momentary advantage, but not for long. The enemy mounts were rested and fresh while their own were weary and worn by the long journey from the river. It was only a matter of time before they were overtaken.

A feeling of hopelessness and despair filled Coffey; it was not so much the imminence of capture which depressed him as the knowledge that if he hadn't been so pigheaded none of this would have happened. He had pushed their luck beyond reasonable limits and now it looked as if his impetuousness had backfired badly. He reined in his camel, calling a halt. Might as well see if it's been worth it, he thought. Pulling down his face cowl, he looked at MacAngus in the pale light of the early morning. Sweat carved little rivulets of moisture through the dust caking the sergeant's face.

'How is he?' Coffey demanded, nodding to the motionless figure strapped to the baggage camel trailing in MacAngus's wake.

MacAngus shook his head, his face sombre and grim, and Coffey felt alarm spreading through his body. Dammit, the man couldn't have died after all they had gone through. Without a word, he kicked his camel forward, reaching down to seize the negro's hair in his fingers. He jerked the head upwards, staring into a face caked with dust. An ugly sore seared the throat where the harsh rope had burned the skin. The eyes were opened, staring sightlessly at the sky. Coffey cursed under his breath. They had been too late. That last act of deliverance had ended the black man's life.

Letting the head fall, he took out his knife and carefully cut the bonds holding the man to the saddle. With a muffled thud, the corpse slid from its perch and collapsed to the ground in a small cloud of dust.

Lieutenant Benson glared at Coffey, hate and fury blazing in his small pale eyes. 'You bloody fool. I told you it was insane to help this man. We've risked everything, and for what?'

Coffey wheeled away without answering. It was senseless talking to Benson. He would never listen to reason.

Lieutenant Driscoll smiled at him sympathetically. 'I hate to say this, old fellow,' he muttered, 'but unless you do something drastic, I'm afraid those beggars will overtake us before lunchtime.'

Coffey's eyes narrowed as he studied the column of dust smearing the sky to their rear; caught by the wind, it drifted eastward, forming a hazy orange blur that hovered above the sand-dunes like wispy lace. Driscoll was right. It would be a miracle if their camels lasted even that long, the pace they were setting. Something had to be done to slow the Dawasir down, and since he couldn't do it himself, and since Driscoll was too important to their survival, and since Benson was inept and inexperienced, there was only one candidate left that Coffey could see. He looked at Sergeant MacAngus, feeling a momentary surge of guilt at the thought of what he was about to ask. MacAngus was more than Coffey's sergeant. He was also Coffey's friend.

'Mac,' Coffey said in a soft voice.

The sergeant stared at him, his eyes calm and composed.

'Somebody's got to draw them off.'

'Aye.'

MacAngus seemed unsurprised by Coffey's statement. Fumbling inside his robes, he stuck a battered cheroot between his lips and lit it carefully, holding on to his camel's back with his free hand.

'In Afghanistan,' he said in his slow drawling way, 'the natives used to play a game called Shu-shu Kairi. There's a move in Shu-shu Kairi where you think your opponent's going one way when really he's heading some place else. Now a man wi' his wits about him might lead them bastards a merry dance, I'm thinking.'

'Can you do it, sergeant?' Coffey demanded gruffly.

MacAngus stared back at the way they had come, his eyes slitted against the sun. He nodded without speaking.

'And afterwards?'

'Och, I'll catch ye up in my own good time, sir.'

'How will you find us?'

MacAngus chuckled. 'Lieutenant, I could find ye in a tubful of porridge wi' nowt but a spoon to dig wi'.'

Coffey watched unhappily as MacAngus dismounted and began to cut himself clumps of spiky camel thorn. The sergeant's features glistened with sweat as he hacked and tore at the obstinate roots, dragging them out of the scorched arid earth. When he was satisfied he had enough, he tied them into a bundle and fastened the bundle to his saddle, dragging the tangled vegetation behind his mount. He did everything with a sense of slow easy purpose which made Coffey want to throw up. He felt ashamed of himself, asking his sergeant to risk his neck in such a manner, but MacAngus's face remained expressionless as he remounted and turned to look at them.

'Ye'd better keep them animals steady, sir,' he ordered. 'Watch the dust, and when ye see them bastards take off after

79

me, move like the blazes out of here. I'll be along right after nightfall.'

He set off toward the east, dragging the ragged bundle behind him. Dust rose on the air, trailing in his wake in a churning twisting column. Watching him go, Coffey felt a choking sensation deep in his throat. If anything happened to MacAngus, he knew he would never forgive himself.

The next few minutes were anxious ones for all of them as Coffey studied the dust clouds through his field glasses, training them first in the direction of the pursuing Dawasir, then switching with a faint feeling of unease to the miniscule figure of Sergeant MacAngus vanishing steadily over the skyline. His nerves tightened as the seconds stretched and sweat broke out between his shoulderblades, trickling down his spine.

Still Coffey waited. Then with a sense of triumph and relief he watched the Dawasir dust-cloud swing to the east as the riders turned their mounts toward Sergeant MacAngus's decoy. 'They've taken the bait,' he hissed.

A murmur of excitement rose from Lieutenant Driscoll but Benson spat on the ground. 'You lucky bastard,' he whispered coldly. 'If there was any justice in this world, your head would be decorating a Dervish lance by now.'

Coffey looked at him in astonishment, the elation freezing in his throat. Lieutenant Benson was disappointed, he realised; he would have welcomed even the prospect of capture for the simple pleasure of seeing his enemy undone. The awareness unsettled Coffey. It offered a chilling indication of the extent of Benson's hate.

MacAngus rode hard through the long hours of morning and into the afternoon. He knew his camel was tired, and he knew too that a tired camel was a dangerous liability. They were not the sturdy denizens of the desert everyone believed. Camels were reliable as long as conditions were easy, but treat them bad and like as not they would drop dead at your feet. MacAngus couldn't afford that. He knew if the Dawasir caught him, they would never let him die peaceably. He had to maintain a lead, at least until he reached the mountains. He could see the mountains a long way off, sharp craggy peaks bursting out of the desert floor, and he steered toward them, following his course with the unerring instinct of a stag heading for water. Twice he paused to drink from his *guerba* and study the dust-clouds behind. His pursuers were gaining, no question; the distance shortened each time he looked but MacAngus did not feel alarmed – he had an inherent trust in his own judgement and this country was no different to the ragged wildernesses of Khyber and Afghanistan.

As he headed north-east, the terrain began to change in slow subtle ways. The flatness broke up, swelling into a series of dark brown humps etched against the sky. The wind blew fierce and surprisingly cool. Southward, MacAngus spotted the rolling sand-dunes of the Erg Tesnou. The landscape looked like a rumpled tablecloth with the sun's rays etching deep shadows along its feathery crests.

MacAngus did not resent Coffey sending him off alone. The facts were clear. Their camels, weary and dispirited, could never outride the fresh mounts of the Dawasir. Only one man could give them the respite they needed, and he was that man. Coffey knew. Coffey's instincts were sound. MacAngus liked Coffey. He saw in Coffey a creature much the same as himself, a man destined to struggle for his very existence, penniless and desperate.

But Coffey had one advantage MacAngus couldn't lay claim to. A clean slate. Coffey was not a wanted man.

Riding eastward a mile in front of the Dawasir slavers, MacAngus thought about the Scotland Yard detective searching for him among the expeditionary forces on the River Nile, and reflected on the night, fifteen years earlier, in the little Ayshire town of Kilbirnie, when he had taken on the Procurator's son in an alley behind the Gaiety dancehall. He couldn't even remember what the quarrel had been about, that was how ridiculous it had been. The fight had started fairly enough, the two of them sizing each other up, trading blows, kicks, insults, and then to MacAngus's surprise, the Procurator's boy had pulled out a knife. The end had been quick, brutal, sordid, and MacAngus had been running ever since. Sometimes he wondered if he would ever stop running. For a while the army had offered refuge, sanctuary, anonymity. Now it looked as if even that was coming to an end.

MacAngus's past was not something he dwelled on often, seeing in its memory the paths to which madness lay. He wanted to forget. God knew he had tried hard enough. But a man couldn't seal off, as he might seal a brandy flask, the unpalatable parts of his own experience, for every act he performed, every thought he entertained, contributed in some small way to his sum total as a human being. That was the bitter part of it, MacAngus thought, and he knew with a fatal certainty that the past and the present were bound together, that though a man might turn his back, seeking solace, seeking escape, his guilt was like an illness, regressed but not defeated; it would return at the moments he felt lowest, like the fear of impending death.

The idea depressed him, and for survival's sake he turned his mind elsewhere, making his brain go blank as he steered his camel eastward through the long afternoon until at last, when nightfall came, dowsing the incredible heat of the day, he had reached the first rugged slopes of the foothills.

He rested his animal, cutting loose the trailing bundle of camel thorn and, taking the *guerba* from the saddle-horn, drank copiously, saturating his body with liquid. He no longer felt any sense of danger, for he knew no man could match him in the mountains. He soaked his face cloth with water and rubbed it over the camel's nostrils, talking soothingly as he did so. The rocks gathered around him, their features merging in the heavy stillness of the desert night, their outlines framed against the stars, sheltering, comforting. He led his camel up the steep ragged slope until he found the spot he was looking for, a narrow ravine cluttered with spiky scrub. When he was satisfied the beast was suitably concealed, he groundhitched it to a boulder, leaving just enough line so it could reach the scattered clumps of vegetation if it needed to without wandering into the open.

Then he began to climb, bearing away from the draw, hearing the soft shuffle of the incoming riders and the almost indistinguishable murmur of voices on the cool night air. They were close. Maybe a hundred yards or so. The slope grew rougher, the outcrops more uneven, and he slowed his pace as he pressed on steadily upward. Small bushes grew among the rocks, catching at his feet, scratching his ankles; there was a sense of unreality to his flight, a feeling that only true substance was the harsh earth beneath his sandals, that the sweep of stars, the misty contours of the adjacent hills were simply an illusion. Deliberately, he showed himself in the moonlight, knowing how well the pale rays would pick up his blue *gandoura*. He heard the dull crack of a rifle somewhere to his left. The bastards had seen him. Good.

Crack – crack. More shots. MacAngus grinned behind his face-cloth as he danced across the twisting network of rocks. Damn fools were as excitable as children. He could hear them chattering away, barking at their camels to kneel and allow them to dismount.

The slope ended on a small plateau, wide enough for a cavalry squadron. MacAngus paused, looking back. He could see his pursuers scrambling up toward him, their pale robes gleaming faintly against the contours of the mountainside. He was breathing hard, his blood pounding rhythmically through his temples, savouring the excitement of the moment, feeling no sense of alarm, only a strange and indescribable elation as if never had he been so alive, never had his senses been so keen, so sharp, so vibrant.

The Dawasir were moving in an uneven huddle, wrestling their rifles and spears through the tortuous maze of boulders. At the foot of the slope, almost hidden by the darkness, their camels waited, guarded by a solitary figure crouching in the shadows, cradling a long-barrelled rifle in his arm.

Grinning savagely, MacAngus turned and swung across the plateau, making for the rocks above. The gradient was steeper here, the contours blending to form a series of fractured cliffs which sometimes blocked his way, sometimes crumbled one into the other. He found a narrow chimney and squeezed into it, the folds of his robe strained tight around his thighs. He knew his dark *gandoura* would merge perfectly with the shadows, and he was standing there motionless, struggling hard to control the level of his breathing, when the first warrior came panting up the incline. MacAngus saw the man's face, the swarthy cheeks and long hooked nose. He saw the chin heavily coated with beard stubble and held himself tight, feeling his ribcage battle for air. The moment seemed elongated, as if he had reached a point in time where the world hung suspended. He waited, the harsh rock pressing against his spine and skull, the coolness of the evening bathing his glistening features. The Dawasir peered around, his eyes glittering fiercely, then he scrambled stubbornly on, picking his way through thorn clumps and slivers of sandstone toward the starlit summit.

The other came in dribs and drabs, stopping from time to time to check out gullies, cracks, vegetation clusters, and MacAngus watched them, his muscles tense, his body rigid, his breathing now gentle and rhythmic, all of him absorbed into the shadowy body of the jagged fissure.

He waited until his pursuers were well above him before he left his place of concealment and crossed the plateau at a run. There were no shots, no cries of warning. His flight had gone unobserved. Down the slope he slithered, making good time with the gradient steadily slackening. Then, as he approached the bottom, he slowed his pace. He could see the camels just below, and the Dawasir warrior guarding them sitting on a rock, breaking a piece of thorn between his fingers.

Stealthily, MacAngus moved closer, his sandalled feet making no sound on the desert sand. His hand slid down, drawing the knife from inside his robe. He could see the spot where his blade would go, in the tiny hollow between the man's collarbone and the side of his neck. It would be a clean death, swift, neat, silent. But just as MacAngus was about to strike, a sliver of starlight lit the tribesman's face revealing, not some grizzled warrior from the Gilf Kebir, but a young boy with smooth cheeks and almond eyes. MacAngus hesitated, weighing up the consequences of his act. Quietly he sheathed the knife and picked up a small rock. When the boy had turned back on his perch, MacAngus rose swiftly, crossed the open in one fluid movement, and without pausing, brought the rock down on the herder's unprotected skull. With a muffled groan, the boy pitched senseless into the dust.

MacAngus moved about the Dawasir beasts, kicking them to their feet. Roaring and protesting, they began to trot angrily across the open *reg* floor. Shots rang out as MacAngus mounted, and he laughed crazily as he slapped the animals into a run. There were more shots, ripping the air above his head, then, yelling and yippeeing, he turned, back the way he had come, ferrying his new-found camel herd into the distant reaches of the desert night.

The wadi was shallow, protected on both sides by ridges of crumbling red rock. In places, the ground was dry and fur-rowed, forming twisting channels where streams would flow when the rains came. Northward, a series of sandy cataracts spread into the desolate flatness of the empty *reg*. In the wadi's bed, parched scrub grew in ragged abundance. Here, Coffey had called a halt. Through the scorching heat of the afternoon and well into the darkness hours they had crouched in the gully's bottom, resting their camels, resting their bodies, wait-ing patiently for MacAngus's return.

Coffey lay with his head against his camel saddle, staring at the stars. He was taking a risk and he knew it. Too much time had elapsed already. But Coffey was determined to give MacAngus every chance. He owed him that, they all did.

Hearing a sound, he looked up to see Lieutenant Driscoll approaching. Driscoll had pulled down his face-mask and his cheeks looked pink in the milky starlight. Coffey knew Driscoll disapproved of his lingering, but in that curious off-handed way accepted it as he seemed to accept everything else in life, with an almost Arabic sense of fatalism.

'Mind if I ask, squire, how much longer you intend to go on waiting here?'

When Coffey didn't answer, Driscoll squatted down at his side, dusting the dirt from his robe. 'I don't wish to sound an alarmist, but even if your sergeant does manage to shake those beggars off, which I doubt, how do you expect him to find us in this little lot?'

'He'll be here,' Coffey insisted stubbornly.

'My dear fellow, I want him to survive as much as you do. Apart from anything else, he's an excellent man to have around. But the fact remains that he's taking on the Dawasir on their own terrain. To be blunt, it matters little how good your sergeant is – I'm afraid his chances are pretty damned slim.'

'You don't know Mac,' Coffey said. 'He can move like a ghost through the desert. No Arab I ever met can match him. He'll be here, you can count on it.'

'Known him a long time, have you?' Driscoll muttered, fingering the narrow line of scar tissue which ran through his beard; sand coated his hair, making him look strangely youthful in the starlight.

'Long enough.'

'I thought so. That other fellow . . . Lieutenant Benson . . . you've known him too?'

Frowning, Coffey peered beyond Driscoll to where Benson's murky outline rested among the shrubs. 'Benson's a more recent acquaintance,' he said, 'he arrived at the railhead from Sandhurst six weeks ago.'

'He doesn't appear to like you much.'

'The feeling's mutual.'

'So I gather.'

'I tried to tell the colonel that. You heard his answer.'

Driscoll's lips tightened into a thin smile. 'Would it be presumptious of me to ask what this antagonism is all about?'

'It's a question of breeding. His breeding, my lack of it. Benson regards it as intolerable finding himself junior to a man he would normally employ as his coachman.'

'Meaning that you're not a gentleman.'

'Precisely. You see that scar on his cheek? And the gap between his teeth? I gave him those in a scuffle at the railhead. Every time he looks in the shaving mirror he remembers that fight and hates me even more.'

'Extraordinary,' Driscoll whistled, shaking his head.

Coffey studied him curiously. Driscoll was a strange one, he thought. With his wild eyes and bearded features he looked every inch a Dervish savage, yet his manner and bearing suggested a background of gentility, of lineage, privilege. 'What about you?' Coffey asked.

'How do you mean?'

'Why do you risk your neck like this. Benson and I have little choice, but this is your own idea.'

Driscoll laughed. 'I can't resist playing the hero, I suppose.

86

It's the drama of the thing that appeals to me. In the blood really. I should have been an actor.'

Coffey's lips twitched. 'I couldn't imagine that. You acting.'

'You're quite wrong. I've wanted to be an actor since I was four years old. I've always known it's where my true vocation lies. They stuck me in our village variety show dressed as a tramp. I had to walk across the stage and drop my pipe. Of course I was too young to understand what was going on, but when the audience started applauding I just stopped in my tracks and stood there entranced. In the end, they had to lift me off over the footlights. But I knew then, with absolute certainty, that was what I was truly meant for.'

Coffey chuckled. 'Why didn't you follow it up?'

'My father insisted I joined the army. Sort of a family tradition. Besides, look at this face of mine. Hardly the right equipment for a successful leading man, is it? I was quick to realise the theatre held little promise for a fellow of my physical attributes, so I decided to stage a little drama of my own. I've been doing it ever since, dressing up in outlandish costumes, taking part in improbable masquerades.'

'One of these days,' Coffey warned, 'your luck's going to run out.'

Smiling, Driscoll nodded. He was about to speak again when suddenly he froze. For a moment he lay perfectly still, then he rolled over in the dust, lying on his stomach with his ear cocked, listening intently.

'What is it?' Coffey hissed.

'Someone's coming.'

Coffey scrambled to his knees. He heard the sound of camel hooves on the soft crumbling earth. The snick of a rifle bolt echoed in the night as, fifteen feet away, Benson cocked his weapon and laying waiting, his pale eyes glaring into the darkness. Coffey drew his pistol and slithered to the wadi's rim, his heart thumping furiously. 'How many do you think?' he whispered.

'Sounds like a whole bloody army,' Driscoll said.

'The Dawasir?'

'Can't be anyone else. Sorry old boy, looks like you've muffed it.'

Coffey drew his breath. Everything looked black. Even the stars looked black. He saw the animals rearing into sight; then a figure swung into view, tall, angular, familiar. 'Mac!' he exclaimed with relief.

It was true. MacAngus was hurrying the camels along, shepherding them forward like a herd of cattle. He reined in his own mount and spat on the ground, grinning at Coffey crookedly.

'I thought ye could wi' a few extra beasties, lieutenant,' he said.

SIX

Victoria Routledge scooped up a handful of salty earth and dropped it into the muddy pit in front of her. She watched the dirt sink slowly to the bottom and thin flecks of coarse-grained salt rise like bubbles to the surface. Eventually, in the heat of the sun, they would form a crust which she could scrape off and mould into salt blocks for the storage of food and other necessities, a function she had learned well during her thirteen years of captivity, for she had performed the ritual every morning as part of her daily chores.

She was a tall girl, statuesque in the classic manner, though with a strong expressive body which seemed at times almost incongruously perfect on such an elegant frame. Her face, tanned to a dusky gold by the desert sun, carried an air of innocent purity only mildly alleviated by her sensual mouth.

Beyond the salt pits the village lay in an uneven sprawl of mudbaked cubes and sand-coloured turrets. The buildings were rough and uneven, and in places seemed to merge with the earth itself.

Turbanned traders crouched in the marketplace, exhibiting their wares on palm-leaf mats. Donkeys clustered the animal pens, and straw-hatted slaves stood pounding grain into powder with long flat sticks.

The Dervish stronghold held no surprises for Victoria Routledge, for she had grown to maturity amid its arid confines; from the moment of her capture at the age of fifteen – an event she recalled with terrifying clarity – she had been condemned to the lowest order on the social scale. Her life and destiny had belonged to her owner, the village Emir, and she had been forced to exist like a nameless ghost, dutiful and servile, demanding nothing, obeying everything.

Victoria had accepted her role with a display of passivity engendered by lack of choice. She had worked hard because it was her nature to do so, and was respected greatly for this by the Dervishes, for though slaves were plentiful, and though new ones could always be acquired by raiding the scrublands of the south, good workers were rare, and assumed almost the status of nobles among their lowly companions. Not only was Victoria allowed the freedom of the village, but even the freedom of the surrounding countryside, and many times she could easily have run off, though what good it would have done she could not imagine, with more than 150 miles of blazing desert between her and safety. Nevertheless, she dreamed continously of escape, and for hours would stare across the empty flatlands thinking of a world she could scarcely remember – cobbled streets, gaslit cafés, hansom cabs, flouncy dresses. In a girl of more temperate nature the isolation of Hamira would have had a profound psychological effect, but Victoria's character had been honed by the rigours of nineteenth-century English society, and though outwardly she embraced the savage environment in which she found herself, she held fiercely and determinedly to the memories of her former life, as if only through them could her true identity be preserved.

She used a stick to skim off the yellowish crust, her hands working deftly as she pushed the coarse substance into the sunbaked moulds, smoothing out the lumps to keep the texture consistent. When she had finished storing the last of the salt blocks in the earthen vat, she gathered up her things, rose from where she was sitting, and made her way through the rabbitwarren of streets to the central marketplace. A group of women with tattoos on their chins sat cutting up tomatoes in the sun; their robes were indigo blue, and in places where the dye had run, their skins had tinted a dark plummy colour. Children trotted gaily through the alleyways, barefooted and dressed in rags, their wiry hair plastered with henna. Chickens scratched at the dry dusty earth looking for leftover particles of food. A priest, green-turbanned to show that he had made the pilgrimage to Mecca, walked along in front of her, his gloved hand supporting a hooded hunting falcon.

As Victoria crossed the square she spotted a young man watching her from under a mudwalled archway. He wore a long white jibbah and a woolly skullcap. His face was narrow, his jaw unusually extended, making his features appear elongated. He stared at Victoria with moist soulful eyes, and she felt a flash of anger stir inside her. The young man's name was Shilluk, and for several weeks now he had followed her everywhere, studying her movements with all the yearning of a lovesick camel. Victoria knew that Shilluk, a young nobleman of the Garu caste, had already approached the Emir with a view to buying her, and although the Emir had so far refused (Victoria was a good worker and he had no wish to lose her), she was uncomfortably aware that if Shilluk kept increasing his offer, sooner or later the Emir might relent.

Victoria had no desire to change masters. Her position was lowly, but as the Emir's property she was protected by law and never molested. Her body remained inviolate. With Shilluk as her owner, she knew that her inviolability would come to an end. She recognised the craving in the young noble's eyes and it worried and disturbed her.

Leaving the marketplace, she entered an arched portico which led to an inner courtyard; it was the workshop of the village artisans where, since her father's release from the abominable prison block eight years before, he had worked as a joiner and carpenter. Victoria could scarcely believe the change which had taken place in her father since his captivity. Once he had been a fleshy man, full-bodied with the excesses of indulgent living. Now he looked at times like a living corpse, his skin dried and cracked by the desert sun, stretched over the skeletal spareness of the frame beneath. She understood only too well the horrors he had endured in his prison hellhole, and even now, though the Dervishes trusted him warily, they kept his wrists and ankles firmly shackled with heavy chains.

He was chiselling a piece of wood as Victoria entered. The rest of the courtyard was deserted, the other workmen following their customary practice of sleeping through the hottest part of the day. There was glint in her father's eyes Victoria had seldom seen before. He looked flushed and elated, as if filled with some secret knowledge he could barely contain. When he saw her coming, his features lit up exuberantly. Then he spotted the look on her face and his expression changed to a frown of concern.

'What's wrong, Victoria?' he demanded quickly.

'That Shilluk,' she said, 'he's following me again.'

Routledge put down his chisel and moved into the centre of the courtyard, rubbing his palms on his loose-flowing robes. 'He's getting to be a menace, that one. According to Cassato, he's sent north for an albino camel so that he can increase his offer to the Emir.'

'Will the Emir acept?'

'Hard to tell. Owning an albino would make the Emir quite a celebrity. On the other hand, he's a wily old beggar. He knows how much Shilluk's pining for you and he's determined to push up the price as high as he can.'

'But father, what are we going to do if the Emir agrees?'

Routledge ran his fingers over his face. The gauntness of his features conveyed an impression of encroaching death. His eyes seemed to bulge in their sockets as if some hidden pressure inside his skull was forcing them steadily outwards. Deep lines creased the corners of his mouth and the skin flapped dryly below his throat and chin. 'There's only one thing we can do, Victoria. We must try to escape.'

Victoria looked at him with exasperation and moved under the heavy stone arches, away from the sun. For years her father had talked of escape, ignoring realities, referring to the one blind dream he could still cling to as a man in a famine might harbour inordinate fantasies of plenty.

'You know it's impossible,' she sighed. 'How far would we get across that desert with you in chains? They'd run us to earth in no time, and the penalty for running away is immediate death.'

'We could steal a couple of camels. Travelling by night we could steer by the stars. If we head due east we're bound to hit the Nile. There, we could buy fresh mounts and make our way to the Egyptian border.'

92

'Buy? What does that mean, buy? We haven't a single possession in the world we can call our own.'

Suddenly the excitement came back into Routledge's face. Its intensity startled Victoria. He peered at her, smiling secretively.

'I wouldn't say that, Victoria. I wouldn't say that at all. We have a great deal to bargain with. A week ago, two days ago, I wouldn't have contemplated escape. Now, I can think of nothing else.'

'Father, what are you talking about?'

'Come over here. I have something to show you.'

Mystified, Victoria followed him to the corner where the tools were kept. Routledge fumbled among the shadows for a moment, then he dragged out a heavy bag, almost the size of a small flour sack. Unlacing its top, he tipped some of its contents on to the bare earth floor. Victoria frowned as a number of large stones, light green in colour, scattered across the ground. When she picked one of them up, its surface felt oily to her touch. 'What are they?' she asked.

Her father grinned at her, his eyes dancing wildly in the devastation of his face. 'The biggest fortune you're ever likely to see in your entire life,' he whispered.

'What? These little stones?'

'Not just stones, Victoria. Diamonds, brought up by caravan from Central Africa.'

'Diamonds?' Victoria echoed increduously. 'This size?'

'That's right. Aren't they marvellous? The idiots are using them on their drill-tips to bore holes in metal and timber. Can you imagine it?'

'Father,' Victoria muttered in a wary voice, 'are you sure about this?'

'I tell you I've handled enough diamonds in my time to recognise the real thing when I see it. Never have I come across gems of such quality. Why, Victoria, if these ever got on to the market, they'd throw the diamond world into a turmoil.'

Victoria stared down at the dull greasy stones, mesmerised. In thirteen years of slavery she had grown to accept the unexpected as a natural part of life. But nothing like this had ever entered her mind. Diamonds. Why, they were enormous!

A new thought occurred to her, something she had never dreamed of before. What if she returned to her own world as a woman of wealth and influence? Surely it would give some kind of sense to the wasted years in between? Her life with the Dervishes could be viewed as a kind of penance, a period of servitude justly and amply rewarded. The idea caused a sudden feverish vitality to flow through her.

'What you see in this sack,' her father went on eagerly, 'is almost impossible to evaluate. These gems are priceless, Victoria, priceless. If we can only get them out of here, everything we've ever wanted will be ours for the asking. On the Nile we'll find Greek merchants who will recognise their value. We'll be able to get these chains removed and buy fresh camels to carry us into Egypt. And once back among our own people . . .'

He smiled, leaving the sentence unfinished.

Victoria knew the desert was more than a hundred miles across. Between them and the river lay trackless sands and bands of savage tribesmen. She hadn't the heart to tell him they would never make it. And yet, with riches like these in their possession, surely any risk was justified? She let her mind drift to the world beyond the Sudan, savouring the simple pleasures of a life she had almost forgotten. She thought of the circumstances which had brought her to this sorry plight, circumstances which seemed in moments of reflection like a fractured dream she had scarcely been party to.

As she stared into her father's feverish eyes, she felt her mind drifting back with a curious and elusive persistence to that fateful day she had first set foot in this wild and arid land thirteen years before.

The sternwheeler's engines throbbed beneath Victoria's feet as she sat on the deck looking out over the rippling river. An Arab nuggar with its huge triangular sail bobbed in the paddleboat's wash and she could see the sailors, robed and turbanned, waving at her in the sunlight. Smiling, she waved back, filled with a buoyant sense of anticipation. This was her first glimpse of the world beyond England and from the beginning she had been fascinated by the strangeness of it all, the veiled women, the ragged leather-skinned men, the camels, the goat herds, the khaki-clad soldiers. She had left the damp dreary streets of London, had travelled across an entire continent to the very edge of the great Sahara, and now at long last she was going to see her father.

Victoria had been only four the day her father had walked out of her life, an event that had caused her to suffer a crisis of identity from which she had never recovered. Charlton Routledge had frittered away his family's fortunes on a series of disastrous business adventures which had resulted in financial ruin, and dismayed by his own ineptitude, he had chosen to enrol as a voluntary missionary in the Episcopal Soldiers of St John. Victoria's last memory of her father had been of waking in the early hours of an October morning to find him bending over her cot, of seeing tears glistening on his cheeks, of feeling his moustache tickle her cheeks as he had lifted her from the bedcovers to kiss her lightly on the forehead.

'Goodbye, little one,' he had whispered. 'Some day you'll find that even the weakest of men may display within his soul a glimmer of nobility.'

Victoria's mother had died when she was barely eight years old, and at the decision of her father she had been admitted at once to Hardy's Proprietary Ladies' College in central London, hating it almost from the beginning. She had hated the dusty corridors and vaulted ceilings, the air of constriction and decay. She had hated the way its girls had been taught their places in life; somehow the very idea that a woman should always be amenable, dutiful, inoffensive and attentive, that the highest point of attainment to which she could aspire was the blessed state of matrimony, had seemed to Victoria the most outrageous assumption man could devise, and she had developed a profound distaste for the role she was being groomed to undertake.

Inevitably her dreams had centred around the one person she had ever loved, her father. In her mind she saw him in the distant Sudan, his handsome features baked red by the sun, the Arab tribesmen bending in prayer as his rich bass voice incanted the words of the Christian message. She forgot his disastrous business ventures, the squalor of his marriage, and pictured instead the most noble of human creatures, a man so proud and pure and good he represented the pinnacle of her hopes and ambitions.

When at last Charlton Routledge, no longer able to meet the payments required to keep Victoria at school, had sent for her to join him in the Sudan, she had been overwhelmed with joy. But now that she was on the final leg of her journey to El Serir, she began for the first time to experience a feeling of strange apprehension. Eleven years had passed since she had last seen her father. She herself had changed beyond recognition. Perhaps he too had changed. Perhaps her childhood memories had been coloured by emotion, forged by the yearning emptiness of the life she'd lived.

Her first glimpse of the city was hardly reassuring; the river curved, and as they swung into the central current she saw a cluster of brown and white buildings shimmering in the heat. A stone wall, nearly ten feet high, surrounded the outer perimeter, protected at each corner by rudely constructed gun turrets. Wooden jetties jutted across the water, and on their platforms throngs of robed figures stood waving at them excitedly. The entire waterfront seemed to swarm with black-gowned native women who emitted high-pitched yodelling noises as the steamer drew alongside. An assembly of convicts with heavy chains on their legs began to unload the cargo, stacking packing crates and baggage alike in untidy profusion under the palm trees. Whistles screamed, horses whinnied, and the ear-stunning bawl of the incessant yodelling went on and on as if nothing in the world would induce the perpetrators to stop.

Victoria's belongings were placed in an open carriage and she was driven through the streets by a coachman in a dirty jibbah and woolly skullcap. Clumps of coarse brown grass edged the sandy track which wound between the mudwalled buildings and skirted the tower of a solitary minaret gleaming in the sun. The town looked more solid at its centre, with terraced houses, tall mosques and intricately carved balconies. As they drove, beggars thrust their hands through the carriage doorway, and children danced laughing in their wake.

The mission was situated in the main square, next to the Christian church. It was not a large house by European standards, but it stood three storeys high, which made it a giant in El Serir. Victoria was met at the door by a servant who carried her baggage up to her room. She watched him place the trunks in the centre of the floor.

'Where is my father?' she asked.

'He is upstairs, resting,' the man said in broken English. 'He always rests during the heat of the day.'

Victoria waited until he had gone, then she moved to the window and opened it, looking down at the square outside. Camels stood preening themselves in the sun while their driver, an emaciated man with the negroid features of Central Africa, sat twisting ropes from palm-frond fibres. Beside him, veiled women crouched on mats, cutting up tomatoes for drying in the sun. Under the shade, a baby snored peacefully in a cradle suspended from two tall poles.

The sights and sounds of the marketplace filled Victoria with a strange sense of remoteness, and she closed the window uncertainly. If only her father had been here to meet her. She needed a friendly face, a sympathetic voice. She had waited so long, had dreamed so much of this moment she could not bear to postpone it any longer.

On an impulse, she left the bedroom and climbed the stairs to the floor above. The corridor was narrow, the ceiling high and vaulted. Flies clustered the corners or gathered in dark profusion around the open windows. Her feet made hollow flapping noises on the bare wood floor.

Sounds came drifting faintly from a room at the far end of the passageway. Human sounds. She could not identify them, but she moved forward and tapped lightly on the door. No answer. She held her breath. What should she do? Go back to her room? It seemed unthinkable. She needed her father now, needed his comfort and reassurance. Alone, she was lost, frightened, bewildered.

Gently Victoria undid the latch and slipped into the bedroom. Here the floor was tiled with shiny slabs to convey an impression of coolness. The window shutters were closed in spite of the heat, and around the great bed, mosquito curtains hung in a heavy grey canopy, blotting from her sight the figure which lay beneath.

97

Breathlessly, she crossed the room and reached for the nearest curtain. The sounds she had heard were louder now, sharp mewing noises rising in a steady crescendo. Victoria drew back the mosquito net and gasped, frozen into shock. A man lay on the bed, facing upwards. His pale plump body was glistening with sweat, his lips drawn back in a snarl of pain or ecstasy. Crouched above him, a young negress, furiously impaled, rolled her hips in an undulating rhythm. Her plump breasts shimmered in the pale light from the shuttered window and sweat ran in rivulets down the sweeping curve of her stomach to the tangle of pubic hair between her thighs.

Seeing Victoria she stopped, staring at her with calm yellowish eyes. The man too, sensing the intrusion, looked up with a sickly grimace. Victoria felt bile rushing into her throat. She let the curtain drop, and, turning, dashed from the room. Tears flooded her eyes as she scuttled downstairs to the floor below and ran to her window, gulping in lungfuls of the hot afternoon air. It wasn't possible, surely. That man could never have been her father. The vision she'd harboured all these years, the image etched into her brain seemed suddenly grotesque and childlike. She rubbed her face with her hands and swallowed back the tears threatening to engulf her. How cruel, cruel that her long journey should have ended in such a sordid manner.

She stood for several minutes before she heard the door open gently behind her, and a soft voice say: 'Victoria? Victoria, is it really you?'

She turned slowly. He was standing just inside the room, dressed in an Arab jellaba and a pair of leather sandals. Gone was the stately strength she had visualised in her daydreams, the air of compassion and dignity. This man was small and fat, with heavy folds of flesh hanging beneath his chin. His moustache had vanished, and somehow its absence seemed to emphasise the weakness of his mouth. His skin was drawn, and there were tiny blue veins across his nose and under his eyes. It was a face which held all the marks of dissolute living.

He stared at her with embarrassment. 'I had no idea you would arrive today. Major Johnson was supposed to telegraph me from Berber.'

'He tried to do so,' she told him coldly, 'but I understand the line had been cut. Dervish rebels, the engineer said.'

'Ah yes,' her father muttered, running his fingers through his hair, 'those Dervishes. They're making life pretty damned miserable for everyone these days.'

Somehow the disappointment she felt made her cold and hostile, and all the things she'd wanted to say, the deep intimate personal things she had saved up since childhood seemed locked inside her, unassailable and remote.

He started to cross the floor, then catching the look in her eyes, stopped and stood staring at her unhappily. 'Well, you're looking splendid, Victoria,' he declared in a brave voice, 'every inch a young lady, I must say. And so like your mother. When you . . . when I saw you standing there, I thought for a moment – it was almost as if she'd never died.'

His voice faltered and faded away as Victoria continued to glare at him mercilessly. Was this the man who had lifted her from her cot as a child, whose moustache had tickled her cheek, whose gentleness had filled her life with such warmth?

He sighed, rubbing his palms down his long white robe. 'You must not judge me too harshly, Victoria. It's not easy for a man living alone.'

'You judge yourself, father,' she said.

'I am not strong, Victoria. I try to be, God knows I try. I do my best to fulfil the obligations of my calling, but in El Serir the temptations are many.'

'Who is the woman? Does she live here?'

'She is a Yambarri, a prostitute from the Albert N'Yanza.'

He blinked at her. 'Don't look so disapproving, Victoria. It's a perfectly respectable profession in the Sudan. Here, the pleasures of the flesh are never despised. Strong drink is a violation of everything godly, but sexual abstinence is rarely considered a virtue.'

'But you are a Christian. A man of the church. It is your duty to provide these people with an example. They are not trying to convert you to their way of life. You are here to convert them to yours.'

He nodded regretfully. 'You are right,' he admitted. 'I censure myself a thousand times a day, but the result is always the

99

same. The Lord has filled me with hungers which cannot be assuaged. I dream always of a purer soul, a more virtuous spirit, but the devil seems to drive me until I can no longer help myself.'

He moved toward her, taking her in his arms, and this time, though she kept her body stiff and unyielding, she did not protest. He kissed her gently on the lips and pushed her face against his chest and she felt the tears trickling down his cheeks and dripping on to her temple.

'Perhaps now, Victoria,' he whispered softly, 'perhaps with you here we can help each other. Your virtue may cleanse my guilt and, who knows, in the end we may both be saved.'

SEVEN

Once the initial shock of her arrival had receded, Victoria found that life in El Serir presented a fascinating contrast to the monotony of her years at Hardy's Proprietary Ladies' College. There was little to occupy her time beyond her studies (which her father insisted she continue) but a great deal to occupy her interest. She discovered that the area around the town perimeter, a flat bleak plain peppered with thorn bushes and rocky outcrops, was swarming with wild life. While out riding she would glimpse herds of fleet-footed gazelle, convoys of sand grouse and bustards, crocodiles, lizards and once even a maverick rhinoceros. Hare tracks littered the sandy ground and the low scrub was alive with scorpions, snakes and occasional bands of ostriches which scattered wildly at her approach, their feathery tails fluttering in the shimmering hot air.

Along the river bank, mud villages clung to the arid earth and the slow-moving current hummed with traffic – steamboats, gunboats, barges, white-sailed dahabeeyahs, even humans clinging to inflated animal skins.

The people fascinated Victoria. She would watch the women for hours breaking date stones into powder to mix with their dough for baking into bread. She would watch the craftsmen making rings and armlets, turning out perfect circles with nothing but the crudest of hand tools. She would watch the camel riders drifting in from the adjacent desert, showing off their skill in the saddle by charging and countercharging in front of the city walls.

The handful of European women who occupied El Serir,

officers' wives for the most part, did their best to recreate at least a semblance of the world they had left behind with coffee mornings, tea-parties and sundry social get-togethers, and five months of Victoria's life sped by in this pleasant and leisurely fashion. By the time she was fifteen she was showing signs of developing into an alluring young woman, and had already become quite adept at avoiding the attempts of the younger subalterns to steer her into secluded corners at regimental dances.

Her father, she quickly discovered, was not a bad man in himself, merely a weak one who seemed unable to abandon his indulgences of the flesh. She seldom asked herself if she loved him, but as the weeks went by, a guarded affection began to develop inside her, born out of pity rather than respect.

'My life is nearly over,' he told her one day. 'Though I am not old, I have already passed the point of no return. I can no longer delude myself that change is possible. I must resign my mind to my own depravity. But one thing I know. Having you here these last few months has given me something I have never experienced before. Not hope exactly, but a kind of fresh awareness, a sense of transcendence, as if there might yet be the possibility of salvation, even for a sinner like me.'

Victoria's eyes moistened as she listened. She knew her father wanted nothing in the world so much as her admiration and regard, and though she felt unable to give either freely, she did offer something else, compassion and understanding.

For Victoria, the rhythm of life at El Serir seemed a glorious release from the austerity of her life in England, and she embraced it happily, immersing herself in the city's social whirl with a blissful disregard for the rumbles of discontent which passed daily up and down the countryside. A new leader had arisen among the Sudanese people. Born the son of a boat builder, Mohammed Ahmed Ibn Al-Sayid Abdullah, he had assumed the role of the Chosen One, the Mahdi. He claimed to hear voices telling him to overthrow the Infidel and convert the world to the Moslem religion. The Mahdi's message was simple – deny pleasure and prepare for the world to come. The Sudanese believed he was the true descendant of the Prophet, and his followers deliberately sought death in battle in the hope that it would guide them straight to heaven.

Six months after Victoria's arrival, the Mahdi brought the entire country out in revolt. The telegraph was cut, traffic was blocked on the river, and native runners reported that the capital, Khartoum, was beseiged by sixty thousand warriors. The pleasant jaunty air of the little garrison town vanished completely as defences were strengthened and provisions shipped in by steamboats running the enemy blockade.

One morning Victoria rode out to the open *reg* where troops were mining the city surrounds, their serge jumpers and yellow cord breeches wonderfully colourful against the desert floor. A rider came pounding furiously toward her, reining in his mount in a thick cloud of dust. She recognised Major Smiles, a handsome young Englishman serving with the Egyptian brigade. 'What are you doing out here?' he shouted. 'Don't you know it's unsafe to leave the city walls?'

'It's too hot in the city,' she complained. 'It's like a furnace when the sun gets up.'

'Return at once,' he ordered curtly. 'Scouts have reported a force of twenty thousand Dervishes advancing this way from Khartoum. They'll be within striking distance by sundown.'

Victoria felt a nauseous sensation creeping upwards from her stomach. Her hand reached out, gripping her pony's bridle. For weeks she'd tried to stay aloof, ignoring the tension, ignoring reality. Now it looked as if reality was about to catch up with her.

The Dervishes did not attack that evening, nor the next evening, nor the one after, and for three days the town waited in a fever of anticipation and fear. Patrols were sent out and failed to return. Their heads were discovered each morning impaled on stakes outside the city walls. Then, on the dawning of the fourth day, Victoria awoke to a strange throbbing sound. For a long time she could not discern what it was, until at last the truth dawned upon her. Drums. Not one drum, nor a dozen, nor even a hundred, but thousands and thousands, pounding rhythmically a long way off, five miles, ten miles, growing louder, coming closer.

Pulling on her robe, she crept upstairs to the rooftop terrace and stood at the parapet staring across the mudwalled buildings

103

and the city ramparts to the great sweep of the desert beyond. Not a movement stirred over the desolate pancake of sand. There was nothing to see but the empty *reg*, its orange textures strangely muted in the pale light of the early morning.

Shivering, she drew the robe tightly around her shoulders as she heard her father enter the terrace behind her. He was wearing his Arab jibbah and she guessed he had just got out of bed. His throat and chin were coated with beard stubble.

'Victoria, are you all right?'

'Listen,' she whispered.

He nodded grimly. 'They're here at last.'

'Will they attack?'

'If Khartoum's anything to go by, they'll try to break through our defences and if that fails, they'll lay siege to the city walls.'

'How long can we hold out, father?'

'Well, the Dervishes don't entirely control the river and until they do we can ferry in supplies and reinforcements. Our position's not untenable yet. Still, at moments like this a man needs all the support he can get.'

Reaching inside his robe he drew out a small whisky flask and swallowed copiously. When he had finished, a faint whistling sound emerged from the back of his throat. His face looked sad as he re-corked the flask and slipped it inside his pocket. 'Victoria, please believe me, if I'd had any idea . . . if I'd only known how things would turn out I'd have kept you at Hardy's somehow.'

'Please don't apologise, father. The last six months have been the happiest in my life. I wouldn't have missed them for the world.'

'Do you really mean that?'

She saw tears welling up in his eyes, and on an impulse she stepped forward and kissed him lightly on the cheek. He seized her, pressing her tightly against him.

'I must get down to the clinic,' he exclaimed hoarsely when at last he let her go. 'If the fighting starts, there'll be casualties. I'll be needed. Do not, under any circumstances, Victoria, leave the security of the house.'

Smiling, she promised she wouldn't, and after he had gone

she stood at the parapet reflecting on the strange contrarieties of fortune which had brought her to this isolated outpost to be surrounded and threatened by savage primitive men. The sun rose steadily and its heat strengthened, and then, just before seven, the drums stopped and a brooding silence settled over the countryside. Victoria squinted into the blinding glare. The horizon shimmered eerily, and as she watched she spotted a dark stain spreading across the orange sand. For a moment she took it for a freak of the light – it looked like that, a shadow cast by a passing cloud perhaps, but then she realised the stain was moving; slowly, steadily, it was advancing inch by inch, foot by foot toward them.

Victoria's breath seemed to chill inside her body. The moment she had dreaded had arrived at last. In a curious way she felt almost relieved, as if the strain of waiting and wondering had stretched her nerves so much that now, able to view the thing she had feared clearly and coolly, some of her terror had diminished. The stain on the desert floor disappeared behind a line of sand-dunes and for almost fifteen minutes she waited in silence, wondering if she had made a mistake. Then it rose into view again, much closer this time, so close she could see at once it was not a stain at all but a surging mass of men – men with blue-black faces and ragged jibbahs who carried before them yellow and white tapestries which rippled in the wind.

A strange wailing sound reached Victoria's ears. The Dervishes were singing as they marched, a mournful lament that had no tune to it, but which carried within its strains an eerie unreal quality that could not fail to chill the blood. They were not moving in an unbroken line, she saw now, but in separate squadrons, linked together to form a continuous barrier. The sunlight glinted on their weapons and on their dancing, fluttering standards.

Around the town all movement had come to a standstill. Soldiers – Egyptian, British and Sudanese – stood in silence on the outer walls and watched the slow implacable advance of the men they would soon have to kill. With every minute the sun climbed higher and Victoria felt perspiration trickling between her shoulderblades, running down the length of her spine.

The squadrons of white-robed men spread out, expanding further across the *reg* as they settled into combat formation. They were motionless now, as a line of horsemen took up position in front of the forward ranks. The Baggara cavalry. Victoria caught her breath. They were going to charge the walls in an attempt to forge an opening for the Dervish infantry. It seemed insane. Suicidal madness. Only a lunatic would present that broken wave of humanity to the fury of the Egyptian guns.

She stood watching as the cavalry formed itself into a barrier of brightly flashing swords. A heavy silence descended over the city, broken by the occasional snicker of a horse or the click of a rifle being loaded. On the plain, the mounted skirmish line stood poised and ready.

There was no apparent order, no shout, no shot to break the stillness of the morning, but at the same precise moment the Baggara horsemen, moving as a single man, broke into a charge. Victoria held her breath as across the plain they thundered, spreading like spilling oil over the crumbling earth, their robes streaming in the wind. The roll of hooves was like a rattle of thunder in her eardrums, and above it she could hear the hoarse cries of the riders themselves, distorted, distant, too muted and indistinct to be construed as threatening.

Then – boom-boom, boom-boom – the Egyptian Nordenfeldts opened up and Victoria saw great fountains of earth belch into the sky. Men and animals were tossed aside like discarded toys. Shells shrieked and exploded deep in their ranks, gouging terrible gaps in their frontal array, but nothing seemed able to stem the sheer inexorability of that white-crested tide.

Rat-tat-tat-tat-tat-tat-tat, scything machine guns cut down riders and horses alike. Animals screamed and thrashed in agony. Men rolled in the dust. It seemed impossible to conceive that any living thing could survive that awesome hailstorm of lead, yet still the charge came on; three hundred yards, two hundred, a hundred and fifty.

Victoria's heart hammered against her chest as the foremost warriors drew within eighty yards of the outer wall. She could see them quite clearly now, their features contorted beneath

106

their jibbah cowls, their arms outstretched, slicing wildly at the air with their wicked curved swords. Turn back, she thought tearfully, forgetting for a moment that this was the enemy bent on her destruction, seeing only a helpless flood-tide of humanity and a carnage that was beyond belief.

A rider crested the outer wall, his mount rising high as it took the jump at full gallop, and coming down on the other side its legs folded as horse and rider collapsed in a confused tangle of hooves and limbs. Egyptian soldiers raced swiftly in, bayonets at the ready, and Victoria shut her eyes as the warrior was dispatched struggling to free himself.

Another rider breasted the bulwark, landing unharmed this time and galloping furiously into the empty streets. Before he had gone twenty yards a Sudanese infantrymen blew off the back of his skull with a single rifle shot.

Three more horses came over the wall, then a full half-dozen, and suddenly the enemy were rampaging through the town and men were shouting in all directions as a great fusillade of shots rang out, tipping the riders from their saddles, leaving the terrified mounts to stampede unchecked through the twisting labyrinth of alleyways.

Victoria saw one of the wounded Dervishes rise to his feet. He had been shot in the side and blood was seeping through his dirtstained jibbah, but the bullet scarcely seemed to slow him down at all as he sprinted like a dart across the sandy ground. A shot, sharp and discordant, split the battle-filled air, and with a scream of pain the man crumpled lifeless into the dust.

Beyond the perimeter the rattle of gunfire was almost deafening as the Baggara cavalry, destroyed almost to a man, finally broke into disarray.

The Dervish infantry began to lay down its own barrage of rifle fire, bringing an instant response from the Egyptian guns, but while the Dervishes were practically out of range, most of their shots falling miserably short, the heavy Nordenfeldts of the Egyptian brigade continued to blast their carefully ordered squadrons into mangled heaps of dead and dying men.

Throughout the morning, the merciless pounding of machine guns and artillery forced the Dervishes steadily back; wild-eyed, ragged, imbued with an impassioned belief that nothing in the world offered anything so glorious as this moment of destruction, they regrouped and returned to the fray, but the slaughter was unbearable, and soon the plain was littered with corpses amongst which the vultures had already started to scavenge.

At noon the Dervish army was forced to withdraw. Their losses had been frightful. Even their fanatical belief in immortality could not sustain them under such an onslaught. Now they were digging in beyond the range of the heavy guns, raising the black hummocks of their nomad tents in the outlying desert.

Drained and shaking, Victoria made her way inside and vomited quietly in the bathroom. She knew they had reached an interlude, a brief pause in hostilities while strategies could be re-aligned, policies re-considered. The battle for El Serir was over.

The siege of El Serir was about to begin.

The next six weeks became a nightmare of misery and degradation. After its first débâcle, the Dervish army did not attempt a frontal assault again. Instead it settled in around the city, blocking its defences on three sides. Only the river still offered access to the north, and even then the boats had to run the full fury of the enemy guns. At first six steamers operated a shuttle service between El Serir and Berber, ferrying in supplies and vital equipment, but one by one the Dervishes blasted the craft out of the water until at last the city commander called a halt to the reckless blockade-running, keeping his one remaining vessel moored safely to the dockside.

Toward the end of the fourth week a new threat imposed itself upon the city. Starvation. Victoria had known hunger before but always it had been the transitory kind; now, for the first time in her life, she learned what it meant to live in the uncertainty of ever tasting food again. The old, the weak, the sick died daily, their bloated bodies littering the alleyways and marketplaces. The stench haunted Victoria's senses until she believed she would never be rid of it. The air was black with carrion kites which came in their scores to feast on the corpses. They became so gorged they could not fly, and the

Sudanese soldiers caught and devoured them avidly. Victoria and the other civilians had to make do with what they could scavenge. Dogs, rats, mice, even cockroaches became sought-after delicacies for the cooking pot.

When she peered at her reflection in the mirror Victoria was amazed at the skeletal gauntness of her features. This would be how she would look in death, she thought, shrivelled and shapeless, her contours etched to the angular outline of her bones. Only her eyes seemed alive. They stared back at her with the glazed apathy of hunger, drained of vitality, strength, hope.

One morning, as she was standing on the roof terrace, she heard her father calling her to the room below. Listlessly she turned from the balcony, descending the narrow stairway. Her father had aged through the long weeks of privation. The face which had displayed the indulgence of dissolute living now looked haggard and drawn. He was already an old man, she thought.

With him was Major Smiles. By some miracle Major Smiles had managed to hold on to his handsome looks, though his cheeks had sunk into deep craters on each side of his mouth.

'Come in, child,' Victoria's father said, 'I want to talk to you.'

She moved toward him and he slipped an arm around her shoulders. 'There is still no sign of a British relief force,' he said. 'The Egyptians are safely ensconced in Cairo and our soldiers are weakening every day. Soon they will reach the end of their endurance and when that happens, the city will fall. If we are to survive we must act quickly. The last riverboat is still lying in the harbour. Major Smiles has had its hull barricaded with metal sheets. He has loaded one of the Maxims on board and two heavy machine guns. He intends to run the blockade as soon as darkness falls, forcing his way downriver to the Egyptian lines.'

'But look what happened to the supply boats,' Victoria muttered.

'We are aware of that,' her father said. 'Nevertheless Major Smiles believes, as I do, that a fully armed steamer, suitably reinforced and defended, will be more than a match for the

Dervish forces along the bank. If we remain here it will result in certain death or capture, and you must realise Victoria, what those heathen scoundrels will do to any white woman who falls into their hands.'

Victoria did realise. She had thought about it often, asking herself how she would react to a Dervish intent upon violating her. She had made her decision. Her body was a sacred thing. She would fight to the death.

'What about the townspeople?' she asked.

'We can't take everyone,' Major Smiles explained. 'We have only a limited amount of room. When the town falls, the Sudanese who survive will have the choice of joining the Mahdi's army or being sold as slaves. The Europeans will have no such choice. We must give them preference. Only white civilians will be evacuated. I shall command the vessel with a small number of troopers to man the guns.'

'We leave one hour after nightfall,' her father told her. 'Go quickly and prepare, Victoria. Remember too heavy a load will be nothing but an encumbrance, so take as little as you can.'

She packed in a daydream, going through the motions with an almost mesmerised lethargy. She longed to lie down, to close her eyes, drift peacefully into sleep. Even the prospect of escape did not excite her. Hunger had destroyed her capacity for emotion, and a paralysing lassitude pervaded every part of her body so that tasks which would normally have taken minutes to perform, now seemed to take hours.

At nightfall they assembled on the jetty, the small group of Europeans clutching the few meagre possessions they could carry. The steamer was already churning out smoke and Victoria could hear the low throb of its engines pulsing steadily away. Around the deckrails, corrugated metal sheets had been fixed to form a barricade, and through one of the narrow openings Victoria could see the blunt nozzle of a heavy machine gun.

Clutching their bundles, they filed up the gangplank and Victoria followed a Sudanese soldier to the cabins below. There were people everywhere, checking on friends and relatives, reassuring each other the danger would be minimal.

110

Until now Victoria's fear had been deadened by hunger. Suddenly a feeling of terror engulfed her. In a moment or two they would be out in the open, away from the protection of the city's artillery. There would be no one to help them if things went wrong. They would have to rely on their own resources.

Her cabin was small, the smallest on the vessel, but she was lucky enough to have it to herself. The others were crowded, five or six to a single berth, while her father, with some of the other men, had been forced to seek refuge in the boiler-room.

There was a narrow bunk just inside the door and a single porthole which had been boarded up with metal strips. An oil lamp hung from the roofbeam, but they had been warned to keep lights to a minimum so she left it unlit and sat in the darkness, waiting for departure.

An hour later she felt the hull vibrate as the heavy sternpaddle began to thrash at the water. Her muscles tightened as they steered away from the jetty into midstream. She heard a fusillade of sharp popping sounds, like firecrackers going off at a carnival, followed by a series of metallic 'pings' rattling against the steamer's hull.

Then the entire vessel seemed to shudder as – boom-boom – the thunder of the heavy Maxim gun echoed ominously through the confined cabin-space. Victoria gripped her hands together, the fingernails biting deep into her flesh. What if the Dervishes had blockaded the river lower down? She dismissed the thought as absurd. The Nile was too wide for any army, no matter how well-equipped, to harness its flow with ropes, dams or boats.

Rat-tat-tat-tat-tat-tat-tat. Up above, machine guns opened up and Victoria heard the spent cartridge cases rolling about the deck. She thought of Major Smiles moving behind the gun crews, directing their line of fire with the cool authority she had come to expect, and suddenly all the tension seemed to flow out of her. How could they come to harm, she asked herself, with such a capable man in command?

Within twenty minutes the firing slackened to occasional spasmodic outbursts. At the end of an hour it disappeared entirely. Soon, there was only the soft shuffling of feet on the deck above and the sensuous throbbing of the engines as they butted their way northward through the oppressive silence of the Sudanese night.

A soft knock on the door woke Victoria from an uneasy sleep. The cabin was filled with diffused light which she realised came from the sun's rays striking between the metal strips on the hull. 'Come in,' she called, stretching luxuriously.

It was a Sudanese trooper, carrying a coffee pot and two tiny wheatcakes. Victoria stared at them in mute disbelief. She had gone so long without food that anything edible, no matter how small, looked like a banquet. The grain must have been stored on board throughout the siege, she realised. She waited until the trooper had left the room, then scrambled from the bunk and crammed the first of the wheatcakes into her mouth, almost retching as she swallowed without bothering to chew. The second followed just as quickly, then she licked her fingers and licked the tray where the cakes had lain. Sitting down, she filled the little bowl with steaming black coffee and cradling it between her palms, sipped the life-imbibing liquid. The nourishment revived her and she experienced, for no apparent reason, a surge of happiness and well-being.

She straightened her hair as best she could and went up on deck, blinking in the morning sunlight. People flocked to the rails, watching the banks glide implacably by. Sudanese soldiers moved to and fro, going about their duties with the languid calmness of men at ease with the world. The banks themselves looked deserted, their brown rims cluttered with vegetation.

She saw Major Smiles smoking his pipe at the bow. He waved to her and she wandered toward him. 'Sleep well?' he asked.

'On and off. I kept waking up and thinking I was still in El Serir.'

He grinned. 'Don't worry, that's all behind you now. We're making good time. Got a clear river ahead too. Two more cataracts before Halfa, then we'll be in the clear.'

She peered beyond him at the current ahead. The water looked deep and cool beneath the warmth of the lifting sun. Driftwood bobbed and dipped in their path.

'Was there much resistance on the bank?' she asked.

'Oh, they did their best to sink us, but we soon put paid to that.'

'Nobody hurt?'

'Two troopers hit by flying shrapnel. Nothing serious.'

'Thank God.'

With the cessation of danger, her spirits were rising. 'It's such a relief to be away from the stench of death.'

He nodded. 'We're the lucky ones,' he grunted.

'What about the others? Will they surrender?'

'Probably. The commander was seeking terms before we left.'

'I hope to God they're all right.'

Major Smiles didn't answer. His lips tightened on his pipe stem and he puffed for a moment in silence, his eyes dark and sombre. Victoria knew what he was thinking. The Dervishes were hardly noted for their leniency; whatever fate befell El Serir's residents it would not be a humane one. Then to her surprise she noticed he was straining forward, squinting hard across the narrow bow.

'What's wrong?' she asked.

'Something's out there,' he whispered.

Victoria narrowed her eyes. The flotsam seemed to disengage and in the shimmering sunlight she spotted the outline of a small boat bobbing gently toward them. It carried no sail and its gunwale was chipped and broken. Splinter holes ravaged its hull where bullets had torn at the woodwork. It listed to port as it swung broadside on, scraping along their bow.

'Is it empty?' she asked.

Major Smiles leaned forward, shading his eyes against the sunlight. The lookout on the bridge shouted a warning, bringing the passengers to the deckrail. Victoria felt a sense of deep foreboding. Something about the boat frightened her, though she could not say why.

'It's not an Arab vessel,' Major Smiles muttered. 'Looks like one of ours.'

She gripped the rail, her knuckles showing white through the skin. The craft swayed closer, and peering down Victoria spotted a cluster of motionless figures sprawled about its interior. She glimpsed a silken gown, a scarlet tunic, a piece of lace on a velvet sleeve. 'Oh my God,' she whispered, 'I believe there are women on that boat.'

'Bring her alongside,' Smiles shouted, his voice crisp and authorative; in a softer tone he added: 'Move back, Victoria. Some of those people may still be alive. We'll need all the room we can get.'

Shivering, Victoria edged her way to the steamer's rear. She stood watching as soldiers brought the boat alongside and an Egyptian sergeant prepared to scramble down the rope-ladder and investigate. Along the rail, the passengers craned their necks. The sergeant reached the bobbing vessel and stepped gingerly on board. He used his arms to steady himself, swaying wildly as the boat bobbed and dipped under his weight. Stooping, he examined the figure of a woman in a green shawl, lifting her hat veil to peer at her face. On the steamer deck the passengers waited in sombre silence. Victoria knew what they were thinking. If things had gone differently at the river blockade, they too could have been floating lifelessly like the corpses below.

Something happened in the little boat Victoria could not quite discern, a flurry of movement, a tiny scuffle, brief but intense. She blinked hard as the sergeant slowly straightened. Gracefully, he turned to look at the spectators on the riverboat above like a man about to deliver a personal address. His face was calm, composed, dignified. Horror swept through Victoria's body as she glimpsed the shaft of a Dervish spear, slippery with blood, protruding from the sergeant's chest. No expression showed on the man's face as he stared for a moment at the thunderstruck onlookers above; then, with an air of precise deliberation, he stepped gently across the boat and began to re-climb the rope-ladder.

It was like a scene dredged from some childhood nightmare. Nobody moved and nobody spoke. They watched as the sergeant, moving painfully but determinedly, dragged himself upward, his body twisting to one side to prevent the spear shaft scraping against the wooden hull.

Transfixed with fright, Victoria watched his desperate lonely ascent. His dark face was sweaty with concentration and his eyes, calm, perfectly controlled, fixed on some indeterminate point toward the steamer's rear. For a moment it looked as if he would actually make it, but as his hand touched the deckrail, blood spurted in a grotesque fountain between his lips and he crashed backwards, jerking convulsively into the swirling current.

As if the sergeant's fall had been a signal, pandemonium broke loose. With wild whoops, the figures which had lain so dormant in the boat's bottom sprang suddenly into life, scrambling like rats up the steamer's side, their faces gleaming savagely above their European clothing. Women screamed and Victoria felt her legs turn weak as she watched bearded warriors, clad in silken dresses and lacy petticoats, leap among the assembled passengers, hacking and slashing indiscriminately.

A shot rang out as Major Smiles dispatched one of the invaders with a bullet to the skull, but not before the man had run through a startled trooper, opening up his torso from breastbone to crotch. Bile rose in Victoria's throat as she leaned back against the deckrail. The Dervishes were killing everyone in sight; men or women, it made no difference, they slaughtered with brutal impartiality.

Victoria's instinct for survival quickly asserted itself. She had to hide. Escape. She could go below but that would be pointless. When the killing was finished on deck, the savages would swarm through the entire ship.

There was still the bridge. Victoria's senses quickened, but one glance told her she was already too late. Wild-eyed warriors were scrambling over the sloping timbers, shutting off the captain in his solitary refuge.

She looked behind her to where the great wheel drummed remorselessly at the current. She saw a barrier, three feet wide, built to prevent the spray drenching travellers on the deck above. Behind was a narrow platform, just wide enough for a person to crouch. It looked dangerous in the extreme - the giant blades were zipping past barely inches away - but it offered the only sanctuary Victoria could see.

Sobbing, she scrambled over the rail and slid behind the spray-barrier, ducking back out of sight. Water sloshed into her face, thrown up by the paddlewheel, and the thunder of the blades blotted out all sound of the slaughter taking place on the deck above.

She scarcely knew how long she crouched there. She lost all track of time. She supposed she was caught by madness of a sort, an eerie reverie wrought by the horror of the moment. Then at some point – she had no idea how long it had been – she heard a giggle, and glancing up, spotted a face grinning malevolently above her. She felt no fear, that was the strangest thing. She did not even protest when wiry tribesmen scrambled over the barrier and dragged her from her perch. She was hauled, quiescent, to the deck where the smell of gore almost made her faint. The planks were slippery with blood. Naked and mutilated corpses lay everywhere, and severed limbs littered her path like gory ornature. The screaming had long since stopped, leaving a silence that was painful to listen to. The odour of smoke filled her nostrils, and with it came something else, the smell of burning meat.

Dazed and bewildered, she stared uncomprehendingly at the bodies of raped women scattered about the deck. One had her breasts hacked off, another had been impaled obscenely on a sharpened stake; all, coated with dust and the salted flecks of dried sweat, carried an air of passivity that went beyond death. It was hard to believe these naked abandoned corpses had ever contained life, for they seemed in Victoria's deranged fancy as devoid of human substance as the blood-stained planks on which they had suffered their outrage.

The men too had been tortured and mutilated. One sat propped against the foremast, his severed genitals thrust into his mouth; he looked incongruous in death, like a cat with a captured bird. Flies clustered the corpses in their millions, their low droning rising above the crackling of blazing timber.

Only a handful of prisoners had been left alive, among them her father, she was grateful to see. He stood in the bow, his face rigid with shock as a Dervish warrior carefully moistened the leather thongs binding his arms so they would bite deeper into his flesh. The only women to survive were the two missionary sisters. Victoria guessed from the glazed looks on their faces that they had been violated.

A Dervish came dancing toward her and Victoria started to scream. It was an involuntary outcry against the horror of the moment, an instinctive protest that in the midst of life death could appear in such bizarre fashion, for there, perched absurdly on the end of the warrior's spear, bobbed the severed head of Major Smiles.

EIGHT

Victoria stumbled through the darkness, struggling to see the trail ahead. The desert lay locked in a hush of silvery moonlight, its surface dotted with boulders and camel thorn. The raiders did not travel in convoy, but spread widely in an untidy rabble, steering a herd of donkeys loaded with plunder taken during the fighting. They belonged, Victoria discovered, to a small war party which had set out to pillage the villages along the banks of the Nile. They looked a sorry lot, scarecrow men in ragged jibbahs and thonged sandals. Some wore helmets and chainmail breastplates, others scarlet tunics and tattered gowns taken from the corpses they had slaughtered. All displayed a callous disregard for their captives' welfare.

The horror of the riverboat massacre had left Victoria feeling stunned and disorientated, but she quickly discovered the savagery she had witnessed had been little more than a prelude, for their captors, devoid of any semblance of human feeling or human compassion, seemed intent on exacerbating their ordeal as much as possible. For eight days they moved across the desert on foot, travelling mainly at night and early morning. At noon they halted, seeking what shade they could find while they waited for the terrible heat of the day to fade. The prisoners were forced to carry part of the warriors' booty. When at first Sister Maria had attempted to refuse, she had been beaten on the soles of her feet for her pains, and now, though she obeyed reluctantly, her flesh was so badly swollen it was all she could do to hobble along like an old crone, with laughing tribesmen spurring her on with lashes from rhinoceros-hide whips.

Secured by her neck to the tail of one of the donkeys, Victoria was forced to trot in its wake, hauling her load through the chill hours of darkness and the blistering heat of the lifting sun. Bobbing from the donkey's rear was the head of Major Smiles. The Dervishes, impressed by Victoria's display of hysteria, had decided to keep the macabre booty where she could view it constantly, and the odour of its decomposing flesh hung in her nostrils like a suffocating cloud.

The men fared even worse than the women for, with their arms tied, they were obliged to carry their loads strapped unevenly across their shoulders. Water was only distributed at noon, and the food, small, flat brick-hard cakes of bread which the Arabs called *khobz* were offered in such a desultory fashion that Victoria often wondered how they ever got fed at all. Their bodies, already emaciated from weeks of enforced starvation, had little strength for the arduous journey, and when, on the morning of the third day, Sister Maria collapsed to the ground in a state of exhaustion, one of the tribesmen slit her throat with the same casual unconcern he might have displayed in dispatching an injured animal.

There was now little doubt what their fate would be if they failed to maintain their progress, but though the captives struggled to remain upright their limbs gave out inevitably and one by one they fell in the sand to become victims of the Dervish swords. Sister Loretta was the next to go. A bearded tribesman carefully removed her load, distributing it equally among the remaining prisoners, then he drew his blade and with an air of casual indifference severed Sister Loretta's head.

Toward noon Mr Robinson dropped and was dealt with in a similar fashion. During the following night, three more men sprawled in the dust and they too were summarily slaughtered and left behind for the jackals and vultures.

Victoria's dress was torn and the shoes she wore, tough leather bootees made in Edinburgh for ladies attracted to the heathery slopes of the Scottish Highlands, had already begun to disintegrate under the rigours of the enforced march. On the evening of the fourth day, she tore off the hem of her petticoat and tied the strips around her feet, forming little

119

cushions to protect the soles from the prickly camel thorn littering their route.

Now that her initial horror had receded a new emotion rose inside her. The will to live. Nothing could destroy her, she decided. Not the desert, nor the barbarity of her captors. She was determined to survive. Whatever happened, she would find a way to endure it somehow, she had made up her mind on that.

On the eighth day, instead of calling a halt at noon, the warriors marched on through the blistering sun and Victoria guessed they were approaching the end of their journey. There were now only four captives left, Victoria the only surviving woman.

Across the *reg* she spotted the rooftops of a distant village. The houses were scattered and disorderly, their mudwalled exteriors little different to the bedrock floor, but it was the first sign of human habitation they had encountered in more than a week and Victoria experienced a feeling of profound relief that the nightmare trek was finally over. As they moved closer, she saw that the village formed a kind of disjointed cartwheel, with the placid waters of a desert oasis at its centre. The dwellings looked angular and primitive; in some places the walls had crumbled completely leaving gaping holes through which she could see the inhabitants.

As they approached she heard a distant yodelling sound and people began to pour into the streets in their hundreds; black-robed women with heavy face-veils, dark-skinned warriors in ragged jibbahs, ancient tribesmen in woolly skullcaps. The clamour of their voices deadened Victoria's eardrums. She tried not to show her fear as she and her fellow prisoners were led along the narrow side streets and into the village square. Here, the houses were more solidly built, some two storeys high, with flat roofs and myriad arches which interlocked in a maze of twisting passages.

The warriors who had brought them were determined to make the most of being the centre of attraction, waving their booty aloft and lashing their captives' shoulders with their vicious whips. Dogs barked as they passed by, and children ran shouting in their wake.

In the centre of the square, palms flanked the rim of the oasis pool and beneath their shade the clumsy caravan was brought to a halt. For the first time in eight days the rope was removed from Victoria's neck and she collapsed to the ground, tears springing quickly to her eyes.

Glancing across the sand, she saw her father squatting in the dust with the other men, his face riven with exhaustion. His wrists and hands had swollen painfully from the tight leather thongs. Victoria reached under her dress and tore off a strip of her petticoat. To the amusement of the laughing throng, she dipped the rag in the water and carefully bathed her father's face. He gasped as the cool moisture touched his skin, his tongue darting out to catch the trickling drops. 'Where are we?' he whispered weakly, his voice cracking in his throat.

'I don't know,' Victoria told him, 'but surely they'll let us rest now. Even they must see that without sleep and nourishment we will all of us die.'

He blinked as she washed his face, his eyes dazed and bewildered. 'How are you, Victoria? Are your feet all right?'

She hesitated. She felt numb from the soles of her feet to her knees. She must look a dreadful sight, she realised. Her dress was in shreds and her hair hung lank and dusty over her grime-smeared face.

'Don't worry about me,' she answered in a firm voice, 'concentrate on yourself, father. I'm a survivor. I'll be all right.'

The hubbub of Dervish voices suddenly rose in a ragged cheer and Victoria watched the crowds part to reveal a coarse-looking man who waddled toward them with the ungainly gait of a pregnant camel. He carried in his hand a tall stick, its tip carved into the shape of a viper's head. His face beneath the turban displayed the fleshy indulgences of easy living, the nose prominent and pulpy, the frontal portion forming a bulbous globe which almost blotted out the upper lip, the nostrils spreading into the chubby rotundities of his cheeks. As he drew closer, a stench of sweet-smelling spices reached Victoria's nostrils, their scent so cloying she almost wanted to be sick.

'It's the local Emir,' her father whispered under his breath, 'the village headman.'

At that moment, for no apparent reason, a woman in a black face-veil leapt forward and smacked the damp rag out of Victoria's hand with a heavy stick. Victoria was so surprised she froze, staring up at the woman in bewilderment.

The woman brought the stick down across Victoria's shoulders, yelling at her in a high-pitched haranguing tone which drummed infuriatingly in Victoria's eardrums. Victoria's uncertainty vanished. Slowly she straightened. She had come through too much to put up with this.

The woman went on shouting and waving the stick under Victoria's chin as Victoria stared at her coldly. Then Victoria drew back her fist, and with all the strength she could muster, hit the woman full in the face. She watched the black-robed figure crash to the ground, the veil ripping from her features. A hush settled over the startled spectators. Their voices faded and silence descended on the village square, broken only by the sound of a dog barking in the middle distance.

Victoria glared defiantly at the dark faces watching her. She saw the woman stretched at her feet, eyes filled with pain and fear. She saw the cheeks of the warriors, wrinkled by the sun, studying her intently beneath their tightly bound turbans. She saw the Emir, his loose lips pursed into a puckered circle which was almost lost beneath the heavy cornice of his nose. Then suddenly he began to laugh. He guffawed out loud, and as if the sound was a signal, the crowd began to roar in unison.

The Emir lifted his staff and bellowed something that sounded like a pronouncement. His message was met by a burst of cheering from the assembled spectators. Four women came forward, seizing Victoria by the arms. She glanced helplessly at her father as the crowd parted and the women led her through the throng of laughing milling people. Away from the waterplace they took her, into the narrow sidestreets where the walls cast blessed curtains of cool shadow. Grinning tribesmen trotted at their side, waving and gesticulating like frenzied children. Victoria made no attempt to resist. Even if she escaped, she reasoned, where could she go? The desert lay in all directions, flat and implacable. She would never survive it alone.

A building loomed up, slightly larger than the rest and set

back from the twisting maze of alleyways. It was square in shape, with an ornate parapet and a huge central roof-doom. Inside, live chickens scratched on the ground, pecking hopefully for scraps of food which might have dropped from the cooking pot. Rush mats had been placed around the walls, and on one of these a half-naked black woman was grinding corn into powder with a stone hand-mallet. She paused when she saw Victoria, but after a quick glance at the women accompanying her, carried on with her labour without a word.

A fire bubbled merrily in a steel bowl at the centre of the floor, its smoke rising through a star-shaped aperture in the roof-globe. One of the women filled a metal pot with water and set it on the fire to boil.

To Victoria's embarrassment, the other women, giggling and chattering vociferously, began to remove her clothing. It had been eight whole days since she had last undressed, and it seemed a blessing to rid herself of the sweatsoaked linen, but naked, she felt vulnerable and afraid.

Wide-eyed children peered in through the open doorway until one of the women, clapping vigorously, shooed them away. She walked back to Victoria and studied her pubis, clucking deep in her throat. The first wispy curls of hair had only recently started to grow on Victoria's groin, but the woman produced a razor-sharp knife and, to Victoria's alarm, began to shave her flesh clean. When she had finished, she polished the skin smooth with a pumice stone, and while Victoria was trying to assess this unseemly affront to her person, the other women dragged forward a heavy metal bathtub with the words 'Made in Sheffield' printed plainly across its top, and filled it with the water that had been set on the fire to boil. When they were satisfied the temperature was just right, they tipped in a jar of sweetly smelling spices and invited Victoria to immerse herself.

Victoria hesitated. After the cruelty of the past few days, she could scarcely believe this was happening. She stared at the veiled faces watching her and they nodded encouragingly. Taking a deep breath, she stepped into the tub and sank into the blissful steaming-hot water.

After she had bathed and dried herself, the women brought

her a loose indigo robe and showed her how to get into it. One of them produced a bowl of porridge-like substance with pieces of roast chicken mixed among it. A small dish of dates was placed at her side, together with a pot of coarse black coffee which left an inch of sediment at the bottom of the cup.

Victoria ate ravenously. It was like the end of a long and harrowing nightmare and as she gobbled down the food she felt new hope springing up inside her.

When she had finished, one of the women tugged at her sleeve and led her across the line of rush-mats into the room next door. It was dark and airless, and around its walls stood a series of *angarebs*, stout wooden frames lashed across with thongs to form Sudanese beds. The woman indicated one and murmured something in a soft voice.

Victoria felt a wave of gratitude sweeping through her. The rigours of the march, the constant fear of decapitation, the long weeks of hunger at El Serir, had filled her with a languor she could scarcely control. With a muffled sob of relief and delight, she fell across the *angareb* and drew the blanket tightly around her. The last thing she heard as she drifted into sleep was the hypnotic throbbing of tam-tams in the street outside.

Something woke her several hours later. She opened her eyes, blinking in the darkness. Through the narrow opening which served as a window she could see the stars shining brightly. The street outside seemed as still as death.

Each of the other *angarebs* was now occupied, she saw, recognising the outlines of the women who had bathed and fed her. They were lying motionless, their bodies rising and falling gently with the rhythm of their breathing.

A cool chill moved through Victoria's body as something familiar assailed her nostrils. It was the odour of body spices, sickly and cloying. A foot scraped on the bare earth floor and, startled, she squinted up through the darkness to see the monstrous figure of the Emir standing in front of her. He was turbanless and sandal-less, his long robe open down the front to reveal his sagging belly and plump hairless thighs. The pale sheen from the window illuminated his erection, glinting on the shiny scar tissue where the ritual circumcision had flayed not merely the foreskin but the organ's entire length.

She tried to scream, the sound catching in her throat. One of the women giggled softly and she realised they were not asleep after all. They had been lying silently, waiting for the Emir's arrival. There would be no help from that quarter, she realised, and panic seared her brain. She struggled into a seated position, casting the blanket aside, but the Emir seized her by the throat, his podgy fingers digging deep into her helpless flesh. She choked and spluttered as he tore at the loose robes covering her body. Then the cool night air touched her naked skin and she almost gagged as he rolled on to the bed beside her.

The odour of his spices overpowered her senses as his hands move over her flinching form, squeezing her barely formed breasts, sliding down the steep curve of her spine to seize the flesh at her rump. Gasping, she tried to struggle, but the sheer weight of his enormous body held her in place as he positioned himself comfortably between her thighs. He was grunting in the hoarse instinctive way of an animal going through some timeworn ceremony which offered neither meaning nor fulfilment.

Desperately she pounded his skull and shoulders with her fists. A searing pain shot through her groin as he forced himself inside her. She threw back her head screaming, and he began to drive his body in a steadily quickening tempo. She could hear the women giggling openly now, making no attempt to cloak their amusement.

His movements grew more frenetic, more desperate, until he was gasping out loud, his rank breath bathing her face as his florid flesh shuddered into orgasm. It was over almost as quickly as it had begun. He seemed to pause, his body going rigid and still. Then, with a deep sigh, he withdrew his penis and rolled heavily on to his side.

She lay in silence, shivering all over, staring into the night. For a while, no emotion confronted her. She seemed devoid of feeling or response.

The night air cooled her fevered skin, and somewhere far off she heard a dog barking mournfully. Beside her on the *angareb* the Emir slid quietly into slumber, his fleshy lips vibrating as he snored deep in his throat. The women too, with the entertainment over, were now sleeping fitfully.

It had all happened too quickly for Victoria to accept. She had been defiled, squalidly and perfunctorily. Used, like a piece of inanimate clay. Her shattered senses began to focus in a new sensation. Hate.

She swung her legs over the bed and padded naked into the other room. The embers of the cooking fire glowed through the darkness. She filled the pot with water and set it on the coals to warm. She was trembling all over, her body going into intermittent convulsions which shook her entire frame.

When the water was tepid, she poured some of it into a wooden bowl and washed herself thoroughly, scrubbing her chaffed flesh as if it would never be clean again.

After she had finished, she set the pot on the flames to boil. For nearly an hour she waited as steam rose from the slowly heating liquid, until at last its surface broke into a cluster of furious bubbles.

Picking up a stick, she hooked it under the pot's wire handle and carried the steaming liquid through into the other room. The Emir was lying on his back now, his mouth still open, the muffled snores issuing softly from his throat. Beneath his monstrous belly, the flaccid penis looked like a dark flower dropped between his thighs.

As if to reassure herself, Victoria said in a quiet voice: 'No one will ever humiliate me again.'

Then, with a deep breath, she tilted the wire handle and poured the pot's contents over the Emir's groin.

NINE

The sound of the old lady chuckling made Kengle start. He shook himself, shifting uncomfortably in the armchair. He had been so enthralled he had completely lost track of the passage of time. Glancing through the window he saw the sky beginning to darken and he looked hurriedly at his watch. My God, he thought, is it that late?

The old lady was studying him with amusement. Her attitude had softened considerably since their initial meeting, he noticed, and he guessed it was probably the first time in her life she had unburdened herself so completely.

'You must stay for dinner,' she said, making it sound like a command rather than an invitation. 'I get so tired of dining alone.'

'I have to get back to London,' he told her, 'I have an important meeting in the morning.'

'Don't be so impatient, Mr Kengle. The things I have to tell you cannot be hurried.'

Kengle felt his inquisitiveness returning. She was right, he thought. Her story had completely absorbed him. He looked at her curiously. 'What happened to your mother after the Emir affair?'

'Well, the Emir wanted her killed of course. That was the penalty for attacking such a noble personage as the village headman. But by one of those curious quirks of circumstance, the villagers decided in a spontaneous burst of logic that Victoria must be mad, and being mad must therefore be protected by Allah.'

'That couldn't have pleased her victim.'

'Not a bit. The physicians said he would never again enjoy the pleasures of the flesh with quite the same enthusiasm. He ranted and raved for her execution but the people remained obstinate. Victoria was afflicted in the head, they said, and by the laws laid down by the Mahdi himself, son of Allah, defender of the righteous, scourge of the ungodly, she was not to be harmed.'

'Did she remain the Emir's property?'

'Officially, yes. But she was taken from his household and put to work under the guidance of the women. She was never again abused or harshly treated, and despite her obvious beauty, no one else attempted to touch her in the carnal sense.'

'What about her father?'

'He fared less happily, I fear. He was kept, together with the surviving male members of their party, in a cramped oven-hot prison block with heavy chains around his neck. Victoria took them food night and morning, but at the end of the first year the eldest of the prisoners died from malnutrition, and four months later the two remaining males were sold to a slave caravan on its way to Nyala. Soon, of their original party, only my mother and grandfather remained.

She paused as the sound of a bell echoed through the corridor outside.

'That will be Evans calling me in to dinner,' she said. 'Will you stay?'

Kengle hesitated. He had things to do in London. Important things. Messy ends to tie up. And yet . . . time seemed to have lost its relevance somehow. Suddenly he knew there could be no question of his leaving, and with a grin, he nodded.

The meal was pleasant and informal. They dined in a large hall decorated with gilded bronze furniture. The walls were embellished with eighteenth-century tapestries and the high arch displayed a delicate ceiling stucco.

Lady Catherine talked incessantly as she ate but she was careful, Kengle noticed, to keep the conversation on a mundane level. Clearly she wanted none of the servants to overhear.

Kengle, for his part, was seething with impatience. He

128

picked at his food, forcing himself to make polite comments from time to time, but only when dinner was over and the servants had finally withdrawn was he able, with coffee and brandy at his wrist, to re-open the subject.

'So your mother grew into womanhood as a Dervish slave? I had no idea.'

'That's hardly surprising. The story was kept a strict secret by every member of my family. You must understand the times, Mr Kengle. For a respectable Englishwoman, such an experience was regarded as the worst kind of social disgrace. After the fall of Khartoum, the British virtually withdrew from the Sudan and for the next thirteen years they had to live with the ignominy of defeat. That is, until the expeditionary force of 1898. Ironically, the Dervish leader, the Mahdi, died only five months after my mother's capture, but he was succeeded by a new ruler, the Khalifa, who was just as ruthless, just as fanatical.'

Kengle swirled the brandy in his glass. 'And the diamonds, the ones your grandfather discovered in the carpenter's shop, they were of course the Churchill collection?'

'That's correct. If Charlton Routledge had not been a Dervish prisoner he would have known about the diamonds already. They'd been stolen from a sultan's caravan on its way to Bambari, and there wasn't a soldier in Kitchener's army who didn't dream of discovering for himself the legendary riches said to lie in Dervish hands.'

'And through all this time your grandfather and this young innocent girl from Hardy's Proprietary Ladies' College continued to exist in a world which must have seemed, to their eyes, utterly foreign and barbaric?'

The old lady smiled. 'Yes, it's hard to conceive of in this day and age. My mother lived with the Dervishes for thirteen years. The British of course imagined she was dead. There were times no doubt when she felt like that herself. But she hung on, stubbornly and defiantly, until at last, when she must have finally despaired of any hope of rescue, there came riding across the desert toward her four men whose lives would become inextricably bound up with her own.'

*　　*　　*

From two miles out, the village looked like a handful of brown sugar cubes scattered across the desert floor. The buildings seemed to ripple into each other, their contours blending in the heat. Coffey reined in his camel and waved the others back. Hamira, he thought, experiencing a momentary sense of jubilation at the thought that they had crossed mile upon mile of hostile desert using nothing more than a battered ship's sextant strapped to Driscoll's saddlehorn, but he suppressed the feeling quickly. There could be watchers on the hillslopes, outriders, Dervish patrols. It was time for caution.

In a little hollow choked with acacia trees they hobbled the camels and held a hasty council of war. 'The difficulty as I see it,' Coffey explained, 'is that there's no way of approaching the village without signalling we're coming. Any attempt to cross that *reg* will raise a dust-cloud a mile high.'

'Why don't we go in at night?' Benson suggested. 'They won't see our dust in the dark. What's more, I'll bet they feel pretty safe in their little refuge. It wouldn't surprise me if they didn't bother posting guards.'

'We can't go stampeding through the whole damned village looking for the woman and her father. We've got to locate them first.'

'Lieutenant,' Sergeant MacAngus said slowly, 'yon village is at least two miles away. Even with field glasses we'll pick up precious little detail at this range. And there are bound to be goatherds out, people wandering, children playing. The longer we hang about, the greater the chances of discovery.'

Coffey settled back on his haunches, chewing at his lower lip. 'You're right. Surprise is the only advantage we've got. We really ought to move at once.'

'Well, we've bluffed our way across 140 miles of desert and nobody's challenged our story so far,' Driscoll said. 'Why don't we simply ride in and ask for a night's lodging? I suggest we choose the six stoutest Dawasir camels, four for us and one each for Miss Routledge and her father, and leave them here under the watchful eye of Sergeant MacAngus. The rest we'll offer to the village headman.'

'You mean a bribe?'

'Well, let's face it, squire, it's very difficult to be

inhospitable to people who come to your home bearing gifts.'

Coffey considered for a moment. He didn't care much for the idea, but it seemed the only reasonable one in the circumstances. 'Very well,' he agreed. 'Our bluff's brought us this far. Maybe it'll work again. Sort out the camels and let's get started.'

He was not a cowardly man, but as they made their preparations he felt fear rising inside him and his muscles knotted with tension as he climbed into the saddle and set off across the desert *reg*, Benson and Driscoll following discreetly, shepherding the spare camels in a ragged disordered line. Coffey slowed his animal to a walking pace, struggling to quell the tremors which were rippling through his stomach. His throat felt dry and he forced himself to sway lazily with the rhythm of his mount as if there was nothing on his mind beyond a natural inherent desire to complete their task as quickly as possible. He recalled stories of how the Dervishes treated their prisoners, of eyes prised out, skin flayed off, parts severed and mutilated, and the tension inside him steadily intensified.

He watched the flat-roofed houses gradually taking shape, their outlines, cube-like from a distance, assuming new textures as they drew steadily closer. Turrets rose in the sunlight, the parapets moulded into crude battlements etched against the sky. Soon he could see streets, narrow and winding, their rough contours almost obscured by dwellings crowding in on either side. The buildings became grander, taking on new definition with terraces and archways and little flights of stairs worn smooth by thousands of sandalled feet.

They got within four hundred yards before the alarm sounded. A small boy tending a herd of goats spotted their approach and set up a series of high-pitched yodelling noises which echoed discordantly on the hot dry air.

'There goes our anonymity,' Coffey murmured.

'Shouldn't worry, old boy,' Driscoll answered in a cheerful voice. 'Too late to turn back now anyway.'

They reached the mudwalled outdwellings and Coffey saw people appearing in the doorways, blackrobed women, tiny children, turbanned tribesmen, all staring at them with expressions of amazement. A few emaciated donkeys stood chewing docilely from battered feeding pails.

Suddenly they were surrounded. It happened as quickly as that; one minute the villagers were studying their approach from the shelter of their doorways, the next they were swarming around Coffey and his companions completely blocking their path. On all sides, excited faces peered up at their own, women in heavy black veils, children with hair-tufts sprouting from closely shaved crowns, dark-eyed warriors wielding spears, swords and long-barrelled flintlocks, all of them yodelling insanely in a high-pitched caterwauling way that made Coffey's senses reel. It was impossible to proceed for the crowd obstructed them at every turn, so they reined in their camels and sat staring down at the sea of bobbing heads while the din rose to a hysterical crescendo.

'What the hell do we do now?' Coffey shouted at Driscoll.

'Sit tight. We can keep this up just as long as they can.'

The sunlight gleamed on brandished weapons and savage faces; Coffey felt as if his brain was bursting through his skull, and only with the greatest effort of will did he manage to hold himself in check, maintaining his composure with an air of steely reserve which owed more to panic than to any true strength of character.

For nearly ten full minutes they sat in silence while the sea of people yelled and swayed and their camels snorted in protest. Then, just when Coffey thought he could stand it no longer, the tumult suddenly subsided and a blessed silence settled around them.

The crowds parted and down the centre of the street came a thickset man carrying a staff carved in the shape of a snake's head. Slowly and imperiously he walked toward them, followed by a group of what Coffey assumed to be the village dignitaries.

'The Emir,' Driscoll whispered. 'Dismount slowly and stand beside your camels. Keep your movements steady and unhurried, and let me do the talking.'

Coffey slid to the ground, feeling a sense of trepidation as he did so. Here, he was no longer rearing above the demented townspeople, but level with them, eye to eye, arm to arm. Struggling to maintain an air of dignity, he stared back at the savage features glaring into his.

132

Driscoll meanwhile was going through the elaborate greeting ceremony. Nobody in the world could be quite as graceful as a Dervish when he had a mind to, Coffey thought, bowing and scraping, delivering grandiose flatteries, and all the time the two men watching each other like hawks.

The people waited in silence, hoping Driscoll's explanation would prove inadequate so they could press on with the more interesting business of severing limbs and heads.

Driscoll indicated the Dawasir camels, conveying by expressive gestures that they were now the Emir's property. When the complex greeting ritual had been exhausted, he eased sideways and without turning his head, said through his face-veil: 'The old boy seems satisfied with our story. He thinks it's unusual to find Tuareg nobles wandering so far east but he's delighted with the camels and he's invited us to spend the night as his personal guests.'

'Thank God,' Coffey breathed.

'There's just one slight difficulty. As a sign of good faith, he's asked to see our faces.'

Coffey felt his wrists turn icy. 'For Christ's sake, can't you talk him out of it?'

'I've tried. I've explained that according to our beliefs, displaying our features would be the worst possible kind of insult, but he's adamant, the fat bastard. Says he doesn't care about that; says it's so rare to meet tribesmen from such a distant country, he'd like to see what we look like.'

'Dissuade him,' Coffey ordered. 'Tell him we've sworn for religious reasons never to reveal ourselves to man or beast. Tell him anything you like, only for God's sake change his mind.'

'I'll give it another try, squire. But if he refuses to listen, you'd better be ready to obey with good grace.'

'Are you crazy? One look at our white skins and he'll know we're imposters.'

'Why should he? We're probably the first Tuareg he's seen in his life.'

'He may be a savage, Driscoll,' Coffey said dryly, 'but he's not a fool.'

'Very well,' Driscoll sighed, 'I'll try the religious argument and see how he responds.'

He spoke again to the Emir, keeping his voice carefully deferential. The man listened in silence, his face placid as he waited until Driscoll had finished then, without bothering to answer, he barked out a command in a sharp guttural voice and instantly, a group of tribesmen seized Lieutenant Benson by the arms. Benson jerked back, struggling to pull himself free, but before he could protest, one of the men had reached up and whipped the blue cowl from his face.

There was a moment of frozen stillness, a moment in which Coffey held his breath. Benson looked startled, his eyes bright, the scar on his cheek crimson against the milk-white skin. His mouth hung open in an involuntary gasp and his teeth, with their V-shaped aperture, gleamed in the sunlight.

Coffey felt his heart sink. Their masquerade was over. There was no disputing it, Benson looked every inch an Englishman. Instinctively, Coffey's hand crept beneath the folds of his *gandoura*, his fingers locating the handle of his Browning revolver.

Then a strange thing happened. The people fell back. On all sides, the crowd receded and a weird wailing sound rose from a thousand throats, hovering mournfully on the air. Coffey frowned, his thumb pausing as it fumbled for the pistol's safety-catch. He was aware that something inexplicable was happening in front of him. The expressions on the faces of the villagers had changed from malevolent and demented glee to an air of universal awe, bewilderment and (Coffey could not be sure about this, but he was practically certain he had analysed it correctly) reverence. Before his astonished gaze, men, women, children, even the chubby figure of the Emir himself, flopped slowly forward and prostrated themselves on the ground. The effect was disorientating to say the least. Suddenly they were the only figures left standing in the entire street, and as Coffey stared in amazement across the sea of lowered heads he thought for a moment they had become the victims of some cruel and elaborate joke, as if the Dervishes, in a spontaneous display of humour, had decided to taunt their captives with a bizarre last salute. Blinking helplessly, he peered over the quiescent figures at Lieutenant Driscoll. 'What the hell is going on?'

Driscoll shook his head. He looked as puzzled as anyone. He frowned down at the villagers sprawled at his feet, then, as he stared at Lieutenant Benson, a glimmer of understanding entered his eyes. 'It's Benson,' he whispered. 'They think he's the re-incarnation of the Mahdi.'

'What?'

'Look at his teeth. That opening in the front is a sign. It's laid down in the scriptures. And the birthmark on the cheek.'

'That's not a birthmark, it's a scar. I gave it to him at the railhead. And his teeth are crooked because I knocked them that way with my elbow.'

'For God's sake, the Dervishes don't know that. Don't you see? They think Benson is the saviour they've been waiting for. They think he's the Mahdi returning to lead them against the Infidel.'

'He's not even the right colour, for God's sake.'

'Who gives a damn about colour? He carries the signs, that's all the Dervishes care about. What's more, if we want to go on breathing, old sport, I suggest we do everything in our power to foster the idea.'

Benson looked dazed and uncertain. He stared down at the bowed heads pressed meekly in the dust. 'You mean, they think I'm some kind of god?' he whispered.

'Well, not a god exactly. More like the son of the Prophet. Among the Dervishes, that makes you a very powerful individual indeed.'

'But I can't even speak their language.'

'Who cares? As long as they think you're the Mahdi, you can say what the hell you like. Nobody's going to argue.'

Coffey thought quickly. What a stroke of luck. A chance in a million. A miracle, he thought. But if they wanted to utilise it, they would have to act quickly. 'Tell them to get up,' he ordered. 'We can't have the whole bloody village lying around like corpses. Ask the Emir about Miss Routledge and her father. Tell him we'd like to see them if we may, as quickly as possible.'

'We'll have to give him a reason,' Driscoll argued.

'Say the Mahdi has heard about the lady's beauty and wishes to view it in person.'

'That's pushing it a bit, squire.'

135

'All right. Say we want to question them about the ways of the Infidel. For strategic purposes, of course.'

'That's better,' Driscoll agreed.

He began to speak in loud ringing tones, and gradually the villagers clambered to their feet. The Emir made a series of statements, but he sounded a good deal less confident than he had a minute or two before. He barked a command, and some of his henchmen elbowed their way back through the tightly packed throng while Coffey waited, humming nervously under his breath. He was trying hard to look at ease but the tribesmen were staring at Benson fascinated, and Coffey had the unpleasant notion that if they weren't suitably restrained they might at any moment decide to hurl themselves upon him out of sheer adoration.

After a few minutes he spotted the Emir's men returning, escorting a wizened scarecrow of a man in a ragged jibbah. The man's wrists and ankles were shackled with chains, and as he shuffled along, he clutched the chains in front of him like some grotesque form of offering.

Walking by his side, moving with a slow fluid grace, was a tall suntanned woman dressed in Arab robes. Her features were stunning in their symmetry, but it was not the woman's beauty which impressed Coffey so much as the innate strength which lay in her face, the muted defiance which seemed to blaze out of her in the presence of the people who had held her captive for so many years.

The couple stopped when they reached the gathering, and Coffey was surprised to see no flicker of emotion in their eyes. Then he realised that in their Tuareg robes, he and his companions looked little different to the hundreds of other warriors who thronged Hamira's marketplace.

To Driscoll, he said: 'Tell them to take those chains off.'

Driscoll repeated the order in a flat voice, and at a word from the Emir the chains were quickly unlocked and dragged from Routledge's body. Routledge looked awestruck for a moment. He stood staring at his wrists with the dumbfounded expression of a blind man given the gift of sight. Then to Coffey's consternation, he began to cry.

His daughter slipped one arm around his shoulders, holding

him close, and with a visible effort, he regained control of himself.

'Can we take them out of here without these bastards trying to stop us?' Coffey asked Driscoll in a low voice.

'Not a chance. Getting out's going to be a damn sight tougher than getting in. Now that they've found the Mahdi, they'll want to hold on to him. The Emir has invited us to stay at his home as his guests. They're planning a little celebration tonight, a festival to herald the imminent downfall of the Infidel. It would be imprudent to refuse. Whether we like it or not, old sport, I'm afraid we're stuck here.'

'Will they allow us to wander the village at will?'

'Possibly, if Benson demands it. No one, not even the Emir, would wish to oppose the son of the Prophet.'

'Then ask them to leave us alone for a while. Say we'd like to acquaint ourselves with Hamira's defences while we contemplate the destruction of the British.'

Driscoll sighed. 'Look, squire, these boys may be perfectly happy to allow us the freedom of the village, but letting us wander unattended is something else entirely. Try and put yourself in their position. I mean, if you heard that Jesus Christ was cavorting around the streets of London, wouldn't you be at least mildly curious?'

'Tell them we must have solitude to concentrate on our next campaign. Tell them anything you like, only for Christ's sake get them out of here.'

'I'll give it a try,' Driscoll said.

As Driscoll repeated Coffey's instructions, Coffey noticed a subtle change in the woman's expression. She had caught the lilt and cadences of their voices, the unmistakable rhythm of the English language. Now she was staring intently at Coffey, her chest rising and falling rapidly.

The Emir, after listening to Driscoll for a moment, began to address the throng in a high wailing monotone. They received his words in respectful silence and slowly, reluctantly, began to drift away, moving into the side streets and alleyways. In the space of a few minutes, the little thoroughfare was almost deserted, though Coffey could see the glimmer of faces peeping at them from under the arches and darkened doorways.

The Emir was the last to leave. After repeating his offer of hospitality and describing the precise location of his home, he turned with an obvious air of regret and began to shuffle back the way he had come, followed by the tiny cluster of village headmen.

As soon as the tribesmen were out of earshot, the girl said in a breathless voice: 'Who are you? What are you doing here?'

'Miss Routledge?' Coffey asked.

She gasped at the sound of her name. Coffey tugged away his face mask.

'Lieutenant Coffey, ma'am,' he told her, 'of the 10th Westmorland Lancers. This is Lieutenant Driscoll and Lieutenant Benson. We've come to get you out of here.'

Slowly she raised one hand, pressing it hard against her lips. Her eyes widened. Coffey understood what she was going through, the astonishment, disbelief. the almost fearful flicker of jubilation.

'In the hills behind the *reg*,' he went on quickly, 'we have camels, water and provisions. With luck, we hope to be back behind the British lines in two to three days.'

'The British are in the Sudan?' her father whispered.

'Yes, sir. Kitchener's army is marching south down the Nile to Khartoum. The days of the Khalifa are already numbered.'

Suddenly, for the second time, the man began to cry. This was no momentary outburst of emotion however, but a full-bodied lament, with tears rolling helplessly down his ravaged cheeks. Coffey stood in a paroxysm of embarrassment. It was the woman, still cool, still totally controlled, who reassured him.

'You must understand, we've waited so long for your coming. In the beginning, we expected you almost every week, and then as the months spread into years, I think we came to regard the very thought of rescue as little more than a ridiculous dream. This is the first time since his capture, for example, that my father has had his chains removed. I'm afraid liberation can be a difficult thing to come to terms with when you don't expect it.'

It took her father several minutes to regain control, and when he did he looked at Coffey in a slightly ashamed kind of way. 'Forgive me lieutenant,' he said, 'I am not usually so emotional.'

'I understand, sir. I've no doubt every one of us would react similarly in the same circumstances. For the moment, however, we need your help. By an extraodinary stroke of luck, the Dervishes appear to have taken Lieutenant Benson here for the re-incarnation of the Mahdi.'

'What?' the woman murmured.

'I know how crazy it sounds, but it's perfectly true. Apparently that hole in his teeth and the scar on his cheek have been predicted in ancient writings, which means that, for the moment at least, we're comparatively safe. The question is, if we can find a way out of here, are you ready to ride?'

'Of course,' the man said. 'We'll do anything you wish. But we can't leave yet.'

'Why not?'

Routledge hesitated. He looked at his daughter, then back at Coffey.

'There's something I must show you,' he said. 'Come with me, please.'

Puzzled, they set off along the street, following Routledge past a mudwalled minaret and around a palm-fringed pool where women in bright robes sat scrubbing their laundry on the rocky bank. Coffey noted the glances cast in their direction and with a sinking heart realised the sheer impracticality of making any move undetected.

Routledge walked with a slow shuffling gait, and from time to time his daughter reached out to steady him, whispering encouragingly. The townspeople followed at a discreet distance, their faces dark and intent.

Routledge ducked under a heavy stone archway and they found themselves in a tiny courtyard with palm fronds at its centre. Around the rim were smaller arches, some with wooden boards across their fronts.

'Better tell your friend to remain in the doorway,' Routledge advised. 'Those villagers are bursting with curiosity and we don't wish to be disturbed for a minute or two.'

Coffey glanced at Benson who, without a word, turned and stood beneath the arch, staring stonily into the street beyond.

Coffey peered around the edge of the courtyard. Among the shadows he could see a cluster of primitive carpentry tools. 'What is this place?' he asked.

'Workshop,' Routledge said, 'I help out here most days. I'm good with a hammer and saw. Been a hobby of mine for years. When we lived in El Serir, I furnished the entire house myself. Tables, chairs, beds, everything. A few years ago the Dervishes moved me from the prison block so I could help the local craftsmen.'

Coffey looked puzzled. 'Surely there's no escape route this way,' he said.

'We can't escape, not empty-handed,' Routledge told him gently. 'Come over here.'

He shuffled under the archways to the corner where the tools were kept. After fumbling among them for a moment or two, he dragged out a heavy bag and began to unlace its top.

'What is this?' Coffey asked.

Routledge winked. 'Hold out your hand,' he instructed.

Coffey did so, mystified. Carefully, Routledge tipped up the sack and spilled some of its contents into Coffey's palm. Coffey rolled the stones about, holding them to the light. Routledge stood watching him, an expectant smile on his face. 'Well?'

Coffey looked blank. 'Well what?'

'You don't know what they are?'

'Look like bits of fractured glass to me.'

'Not glass, you idiot. Diamonds. Uncut diamonds. The biggest you ever saw in your life.'

Startled, Coffey sucked in his breath. He looked at Driscoll and Driscoll stared back, his eyes glittering fiercely.

'Of course,' Coffey whispered. 'These are the diamonds which were stolen from that caravan in Central Africa. The whole British army's on the lookout for them.'

'The fools here are using them for their drilling tools,' Routledge said, 'but I tell you, gentlemen, the gems this bag contains are worth a king's ransom.'

Coffey moistened his lips with his tongue. He was not a covetous man. He had never bemoaned the circumstances which had led him to a life of such stringency. But his senses quickened as he jiggled the stones in his palm.

'Diamonds this size, and in such quantity,' he breathed. 'Why, their value . . .'

'It's impossible to calculate their value, lieutenant,' Routledge said, watching him with secret amusement. He felt a new wave of confidence as he recognised the hunger in Coffey's eyes, as if he had encountered a kindred spirit. 'That's why we can't under any circumstances leave them behind. If the Khalifa ever learned what his people are harbouring here, he could keep this war going indefinitely.'

Coffey nodded. The logic of Routledge's statement was irrefutable. It was their duty to carry these gems out of harm's way. But surely that was as far as their responsibility went? Lack of money had blighted Coffey's life. He had been forced to scratch and scrape, to eke out his miserable existence while other officers sauntered along in comparative ease, supported by wealthy families. Was that just? Supposing they held on to the diamonds? He could pay his debts, all his debts, and remain solvent for the rest of his life. He could secure not only the present, but his entire future. The answer to all his problems lay right here within his grasp. How often did a man get the chance to put his whole world in order on a single twist of fate?

Keeping his voice calm and dispassionate he said: 'Mr Routledge is quite right. There's enough in this sack for the Khalifa to finance a dozen wars if he chooses to. It's our godgiven duty as officers and Englishmen to see that when we break out of here, the diamonds go too.'

TEN

The feasting started at dusk. Driscoll had been right in one respect – the villagers, though they struggled to subdue their curiosity toward Lieutenant Benson, submitted in the end to their natural feelings and refused to leave his side, touching his robes, stroking his cheeks, bending to kiss his sandalled feet. Soon it seemed absurd to keep up even a pretence at privacy and Benson, at Coffey's suggestion, surrendered himself to their attentions with an air of wary unease. What was more alarming from Coffey's point of view was the fact that from all corners of the outlying desert, parties of tribesmen came riding in to witness the strange and wonderous phenomenon of the Mahdi's re-incarnation until, by nightfall, the village populace had swollen to almost twice its original size.

On the other hand, Coffey and Victoria were allowed to wander the streets at will, and Coffey took advantage of the festivities to re-saddle the camels, replenish the water *guerbas* and strap the diamonds to his animal's back.

Victoria stood beside him in the darkened courtyard, listening to the tam-tams pounding on the soft desert air. Voices rose mournfully above the rooftops, and the low shuffle of sandalled feet rustled in their ears as the tribal dancers went through their timeless rituals.

She felt better than she had that afternoon when Coffey's arrival had filled her with such confusion. Now the initial shock had gone, she had a chance to think things out, to consider and evaluate the meaning of this new development. The past was over. She was going home. Soon there would be no more chains, no more slavery. Soon she would be free.

Strangely, the realisation made her feel uneasy. She had dreamed of it so long that now the moment had come she visualised a world whose dimensions were inestimably greater than the one she lived in. Coffey, his face pale and handsome as he secured the diamonds to his saddlehorn, belonged to that other world. In his features lay the inevitable hallmarks of civilisation, an elusive grace, a touch of humour, even – she thought – a hint of arrogance. And yet, in thirteen years of captivity, he was the only one who had aroused in her the faintest semblance of physical awareness, for she had built up a barrier against the sensual side of life, a barrier which had never slipped. Now she felt an unfamiliar response, filling her with strange almost-forgotten emotions.

'That should hold it,' he said, putting the last touches to the leather strap.

'They won't spill out?' she whispered.

'Shouldn't. That bag's tight as a drum.' He grinned. 'This must be the richest camel in creation.'

'What will happen to the diamonds after we get back?'

He hesitated. 'God knows. Property of the Crown, I expect. Isn't that the law?'

The law? She could not countenance the thought of any law, civilised or not, taking the diamonds from her. They belonged to her and her father. They had earned them, suffered for them.

She stared at Coffey, noting his dirt-smeared cheeks, the thin lines down the sides of his mouth, the stubbled chin where he had pulled aside his face cowl. He was a man any woman would be proud to be with, and God knew he was the only creature she had seen in thirteen years who represented even a glimmer of civilised behaviour. 'You haven't told me your name,' she murmured, 'I mean your first name. The one your friends call you.'

He looked at her with surprise. 'It's Stephen,' he grunted.

She repeated it, moulding her lips around the syllables. 'It's a nice name,' she said.

His mouth twisted into a crooked grin. 'What's yours?'

'Victoria.'

'Even nicer.'

'It's strange. Nobody's called me that for years. Apart from father.'

'Not even the Dervishes?'

'I'm a slave. Slaves aren't worthy of a name.'

'Well, you won't be a slave much longer. Once we reach the ruined fortress at Malawa, there'll be two troops of cavalry waiting to escort us to the river. After that, it'll be Cairo for you, then back to England.'

She breathed deeply, filling her lungs with the dry night air. She could see the stars framed in a perfect square above the courtyard's rim. The drone of tam-tams lingered in her ears as the tension gathered inside her.

'Father was right, wasn't he?' she whispered. 'About the diamonds falling into the wrong hands? About what the Khalifa could do if he realised their true value?'

'That he was,' Coffey said.

'So it's our clear and sacred duty to prevent them being used against the British army?'

'That's right.'

'But what happens after we've thrown the Dervishes off? Surely then the danger will be over.'

Coffey looked puzzled. 'What are you getting at, Miss Routledge?'

'Call me Victoria, please,' she said. Then she hesitated. 'Lieutenant Coffey, those diamonds don't belong to the Crown. If you hand them over, we'll never see them again.'

Coffey's features hardened. He stared at her in silence, his eyes glittering. Panic seized her, and she gabbled quickly on: 'There are enough diamonds in that saddlebag to make each of us rich for the rest of our lives. All you have to do is forget to mention them in your report. Nobody's asking you to betray your role as a British officer. You'll have done what you had to do, taken them out of the enemy's hands. But instead of turning them in, you'll be keeping them in trust, so to speak.'

She paused, her heart fluttering wildly. Coffey studied her for a moment, his features rigid. 'Who put you up to this?' he demanded. 'Your father?'

'Nobody. I've spent thirteen years of my life in this hellhole. While other girls my age were going to dances and buying fancy dresses, I was living the life of an animal. I've had enough of existing at the bottom end of the social scale. I want to try it at the top for a change. I want to go home with my head held high. And now I have a chance. Can't you see those diamonds are compensation for everything I've gone through.'

She stopped, staring at him defiantly. It scarcely mattered what he thought. She was ready to fight for what was hers. She had done enough of the other thing, she decided. Compliance. Passivity. No more of that. This was too important. This was her entire future.

Holding on to the camel saddle, Coffey peered at her inscrutably. Then suddenly he chuckled. 'You've thought it all out,' he whispered.

'I've had plenty of time for thinking,' she said.

'Well, if it makes any difference, the thought of handing the diamonds over never entered my mind.'

She could scarcely believe her ears. 'You mean . . .?'

'I mean we split them among the six of us, equal shares. To hell with the army. I need the money too.'

He was laughing now, his eyes dancing in the starlight. He was on her side, Coffey was on her side. It seemed a miracle. She felt the tension drain out of her as excitement gathered in her chest. 'That's wonderful,' she exclaimed.

'Is it a deal?'

'It's a deal,' she declared, solemnly shaking his proffered hand.

His face sobered. 'First, however, we've got to escape, and that won't be easy the way those villagers are hanging around Lieutenant Benson.'

'What do you plan to do?'

'We need a diversion, that's the first thing. Once the feasting's at its height, I intend to set fire to some of the buildings. There'll be lots of smoke, lots of confusion. When the panic starts, I want you to grab your father and the two lieutenants and bring them here as quickly as possible. Think you can do that?'

She nodded breathlessly.

'Remember, it won't take the Dervishes long to realise the

145

fire's only a blind, so there'll be no time to waste. Go back to the marketplace and wait for the flames. After we're out of here, then we'll talk about wealth and riches.'

The marketplace was so crammed it took Victoria some time to locate Lieutenant Benson. He was sitting beside the Emir looking dazed and bemused as women selected morsels from the bowls in front of him and popped them into his mouth. At his side, acting as interpreter, sat Lieutenant Driscoll. Next to Driscoll she spotted her father. He too seemed bewildered by his newfound status, unable to accept the sudden transition from slave to honoured member of society.

She stationed herself at a point where she was directly in Driscoll's line of vision as people moved in and out of the firelight, carrying bowls of food and drink. In the centre, women danced crocodile fashion, clapping their hands and moving their bodies to the beat of the drum. Warriors swayed dreamily, their eyes fixed trancelike in the glow of the cooking fires. The dancers faded into the crowd and the village men took over, holding sticks and stamping their feet in the sand. In and out they weaved as the drumbeats quickened, thrusting their staves into the soft crumbling earth then pulling them up again. It was a frenzied dance she had seen many times before and it told a story, though she had never been able to understand what it was.

When the dance finished, a group of singers moved into the space left by the dancers, covering the lower portion of their faces with their hands. Victoria knew the Dervishes considered it the height of indelicacy to display the inside of the mouth, and the singers' gesture gave their voices a curiously muffled effect.

Suddenly a new thought struck her. What if, after all these years of living like a savage, she had lost the ability to behave like a civilised human being? Supposing she could no longer communicate out there? She swallowed hard as she struggled to hold on to the memories of her past, shutting her ears to the throbbing of the drums, the wailing of the lutes, the high-pitched voices of the Dervish serenaders. So engrossed was she that for a moment she did not realise the singing had stopped.

146

She straightened, startled. The entire square had come to a standstill, the people frozen into a mute tableau. She could see their faces, the skins dark, the eyes glittering. Then she caught the scent of fumes, the unmistakable odour of woodsmoke. And with it came something else – tar perhaps, or oil. Coffey had started his fire. Her pulses quickened. Straining her neck with the others, she saw the flames at last. Over the rooftops they rose, the smoke billowing and swelling, growing thicker and stronger by the second. Sparks danced into the air, crackling loudly as the black fumes flung themselves skyward.

He had gone to the new part of the village where the dwellings were timber-built, where the woodwork had dried like tinder in the daily heat of the desert sun. Within seconds the fire was leaping among the terraces like a frenzied animal. Flames billowed through the window holes, multiplying with a terrifying force. The skyline was turning into a solid red wall.

With shouts of alarm, the people stampeded toward the blaze, carrying Victoria along with the sheer force of their momentum. Men yelled and gesticulated, woman wailed, and the deafening clamour of human voices added to the turmoil.

Gasping, Victoria struggled to remain upright in the scurrying torrent of humanity. She spotted Driscoll clutching her father by the arm, battling his way toward her. 'What's happening?' he shouted.

'It's Coffey,' she yelled back. 'He started the fire as a diversion.'

'Where is he now?'

'At the workshop, waiting with the camels. He said to get there as quickly as possible.'

'Right. Look after your father. I'll fetch Benson.'

Victoria held on to her father's elbow. She could feel him trembling as he was jostled by the panicstricken throng. Victoria pushed him sideways, elbowing her way furiously against the tide. A man tried to sweep her from his path, but she drove her shoulder against him, dragging her father behind her. People were cursing, tripping, falling. She scampered over them without a pause. If she hesitated, she knew she would be lost.

The short scramble through the heaving streets was like a nightmare. Flames danced everywhere, transforming the night into glorious day. In places, entire blocks were ablaze, the fire setting rooftops and towers in stark relief as it whirled higher and higher into the sky.

Victoria found the alleyway where the workhouse stood. It was empty, thank God. The great mass of the populace was stampeding on toward the flames. She ducked under the archway and spotted Coffey holding the camels by their bridles.

'Where have you been?' he hissed.

'Sorry. It's like a millrace out there.'

'What about Driscoll and Benson?'

'They're coming.'

'For Christ's sake, they'd better be quick.'

Something clattered at her rear and she turned, startled, as someone ran beneath the archway toward her. Pale robes rustled in the darkness and a face, black as the night itself, appeared through the stifling smoke. It was Shilluk, the young man who had tried to buy her from the Emir. For a full moment Shilluk stood staring at the scene inside the courtyard, his dark eyes taking in Coffey, the loaded camels, her father already struggling behind the hump of the nearest beast. Then, glancing at her swiftly, he turned and scrambled back the way he had come.

'Stop him,' Coffey yelled.

Benson and Driscoll heard his shout as they rounded the corner. Driscoll hesitated, taken by surprise, but Benson lunged furiously, grabbing for Shilluk's robes. Shilluk slithered to a halt, swung to one side and darted around him. Benson grabbed again, but he was already too late. Shilluk easily evaded his clutches and stumbled on into the darkness.

Coffey swore. 'Who was that?'

'His name's Shilluk,' Victoria said. 'He's been following me around for weeks.'

'Lover?'

'No,' she snapped fiercely, 'I told you. He's been following me, that's all.'

'Think he guessed what's going on here?'

'I'm sure of it.'

'Then for God's sake mount up before he sounds the alarm. Benson, you carry Mr Routledge. I'll take the girl.'

It was awkward riding double on a camel. The spinal structure wasn't built for comfort. Victoria crouched behind the hump holding on to Coffey with both hands as they lurched under the archway and into the street beyond. The camel moved with a loping ungainly rhythm and she could feel Coffey's hips hard against her. Then her chest tightened in terror as she spotted blocking their path immediately ahead, a throng of warriors with drawn swords. Shilluk, she thought. He had warned them.

Coffey barely hesitated. He kicked his camel straight into the thick of the mob and Victoria, gulping, saw his hand come out, drawing something from deep inside the folds of his robe. It glinted in the fire's glare and she saw it was a heavy revolver, its barrel grey and deadly.

A man seized at their saddle, holding on with one hand while he swung his sword with the other. With a fractional movement of his forearm, Coffey shot the top of the man's skull away. Victoria saw the savage face freeze into the desperate rigidity of death as he pitched headlong into the dust.

A spear zipped past her head, so close she could hear the whirr of its shaft as it spun through the darkness. Coffey was firing furiously now, driving his camel forward and shooting point-blank into the upturned faces as the crowd fell back before him. Crack, crack, crack, the shots reverberated. Victoria felt a hand grasp at her ankle and she lashed out desperately with her right leg, but the man was suddenly upon her, leaping up, his hands groping for her throat. She screamed, and Coffey swung the revolver in a wild backhanded curve. There was a sickening crunch and the warrior slid with a muffled grunt into the dust at their wake.

Coffey was lashing out in all directions, his arm rising and falling in a dizzy blur as he hacked and slashed with the empty revolver at the swirling throng of faces. Victoria felt sick as she struggled to keep her balance on the dipping, lunging saddle. Then with a stab of alarm she realised she was falling, the ground rushing madly upward to meet her. She sprawled in the dust, the wind knocked from her lungs. At her feet, the camel thrashed out its life in a frantic tattoo of death. From its chest protruded a wicked-looking spear, the shaft decorated with fluttering ribbons.

Terror engulfed her. They were down and completely surrounded. But the tribesmen, bewildered by the confusion, were stumbling around like excited children, trying to make up their minds what to do next.

She saw Coffey crouching in the dust, calmly reloading his revolver, his movements sharp yet unhurried. A Dervish leapt toward him, yelling insanely, his sword slashing through the smoke-filled air. Without a pause, Coffey snapped the chambers shut, drew back the hammer and shot the man dead through the front of the chest.

Driscoll turned toward them, kicking his camel through the bobbing heads.

'Come on,' Coffey shouted, grabbing her arm and pushing her forward.

A man seized her by the throat but Coffey fired in an almost reflex action and she felt the man tumble away, propelled backwards by the force of the blast.

Driscoll's camel skidded to a halt, and she mounted without waiting for the creature to kneel, dragging herself up with an almost demented fury, sobs choking deep in her throat.

Coffey grabbed the camel's tail, firing with his free hand into the buffeting mob. She heard her father's voice rising above the mêlée. 'The diamonds, don't forget the diamonds.'

But it was already too late. With Coffey holding on to the animal's tail, Driscoll kicked its flanks with all his strength, and they thundered furiously into the desert night.

ELEVEN

MacAngus heard them coming through the darkness. Reaching for his rifle, he scrambled down the hillslope to where the trail curved beneath the starlight in a golden arc. He saw the shadows merging, thickening, taking on movement and solidity, the camels strangely distorted as they reared, double-loaded, out of the night. He recognised Driscoll kicking his animal into a crouch. There was a woman clinging furiously to Driscoll's waist. Her hood had come off and her hair was tumbling crazily over her shoulders.

Lieutenant Coffey stood holding on to the camel's tail, his face scarlet as he gasped for breath.

'What happened?' MacAngus asked.

Coffey's chest breathed heavily as sweat trickled down his face gathering in a blob on the end of his nose. 'They cut us off.'

'Anybody hurt?'

'Don't think so. We lost a camel though.'

'What about the old man?'

'Lieutenant Benson's got him.'

MacAngus saw a second camel looming through the greyness. Riding it, he recognised the slim outline of Lieutenant Benson and behind him a small sinewy figure in a dirty jibbah. MacAngus watched Benson and the old man dismount. 'Is Miss Routledge all right?' Benson asked Coffey.

'She's fine.'

'What about the diamonds?' the old man demanded.

'What the hell do you expect? We left them behind. It was like a circus back there.'

MacAngus's eyes narrowed. 'Diamonds?' he echoed.

Coffey stared at him, his flushed cheeks calming as his breathing slowly steadied. He spat on the ground, then in a few terse sentences he outlined the details of Routledge's discovery. When he had finished, MacAngus whistled softly under his breath.

'We can't just abandon them,' Routledge protested.

'I don't intend to,' Coffey told him.

'You're not suggesting we return to Hamira?' Lieutenant Benson's cheeks were pale as death.

'We have no choice.'

'You're crazy. Those stones don't even belong to us.'

'Who do they belong to, Benson?'

'The British Crown, of course.'

'Why? Because they were taken in combat? Well, that's not strictly true, is it Benson? If they belong to anyone at all, it's to Mr Routledge here, and I have a feeling he'll be happy to share them with the rest of us if we can only get them back.'

He stared at Routledge as if seeking confirmation, and Routledge nodded.

'Our job was to rescue these people,' Benson declared in a cold voice. 'That's what we came for. Let's forget the diamonds and concentrate on staying alive.'

'The situation's altered now, can't you see that?' Coffey said reasonably. 'If those diamonds find their way into the Khalifa's hands they could change the tide of this entire war.'

'The Dervishes don't even appreciate their value, for God's sake.'

'Not yet, they don't. But when they see them strapped to my saddlehorn, when they realise the risks we went through to carry them back to British lines, they're bound to guess the truth. They may be primitive, Benson, but they're not stupid. Of course it's important to rescue the Routledges. But what's more important still, for Kitchener, for the whole British army, is to get those diamonds out of Hamira.'

'Why don't you tell the truth?' Benson hissed furiously. 'It's not Kitchener you want those diamonds for.'

'No,' Coffey admitted honestly, 'I want them for me. For us, all of us. But that doesn't alter the fact that it's our duty to

152

remove them from Dervish hands. Mind you, I'm not risking my neck to turn over a king's ransom to the British Crown. When we get them back in our possession, they stay in our possession. All we do is forget their existence. A simple omission in our report, nothing more. There'll be no questions asked, no comebacks.'

'You intend to steal them?'

'Not steal, Benson. Redistribute, that's all. Just think, you'll be a wealthy man.'

'I'm already wealthy.'

'Are you, Benson? Are you really? Your family's wealthy. They'll give you anything in the world you ask for as long as you do their bidding. But have you ever considered how sweet it would be to make your own decisions once in a while, to be your own man, free and independent?'

He turned to the others. 'What about the rest of you? Driscoll?'

Driscoll pursed his lips, whistling softly. 'I don't know, old boy. Strictly speaking, what you're suggesting is illegal.'

'Are you with me, yes or no?'

Driscoll smiled, his lips twisting into their crooked grin. 'I've always had a feeling I had a remarkable facility for crime. How much do you estimate those diamonds are worth?'

Coffey looked at Routledge.

'Millions,' the old man promised. 'They'll have to be cut, of course. They'll be considerably smaller by the time they're ready for the market, but their quality is inestimable. I tell you, gentlemen, those stones are unique.'

Coffey glanced at Driscoll. 'Satisfied?'

'Eminently, old son. I'd murder my own grandmother for that kind of money.'

'Sergeant?'

'I'm your man, lieutenant,' MacAngus whispered.

'That leaves you, Benson. Make up your mind. Are you with us or against us?'

Benson looked unhappy as his eyes flickered from one to the other, seeking support. They stared back at him stonily. 'Very well,' he whispered at last, 'if you've all decided.'

'Good,' Coffey breathed, wiping his face with his sleeve.

Glancing into the darkness, he studied the way they had come. 'We're still faced with the same basic problem though. They've got the diamonds, we haven't. The Dervishes will expect us to head east toward the Nile. But they can't follow our tracks in the darkness so we'll double round and re-approach the village from the other side.'

'We can hardly ride in again, squire. Not openly anyway. One look at our *gandouras* and they'll cut us to ribbons.'

'With a bit of luck there'll be nobody in those streets but women and children. Most of the men will be out looking for us.'

'But for God's sake, we can't spend the entire night searching the place room by room.'

'You're right.'

Coffey looked at the old man. The wind ruffled his hood, fluttering it against his face, and absently he brushed it away. 'What do you think? If the Dervishes have something valuable in their possession, where do they put it for safety's sake?'

'You mean a hiding place?' Routledge asked.

'I mean what's the Dervish equivalent of a bank vault?'

'There's only one place in the village which could substitute for that,' Victoria said. 'The prison block.'

'Why there?'

'It's the only building in Hamira you can actually lock.'

'What about the inmates?'

'It's empty at the moment. Hasn't been occupied for nearly a year.'

'Then that's it,' Coffey muttered, 'got to be.'

'Just one thing, old boy,' Driscoll grunted. 'You're not suggesting we ride in *en masse*, so to speak?'

'No,' Coffey answered, 'I'll go alone.'

His eyes rested on Victoria's face. There was a determined tilt to her chin, an air of steely reserve in the firm set of her features.

'Is there some place the rest of you can hide?' Coffey asked her.

'There's the dyeworks on the opposite side of town. It's a good hundred yards from the village outskirts.'

'Sounds perfect. We'll double back in that direction.'

'One moment, Lieutenant Coffey,' Victoria murmured. 'How do you intend to find that prison block? You've never been in Hamira in your life before tonight.'

'Don't worry about me.'

'I'm not,' she answered simply, 'I'm worrying about the diamonds. Muck this up and we may never see them again.'

Her directness startled him. 'What do you suggest?' he asked.

'Take someone with you. Someone who knows the lie of the town.'

'Your father?'

'My father is an old man, weak and unstable. He's been shackled in chains for the past thirteen years. There's only one person you can depend on to get you in and out again and that person is myself.'

'I can't let you take the risk.'

'Don't patronise me,' she snapped, 'those diamonds belong to me too.'

'It's too dangerous.'

'I've lived with danger all my life. At least this time there'll be some purpose behind it.'

Her reasoning disturbed him. He sensed the power within her, the determination blazing like a defiant flame. He did not like the idea, but her logic was irrefutable. 'Very well,' he agreed, 'we'll go together. But I want it understood that once we get in there, whatever I tell you must be done without question or argument.'

'Ssshhh,' Driscoll whispered hoarsely.

Coffey held his breath and they strained their ears in the desert stillness. Dimly, like a muffled roll of thunder, they heard the pounding of camel hooves on the soft crumbling earth.

'They're coming,' Benson whispered.

'Didn't take the bastards long to pull themselves together,' Driscoll grunted. 'Those Dervishes must have some kind of spontaneous reflex system.'

'We've hung about long enough,' Coffey snapped. 'Transfer the water *guerbas* and let's get the hell out of here.'

* * *

The warriors rode through the desert spread out in a ragged line. Their eyes gleamed with the savagery of men who have seen their most cherished concepts affronted. They carried swords, lances, old-fashioned flintlocks, and as they rode they scoured the earth, looking for tell-tale signs which might denote the passage of people.

At their head rode the Emir, his fat belly wobbling obscenely with the loping movement of his camel. The foremost warriors carried flaming torches which they held as low as they dared, casting a flickering glow across the desert surface. They were excitable men, but there was no sign of hysteria in their movements as they pounded relentlessly through the night. The fire had taken them by surprise, but more bewildering still had been the realisation that the man they had welcomed as the Mahdi had been an imposter, a defiler of the vilest kind. In the name of Allah, it was their sacred duty to exact vengeance. Resolute, they rode with purpose, their attention focused into one overriding aim.

The column slowed as the leaders paused, searching the earth for fresh tramplings. The ground looked rough and uneven in the eerie torchlight. There was a moment of indecision as the camels milled about confusedly, then a man gave a gutteral cry, claiming he had spotted tracks leading eastward. Spurring their mounts, the tribesmen pushed on into the darkness.

As the riders moved off, one figure remained motionless, staring thoughtfully at the desert floor. His name was Abu Ababdeh, a young noble barely twenty-three years old who had already gained a formidable reputation for his judgement and powers of reasoning. Now something made Abu Ababdeh hesitate. He was a primitive man who thought in primitive terms, but he possessed an instinctive intelligence which went beyond the levels of learning, imbuing him with an inherent awareness his fellow tribesmen both recognised and respected. Now, as he sat like a statue in his camel saddle, Abu Ababdeh's eyes drew into narrow slits.

The column was thundering eastward, lost in the fervour of pursuit, but there were no tracks to substantiate that eastward was the right direction. A man with his wits about him might double back and strike to the north. That was assuming always that escape was his major objective. On the other hand, Abu Ababdeh reasoned thoughtfully, drawing out the Emir's fighting force could be the first move on the part of an inspirational commander about to launch an attack upon the village itself.

As Abu Ababdeh pondered in silence, a group of about twenty men disengaged themselves from the main Dervish force and turned back toward him. They were Abu Ababdeh's own followers, men of the Umm Bambara, young and impulsive, obedient always to the wishes of their chosen leader.

As Abu Ababdeh watched them gather around him, their faces puzzled and uncertain, he came to a decision. Wheeling his camel, he barked out an order, and in servile silence the warriors followed him back toward the village of Hamira.

Coffey saw the building ahead. It was larger than he'd expected, its walls cracked and arid, merging easily with the desert floor. The dyeworks' roof was flat, and beneath its surface the tips of timbered ceiling struts stuck out crudely from their dried-mud casings. Beyond it, the land lay locked in a hush of misty starlight to the first straggling outbuildings of the village perimeter.

Coffey reined in his camel and studied the scene in silence.

'Sure it isn't occupied?' he whispered to Victoria, perched behind him in the darkness.

'I'm sure.'

'Sentry perhaps? A caretaker?'

'Nobody.'

Coffey pursed his lips. 'Just the same, I think we should approach with caution,' he said, kicking his camel to a crouch and dismounting. Drawing his Martini from its scabbard, he checked to see it was loaded. Then he cocked it loudly. 'The rest of you wait here. Lay down a line of covering fire if anything happens. I'll wave you in if the building looks safe.'

His palms were sweating as he made his way across the open ground, zig-zagging from boulder to boulder, using what cover he could. He reached a point almost thirty yards from the building's exterior and hesitated, crouching low in the dust, his eyes scouring the dyeworks' windows for any flicker of movement, no matter how slight, which might denote the presence of people inside.

The building stood like a sepulchre, silent and remote. Gritting his teeth, Coffey rose from his crouch and scuttled across the last thirty yards, slamming to a halt against the earthen wall. He was breathing hard, his blood pounding in his throat. He glanced back to where the others waited in their saddles, the men holding their carbines in readiness. He could see MacAngus, his features flat and expressionless, watching him carefully.

Taking a deep breath, Coffey turned and rammed his foot against the timbered door. It swung open easily, the leather hinges making a faint creaking sound. Coffey held the Martini across his chest and glanced quickly through the narrow opening. He could see a massive room, thirty yards long, the floor pockmarked with huge pits. At a cursory glance it looked like a chessboard, but each chamber was filled with a different coloured liquid, black, green, indigo, scarlet, blue, yellow. Above the pits, great shrouds of cloth, already dyed into a multitude of hues, hung across the timbered struts to dry. There was no sign of recent activity, no sign of life.

Relaxing slightly, Coffey lowered the Martini and pushed into the dyeworks' interior. The windows let in slivers of starlight and the odour of the dye-pits hung in his nostrils like the smell of rancid butter.

He waved the others in, watching them guide their camels through the narrow doorway. There was room enough for them all, thank God, which meant that if daybreak came they would still be suitably concealed.

'What happens now?' Driscoll asked, hitching his mount to one of the drying spars.

'The girl and I go into the village,' said Coffey. 'The rest of you wait here.'

'Taking a risk, aren't you, old boy? The whole population can't be out rampaging around the countryside.'

'No, but judging by that glow in the sky, whoever's left behind will have enough on their hands trying to bring the fire under control.'

Coffey looked at Victoria, struck again by the vividness of her beauty.

'Still want to go through with this?'

She nodded.

'Supposing we get caught out there?'

'It's a long way to the river. We might get caught anywhere. At least let's finish what we came for.'

'Very well.'

There was a strength in her he had never witnessed before. He envied her that, her calmness and determination. She was a woman in a million, he thought.

To the others he said: 'We'll get back as soon as we can. If dawn breaks and we've still not shown up, remain out of sight until nightfall then run for the river.'

'What happens when the dyers arrive for work in the morning?' Driscoll asked.

Coffey smiled thinly. 'After a night like this one, I don't imagine they'll be in an almighty hurry to open up for business,' he said.

Victoria moved to her father and held him tightly. His arms slid around her waist, pulling her close, and his eyes glistened as he kissed her gently on the forehead. He started to speak, but something caught in his throat and he turned away in confusion.

Coffey peered at Victoria. 'Ready?'

She drew in her breath, nodding silently, and together they strode off towards the settlement. The shadows gathered around them in weird complexities of purple and grey, and Coffey felt the fear starting deep in his chest, rising in a paralysing wave to freeze his brain and thought processes. It was a crazy thing they were doing, walking in like this. He was gambling everything on the slender hope that the entire population would be drawn to the scene of the fire, that the streets would be empty and deserted. If he was wrong, even marginally wrong, there would be no hope for either of them, trapped in that labyrinth of twisting alleyways.

They covered the first fifty yards at a decent pace, not troubling to hide their movements. From this distance the village looked like an ant hill. Flames still licked from the rooftops and the pungent odour of smoke reached them across the barren landscape.

The first outbuildings reared through the darkness and instinctively they slackened their pace. There was no sign of movement. The rabbitwarren of streets appeared abandoned. Only the reflection of the flames and the distant murmur of people gave any indication that human life existed.

Coffey glimpsed a flicker in the darkness, then the silence was rent by an inhuman wailing noise that arose into a clamour on the stillbound air. Dogs, he thought. He could see the pack loping toward them, their grey shapes streaking across the open ground like a swarm of scurrying rats.

Coffey picked up a rock and hurled it hard. A squeal of pain told him the missile had found its mark. He threw another, scoring again. The dogs broke up in confusion, slinking hurriedly into the darkness.

Coffey moved on, Victoria following, and slowly the houses gathered around them, the streets twisting and turning, following no discernible order or pattern, baffling Coffey with their sheer complexity. Now Victoria took the lead, picking her way with easy confidence. No one there to challenge them, he was happy to note. There was barely a sign of life – an occasional chicken-coop, a tethered goat, a cow, scrawny and undernourished – nothing else.

Coffey felt strange having the woman beside him. He was acutely conscious of her closeness, of how long it had been since he had found himself in such intimate proximity to a civilised female. He had lost the knack, he told himself, of making conversation. He felt awkward in her presence.

'How much further?' he asked, his nerves stretched to breaking point.

'We're nearly there. I brought you the long way round for safety's sake. The other route runs by the site of the fire.'

He nodded approvingly. They turned a corner and he squinted into the shadows ahead. 'It's like a bloody maze in here. Don't those beggars know anything about organisation?'

'They build their houses as they need them,' Victoria explained. 'Hamira's been in existence for hundreds of years. In the beginning it was nothing more than a cluster of hovels around the water hole. Then, as time went by, the buildings gradually moved outwards. Nobody bothered with plans or blueprints.'

Abruptly the road opened, widening into an empty square with alleys running out of it in all directions like the spokes of a wagon wheel. At the centre rose a blockhouse of sorts, its walls windowless and stout, its grounds encircled by a formidable palisade. The palisade was twelve or fifteen feet high, its rim sharpened into a series of jagged points, but Coffey noted with relief that the gate hung open on its hinges. Beyond, he could see the studded metal door of the building itself, sealed with a massive bolt held firmly in place by an old-fashioned padlock.

'Is that it?' he whispered.

Victoria nodded gently.

'What about the guard?'

'There isn't one. Nothing to keep an eye on.'

'Except the diamonds.'

She smiled. 'If they're really in there it would take an army to break through that metal door. The Dervishes know that.'

'Come on,' he hissed, seizing her wrist.

They scrambled across the open ground, darting through the massive gateway. On the doorstep, Coffey studied the bolt and padlock with dismay. It looked as solid as the Bank of England. Victoria was right. They would need a squadron of cavalry armed with battering rams to pound through that little lot, he realised.

Examining the lock, he ran his fingers over its uneven surface. It was rusty with age, probably nearly a century old. If anything was likely to give, it would be the lock itself.

He peered back across the square. There was no sound, only the distant crackle of flames. Dare he run the risk of a shot? They had been lucky so far, incredibly lucky. No Dervishes to be seen, not even children. But a shot? In this stillness, the sound would be alien, unmistakable, hard to ignore. Yet there was no other way. The prison door was built like a fortress. The lock itself was the only weak point.

He reached inside his *gandoura* and drew out his Browning.

'Ease back,' he ordered.

'What are you going to do?'

'Blow this thing apart.'

'They'll hear.'

'We'll have to take that chance.'

Her cheeks pale, she moved aside without a word, edging against the wall. Coffey took two paces backwards and held the Browning out at arm's length, gripping his wrist with his free hand. He aimed the gun at the keyhole, directly where the spring would be. One shot was all he could afford, Two would be pushing their luck. Three – no question about it – would bring the villagers around their heads like a locust swarm.

He squeezed the trigger and his hand jumped as the revolver cracked. The shot was like a cannon going off in the stillness, its echo reverberating through the empty streets. The padlock jumped like a firecracker, smacking wildly against the iron door. He could see the hole where the bullet had gone in, but the lock remained firm.

Coffey swallowed and looked at the girl. He noticed her fists were clenched tight. He hesitated, then fired again. This time there was a metallic clanging sound and the padlock flew from its moorings, slithering across the ground.

'We're in,' he hissed. And slipping the revolver inside his *gandoura*, he drew back the bolt and slid open the heavy door.

Riding through the marketplace, Abu Ababdeh heard the first shot echoing above his head like a distant clatter of thunder. He reined in his mount, raising his arm to draw his followers to a halt. The village lay shrouded in an eerie silence. East, the sky hung copper-coloured above the flickering flames. A cat, startled by the unexpected noise, darted across their path, vanishing into the maze of alleyways on the opposite side of the square.

Abu Ababdeh remained motionless, trying to assess the direction from which the shot had come. Then his camel grunted nervously as a second shot rang out.

The sound ricocheted through the empty streets, hurled from building to building like a careering ball. Abu Ababdeh made his decision quickly. Barking out a gutteral command, he spurred his camel forward and galloped briskly in the direction of the village jail.

Standing in the doorway, Coffey and Victoria felt the first tremor of foreboding. The prison interior looked as desolate as an empty grave. The ceiling was high, the timbered supports rotting with age. The floor was flagged, covered with straw. Rats darted across the filthy surface, their scuffles rising like the murmur of a distant ocean. The stench of refuse and decay pervaded Coffey's nostrils as he moved gingerly inside, his sandalled feet making little sound on the straw-strewn floor. Along one wall, small oven-like compartments had been shut off from the rest of the interior, special quarters, Coffey guessed, for high security prisoners; the cells were too small for men to sit upright so the occupants would have been forced to huddle in the crouch position, tormented by the heat and stench of their own perspiring bodies.

Coffey felt a chill on his stomach as he thought of the horrors these walls had witnessed, the luckless creatures who had found themselves incarcerated here, the long nights of suffering, the days of hellish heat, the slow debilitation of mind and body, the endless lingering death.

He pushed the images from his head, checking each of the cubicles in turn. They were all empty. He moved around the main cell, investigating every corner. Heavy chains hung from the walls, iron rings where prisoners would be manacled during occupation. There was no sign of the diamonds, no sign of anything at all beyond the straw and the rat droppings.

Coffey spotted a ladder leading to a loft above. 'What's up there?' he asked Victoria.

'The overflow,' she told him. 'When the prison got crowded, they pushed the more unfortunate occupants upstairs. It's so close to the ceiling, it gets like an oven in the heat of the day. My father and his friends used to call it Paradise Corner. Nobody lasted more than a day or two.'

'Let's take a look,' Coffey said, climbing the ladder.

The upper storey was marginally cleaner than the one below, but just as empty, just as desolate. Through the shadows, Coffey could see more metal rings on the wall where the prisoners would be shackled. The ceiling at this point was barely three feet high, and he had to crawl on his hands and knees to check the farthermost corners. A few bales of dark cloth lay stacked against the wall, covered with sand and dust. Coffey pulled them out and examined the space behind them. Empty.

'Anything there?' Victoria called from the top of the ladder.

He shook his head. 'We're wasting our time. There's been nobody inside this building for years.'

A feeling of dismay rose through him, a fury directed more at himself than at circumstance, as if the knowledge that they had taken such a risk for no reason was almost more than he could bear. He slithered back toward her.

'Think,' he said. 'Where else might they put those diamonds?'

'There is nowhere else,' she insisted. 'This is the only safe place in the whole of Hamira.'

Coffey was conscious of panic threatening to engulf him. The excitement of the last few minutes had blotted out the natural instincts of fear and apprehension, but now, finding the prison empty, his alarm began to return with astonishing force. They had been crazy coming back to the village like this. At any moment their presence might be discovered. But above his fear rose a desperate frustration. Somewhere near at hand the diamonds were lying, a fortune waiting to be claimed. An hour ago he'd held it in his grasp and all the problems of his life had seemed over. Now, by a savage twist of fate, he was back where he'd started.

'Sssshhh,' Victoria exclaimed, pressing two fingers against his lips.

'What is it?' he hissed.

'Someone's coming.'

Coffey took her arm, pulling her over the ladder on to the creaking timbered floor. Easing forward, he peered down through the open doorway and into the street beyond. Dust rose on the air, and in its swirl a body of mounted men wheeled into view, the ugly grey snouts of their carbines outlined against the stars. Dervishes.

At his side Coffey felt Victoria trembling. 'What will we do?' she whispered.

He glanced back at the far wall. The bales of cloth were still stacked where he had left them. Dust coated their surfaces, and a solitary spider scuttled across the outer casing. 'Come on,' he snapped, and holding on to her hand, wriggled backwards, pulling the bales aside.

'In there,' he ordered.

They squeezed into the narrow space between the bales and the wall, their bodies locked tightly together. Coffey used his free hand to ease the bales back in place. There was barely room enough to breathe, and he could feel Victoria's heart thumping distinctly against his chest.

Feet scraped on the floor below. Voices rose in an indistinct murmur. The light from blazing torches filled the cavernous room, casting rippling shadows across the cobwebbed ceiling.

Coffey reached down, found Victoria's hand and squeezed it gently. She was shaking all over. More voices. Then a sharper, more commanding tone barking out an order.

Coffey heard the ladder creak as someone slowly climbed it. He held his breath, training his eyes on the point where the ladder ended. A figure rose through the gloom, robed and bearded. Coffey could see the man quite clearly. He was clutching a blazing torch. For a moment the Arab remained motionless, perched on the ladder's topmost rung, his head raised just above floor level, his torch lifted aloft, casting flickering patterns across his heavy features. His face looked soft – almost gentle, Coffey thought, watching the man's brow pucker into a thoughtful frown as his eyes settled on the bales of cloth. Grunting, the warrior eased himself over the ladder top, and shifting the torch to his other hand, began to edge slowly toward them. Coffey felt his nerves tense. His fingers left Victoria's hand and crept down his stomach to the folds of his *gandoura*. Reaching inside, he gripped the handle of the Browning, switching the safety catch to 'fire'.

The man crawled nearer, so close now Coffey could see the sweat glistening on his nose and forehead. Gently, Coffey rested the Browning in front of him, and as softly as he could, drew back the hammer. The movement made a muffled clicking sound in the heavy darkness. Coffey waited, watching the tribesman warily. The man gave no sign that he had heard. He was still moving toward the cloth bales with the same dogged determination.

At that moment someone shouted from below. Coffey recognised the voice. It was the same commanding timbre he had heard when the Dervishes first entered. The man hesitated, looking back. He shouted something in reply and the voice barked out an order, harsh and precise. The man sighed and muttered something under his breath. He glanced briefly at the cloth bales, then turned back the way he had come and slowly descended the ladder.

Coffey breathed deeply, filling his lungs with air. He heard a muffled sob of relief choke in Victoria's throat. Letting go of the Browning, he again reached down, gripping her hand. They were safe for the moment, he realised, but for how long? The Dervishes were checking the buildings around the square one by one. He and Victoria were caught like squirrels in a cage. They would have to remain where they were until daybreak. Their chances of escape were terrifyingly slim.

MacAngus stood at the dyeworks door, staring out into the darkness. It was impossible to discern what was happening in the village, but he knew there was Dervish activity out there, he could tell. The tribesmen had returned, some of them anyhow. Coffey and the woman were trapped, their escape route blocked, their retreat cut off. MacAngus swore under his breath. He turned back to the others, sprawled on the ground, resting. In the darkness the camels stood like blocks of stone, their long necks tethered to the drying beams.

'What's happening out there?' Driscoll asked, his voice drained and weary.

'They're back,' MacAngus said.

Driscoll started, and MacAngus glimpsed the tension rising in each of them.

'Dervishes?'

MacAngus nodded. 'Not the whole force, but enough to make things tricky.'

Without a word Driscoll scrambled to his feet and moved to the door, looking out through the narrow opening. He whis-

166

tled softly under his breath. 'They're searching the village house by house,' he whispered.

'How can you tell at that range?' Benson snapped.

'I'm like a cat, I see in the dark,' Driscoll told him, flashing his lopsided grin.

'What are we going to do?' Routledge asked, his hands fluttering nervously.

MacAngus guessed he was thinking about his daughter. He didn't blame Routledge for feeling worried. That was no aimless foolery out there. Something had set those Dervishes off.

'They're coming this way,' Driscoll murmured.

MacAngus felt a tightness inside him as he joined Driscoll at the doorway, gazing out at a cluster of riders facing the dye-works' direction, their outlines hazy and indistinct at the village periphery. One rider moved toward them, easing his camel forward in a slow shuffling walk, the others turned back into the rabbitwarren of streets. MacAngus watched the man guiding his mount across the barren ground, his ancient flintlock rifle resting casually over his thighs.

'Move back into the shadows, sir,' he whispered.

'What difference will it make?' Driscoll grunted. 'He'll see us anyway.'

'Just do it,' MacAngus hissed.

Driscoll frowned. He was not accustomed to being addressed in such a brusque fashion by a mere sergeant, but obediently he edged away from the door and began to untie the camels. MacAngus stopped him with a sharp wave of his hand. 'Dinna fuss yourself with that.'

'For Christ's sake, if he sticks his head through that door he'll spot the animals immediately.'

'There's one of him and four of us. D'ye no think them's reasonable odds for our side, lieutenant?'

MacAngus reached down and drew the long curved sword from his waistbelt. In the stillness, he could hear the rasp of Routledge's breathing and the sound of Lieutenant Benson clearing his throat. One of the camels grunted softly and Driscoll silenced it with his fingers on its nostrils. Outside, the hoofbeats came steadily closer. The man was clearly in no

167

hurry, MacAngus thought, and his hand tightened on the sword hilt as he pressed himself hard against the wall. He made no attempt to look through the opening, but listened instead to the mount drawing nearer.

The hoofbeats stopped. MacAngus heard a soft scuffling noise as the rider dismounted. Clop, clop, the padding of his sandals reached them through the heavy timbered door.

MacAngus braced himself. There was a moment's pause, a breathless moment that seemed to stretch unbearably, then with a little squeaking sound the door swung gently open. MacAngus glimpsed the warrior framed against the starlight. The man's robes fluttered in the wind. His beard looked like a dark veil dangling below his face. He peered into the darkness, his eyes narrowing as they struggled to adjust to the sudden transition from light to shade, widening almost instantly as he detected the huddle of figures frozen in the breathless hush of discovery.

Then MacAngus moved. He drove his sword arm forward, feeling the blade catch momentarily on something hard, a bone perhaps, before sliding smoothly in almost to the hilt. Hot blood gushed over MacAngus's wrist and he twisted the sword expertly before drawing it free.

The warrior was still standing in the same position, his mouth gaping open in a silent exclamation of protest and dismay, his eyes already clouding into the blue-marbled milkiness of death. MacAngus seized the front of his robes and jerked him inwards, letting him fall bodily to the floor.

'Christ,' Driscoll breathed, looking down at the stricken tribesman with an air of distaste.

The man's chest was rising and falling rapidly as he battled for breath. Flecks of crimson stained his lips and splashed the front of his beard.

'Ask him about the diamonds,' MacAngus snapped.

Driscoll looked at him, startled. Without a word he dropped to his knees and spoke rapidly into the warrior's ear. The man's hand lifted in silent entreaty and they watched the life draining out of him like a visible force. He muttered a few hoarse words and a fresh fountain of blood burst inside his mouth.

'What did he say?' MacAngus demanded.

Driscoll glanced up at him silently for a moment, unsettled by the sergeant's authorative tone. Then he said: 'The diamonds aren't in the prison block at all. They're not even in Hamira. The bloody Emir's taken them bloody well with him.'

MacAngus swore. His coarse features were crimson with rage. He chewed desperately at his lower lip as he struggled to come to a decision. The others watched him silently, shaken by the change in the sergeant's demeanour.

'Ask him how many men have followed the Emir,' MacAngus commanded.

Driscoll looked down at the warrior again, but the man's eyes had glazed and his arm had fallen, his fingers bloody and covered with his own viscera, stretched out motionless at his side.

'Ask him yourself, old sport. You'll get nothing more out of this fellow. He's dead, I'm afraid. Like a piece of chopped mutton.'

MacAngus pulled down his head-cowl and rubbed the back of his neck with his fingers. His eyes were bulging with fury and frustration. 'Pick him up, sir,' he said fiercely.

Driscoll's face looked blank. 'What for, squire? I tell you the man is dead.'

'Aye, but we've got to get Lieutenant Coffey and the girl back. Pick him up, for God's sake. And somebody duck out there and grab his camel. We'll need that animal to take the place of the one we lost.'

Driscoll studied him in silence for a moment, then, impressed by the intensity of the sergeant's tone, he reached down without a word and took hold of the warrior's head. Together, they lifted the dead man from where he was lying and carried him carefully over to the dye-pits.

Coffey lay in the stillness and listened to the Dervishes scouring the street outside. He was still holding the girl, his body pressed hard against hers in the confines of their narrow hiding place. Now that the first flush of danger had passed he was becoming increasingly aware of their physical contact.

Despite the perilousness of their position, his body started to respond. He shifted, trying to ease himself back.

'What are you doing?' she whispered.

'Getting more comfortable,' he said.

Victoria had stopped trembling, he was happy to note. She was not one for panicking easily, that much was clear. Coffey approved.

'How long must we remain here?' she asked.

'We can't leave now. The streets are alive with the bastards.'

'But in another few hours it'll be morning.'

Coffey didn't answer, resolving to keep the truth from her as long as possible, but with an intuition that did not surprise him, she said softly: 'We're trapped, aren't we? When dawn breaks, we won't be able to move.'

He grunted, edging back still further so that his arm no longer pressed quite so disturbingly against the softness of her breast. 'We'll get out, that's a promise,' he whispered.

She was silent for a moment, her eyes large and milky grey in the filtered starlight. 'We should never have come back like this,' she breathed. 'We were lucky enough to escape the first time. Luck like that doesn't happen twice in an evening.'

'We'll make it, I tell you. I gave you my promise, didn't I?'

His voice was fierce and insistent but behind its intensity he felt the emptiness of his words and knew she sensed it too. He tried to turn his mind from the danger outside, concentrating instead on the pleasant comforting touch of warm flesh beneath his fingers, focusing his brain on the soft female odour resting in his nostrils, the pliant sweep of her spine where her back curved into the deep swell of her behind.

He had to turn her mind from the hopelessness of their situation. Softly, he chuckled.

'Why are you laughing?' she asked.

'I was just thinking. Here we are wrapped together like a couple of silkworms, yet before today we'd never even spoken to each other.'

She looked up at him through the shadows, her eyes glittering softly.

'Are you married?' she asked.

170

The directness of the question surprised him. 'No,' he answered stiffly.

'Why not?'

He hesitated. Then he smiled. 'Can't afford it.'

'You make it sound like a stockmarket investment.'

'That's what it comes down to in the end. It's what everything comes down to. Money. It takes me all my time to pay my mess bills. If I had a wife to support as well . . .' He shrugged, leaving the sentence unfinished.

She was silent for a moment, then she said: 'Is that why you want the diamonds so much?'

'That's why.'

'Money isn't everything, you know.'

He laughed bitterly. 'Not when you've got it.'

'There are things more important. Being free, for one.'

'Without money? Call that freedom?'

'It's better than slavery. Anything is.'

'It's just another kind. They've got a different word for it, that's all.'

He stopped himself as if he had unwittingly exposed some vital flaw in his nature. She'd glimpsed it too. He could sense the sharpness of her insight. 'Why are you so bitter?' she whispered.

'I'm not bitter. What makes you say that?'

'You're like a volcano threatening to erupt.'

His lips tightened, then all at once the tension seemed to flow out of him. It was like the release of some poisonous fluid. 'You're right,' he admitted, 'I *am* bitter. And I've no reason to be, God knows. I've been luckier than most, a damn sight luckier. But luck itself isn't enough. Not when you're up against a system like ours.'

'What are you doing in the army?' she asked.

'What's anyone doing in the army? It's a good enough career for a young man with limited assets and dubious prospects.'

'But you're not the soldiering type.'

'Why not?'

'You're too . . . gentle,' she said.

Her answer surprised him. To his knowledge, gentleness

had never been one of his virtues. Anger certainly, the bitterness she had so accurately discerned, occasional bursts of murderous rage when the iniquity of his position became too much to handle, but gentleness never.

'Nobody's called me that before.'

'When you live with the Dervishes, gentleness becomes very important. There's something about being a slave that destroys your very soul if you let it.'

'I can't imagine that happening to you. You're too controlled.'

'I'm not as controlled as you think. If you want to know the truth, I'm scared.'

'Nobody would blame you for that.'

'I don't mean scared of the Dervishes. I mean of people. Of going back to a world I no longer belong to. I don't know if I can cope.

'Of course you can. You'll settle into the swing of things, you'll see.'

'But will people accept me out there? Civilised people, I mean?'

The question carried an artlessness, an almost plaintive innocence he found curiously endearing. 'A woman who looks like you,' he said, 'will be accepted anywhere.'

'Am I attractive, physically attractive in a civilised sense?'

Again, her directness startled him. In a more sophisticated woman he might have suspected female guile and strategy but he knew Victoria's upbringing had been uptempered by the wiles of westernised behaviour.

'I find you . . . extremely attractive,' he admitted softly.

She seemed to consider this, staring down at his chest. He wondered what complexities were drifting through her mind. A man could be forgiven for losing his head in such circumstances, he reasoned.

She peered at him again, her eyes unfathomable.

'Have you had many women?'

He laughed softly. 'What kind of question is that, for God's sake?'

'The Dervishes regard pleasures of the flesh as one of the great essentials of life. They seldom drink or smoke, but making love is as natural to them as saddling a camel or milking a goat. They look upon our so-called European standards as puritanical and absurd.'

Something in her voice made his pulses quicken. He lay motionless, his face barely an inch from her own, trying to quell the impulses rising inside him.

'I have never known a man in the true sense, not in the real sense. I mean the "wanting to" sense.'

His breathing seemed to stop, trapped in his chest as if some indefinable force had halted his metabolism. He struggled to keep his face impassive, scarcely daring to believe what she was saying.

'I want to now,' she whispered, 'I want you. . . I want you to make love to me.'

He was filled with a frantic, impossible-to-ignore excitement. His throat tightened and the blood throbbed in his temples, its beat ragged and uneven. Leaning forward, he kissed her on the lips. It was a tentative kiss, gentle and exploratory, but within a second his emotions seemed to career out of control. His instincts had been held too long in deferment, too firmly in check. He heard her gasp as his mouth moved down the steep curve of her throat. Breathless he tugged at the light linen toga, finding her breasts. In the darkness, her skin shone with a pale, almost ethereal gleam.

And then, as the pounding in his skull intensified beyond endurance, a new sound intruded upon his consciousness, a scream too high and shrill to be construed as human, and yet human it was, and hearing it he felt the hairs prickle on his neck as the sound rose, growing louder, harsher, deadening the senses, filling his ears and head and brain with the mournfulness of its lament.

Abu Ababdeh heard the scream at the same moment. He jerked back his camel, listening intently. Around him, his men had frozen and like him were poised immobile, their heads cocked warily, straining to assess the reason for the weird unearthly clamour.

The wail echoed across the rooftops, fading as suddenly as it had started, leaving only the shuffling of the camels and the distant crackle of burning buildings.

Abu Ababdeh knew where the shriek had come from. The dyeworks. He kicked his camel into a trot, and with murmurs of excitement his men followed, surging through the alleyways to the building beyond.

A feeling of unease filled Abu Ababdeh as he rode through the night. Screwing up his eyes he detected, like a faint smudge in the surrounding gloom, a crimson glow, flickering eerily.

Drawing closer, Abu Ababdeh heard murmurs of consternation rising from his men and he slowed his camel to a walk, frowning into the darkness. The glow was taking shape now, clearly discernable at close quarters. A fire. Not a raging inferno like the one behind them, but a small dancing flame just large enough to illuminate the few bare feet around it and throw into striking relief the figure of a tribesman strapped to a wooden frame.

The man's arms were outstretched in the manner of a priest reciting the Koran, and his head was drawn back, fastened to the upright post by a leather thong, the eyes gazing sightlessly into the night. His head and body had been dyed a variety of brilliant colours, purple, blue, indigo, orange, green, all flickering luminously in the pink glow of firelight.

Abu Ababdeh was not an educated man. Though he possessed a natural shrewdness and sagacity of judgement, he had grown to manhood among primitive people and his instincts were primitive also. The sight of the lifeless warrior, his arms outflung in wordless embrace, his robes and features stained into a grotesque complexity of hues by Driscoll and MacAngus, filled Abu Ababdeh with superstitious dread. His eyes bulged fearfully, and behind him he heard the whispers of his men as they drew their camels backward, staring with trepidation at the macabre figure poised before them. Without waiting for their leader to give the word, they wheeled crazily and with cries of muffled terror, pounded back the way they had come.

Abu Ababdeh remained motionless a moment longer. He cast one last look at the purple skull, its teeth bared in a grimace of silent menace, then he too turned his camel and followed swiftly in his warrior's wake.

*   *   *

Coffey listened to the sound of the tribesmen leaving, scarcely able to contain himself. They were riding off to investigate the source of the scream, he realised. For a minute or two at least, the square outside would be empty. It was their one chance of escape.

'Come on,' he snapped at Victoria, and clutching her hand, rose from the place they had been lying and scurried across the timbered floor. He saw the pale flash of her naked breasts as they scrambled furiously down the ladder and through the open doorway.

Gasping, they sprinted through the network of streets, aiming for the open desert, Victoria struggling to draw together the flaps of her billowing robe. All thoughts of passion were driven from Coffey's mind by the frantic urgency of flight.

He heard someone moving toward them and slithered to a halt, drawing Victoria back. Instinctively, his hand groped through his robes, fumbling for the ribbed grip of his Browning.

The rider broke into view, dragging a pair of empty camels behind him. His headcloth fluttered in the wind as he skidded to a halt, swinging his mount sideways between the silent buildings. Coffey recognised the tilt of the head, the heavy set of the shoulders.

MacAngus, he thought jubilantly. The sergeant's face looked flushed in the stillness as he waved them impatiently forward.

Coffey ran to the first of the camels and jerked it into a crouch. He helped Victoria into the saddle, then mounted the second, and with a click of his tongue followed furiously in MacAngus' wake.

TWELVE

The plain shimmered in the heat. Flat as a pancake, it merged into the blinding glare of the sun, losing its density, paling in slow subtle nuances of colour until it was impossible to tell where the earth ended and the sky began. To Coffey's right the outlines of the adjacent mountains looked strangely blue in the early morning.

He lay flat on his belly in the camel scrub, training his field glasses on the vast wave of warriors advancing steadily across the desolate *reg*. They rode in no particular order or formation, but spread instead like an untidy carpet over the endless acres of sand, moving slowly, studying the ground, puzzled that there were no tracks to follow, that the runaways they had pursued so resolutely through the darkness had, with morning, vanished without trace.

Coffey had ridden through the night in a desperate effort to overtake them, but now, with the first heat of the day gathering on the grid-iron of the desert floor, he felt his spirits sink as he counted two to three hundred men. An army, he thought. He could pick out the Emir clearly, his fat form swaying with the uncomfortable persistence of his camel's rhythm. A pale blur adorned his saddlehorn. The diamonds.

Pushing the field glasses into their leather case, Coffey edged back to where the others were waiting. They studied him expectantly.

'He's got them all right,' Coffey confirmed.

'You're sure?' Routledge demanded.

'I saw them dangling from his saddlehorn. However, there are roughly three hundred men out there, and only six of us.'

'Got anything in mind, squire?' Driscoll inquired casually.

'Not a thing, short of fighting our way through half the Dervish army, grabbing the diamonds and fighting our way back again. But I'm open to suggestions.'

Sergeant MacAngus spat on the ground. 'Och, it's not as hopeless as it looks, lieutenant.'

'How's that?'

'When I was serving in Afghanistan, there was an old Pathan warrior called Khaima Rakhri. With less than thirty men he held off the whole British army for damn near seven years. It seems to me if Khaima Rakhri could do it, we can too.'

'Six against three hundred?'

'Pathan style, we can even up the odds.'

'How?' Coffey asked.

Sergeant MacAngus scuffed at the dirt with his toe. 'Well, what we need for starters is a new chain of command. Let's forget the army for a wee bit. I ken you gentlemen cut quite a dash at officer school but when it comes to something like this, we need somebody who thinks like a Pathan.'

Coffey frowned. He had noticed a new confidence in MacAngus since the discovery of the diamonds. 'Are you seriously suggesting . . .?'

'I'm suggesting that until we get them diamonds back, I take over,' MacAngus said simply.

Coffey stared at him thunderstruck. He hadn't been mistaken. MacAngus *had* changed. His manner had never been servile or deferential, but now it had grown presumptious almost to the point of insolence.

'Think it over, lieutenant,' MacAngus argued reasonably. 'What difference does it make who gives the orders and who obeys them? The only thing that matters is who gets rich at the end of the day.'

Coffey glanced uncomfortably at the others. He knew that what MacAngus said made sense. In a situation like this, the sergeant had more experience, more natural cunning. 'This is highly irregular,' Coffey said.

'I ken that, lieutenant. But so is grabbing the diamonds for ourselves.'

'Very well. Until we have the diamonds back, you may assume temporary command.'

MacAngus turned to the others. 'That suit you, gentlemen?'

Surprised, they glanced at each other, then Driscoll nodded, smiling thinly. 'Congratulations on your promotion, sergeant.'

MacAngus ignored the remark. Satisfied with his new status, he was already concentrating on the problem in hand. 'The first thing we must do,' he said, 'is choose our ground to fight on. Them Dervishes are heading across the open *reg*. Now, no Pathan in his right mind would fight in the open. We need to lure them into the mountains so we can use the land as an ally. Also, after we've got what we come for, we have to make sure the bastards don't overtake us when we run for Fort Malawa.'

'How do you intend to accomplish that?' Coffey asked, mystified.

MacAngus squatted on his haunches, drawing a line in the dust with his finger. 'The Dervishes have been riding all through the night, fully loaded. They're moving slow, looking for our tracks, but by sundown their camels will be worn and weary. Now, a shrewd Pathan would give his mounts a rest, send them out empty-saddled to cut across the Dervishes' path.'

'Why?'

'Empty camels move faster than ones with riders on their backs. And they're a damn sight fresher at the end of the day. Now we choose the lightest man we've got. He takes the animals in a wide arc, switching from beast to beast so's they don't get over-tired. He cuts in front of the Dervishes, and when they spot his tracks they take off after him at the double. He keeps on weaving, wearing them down bit by bit. Then he leads them into the foothills. We'll be waiting by the time they get there.'

'How?' Coffey asked.

'We walk,' MacAngus said. 'I estimate them foothills to be no more'n five miles off, maybe even four. We cut across the desert on feet.'

'And afterwards?'

'Och, one thing at a time, lieutenant,' MacAngus grinned.

178

'I like to make up my plans as I go along.'

Coffey considered for a moment. 'Makes sense so far,' he said. 'If it achieves nothing more than tiring out the enemy's mounts, it's worth the effort. The question is, who goes with our camels? Strictly speaking, Mr Routledge is the lightest, but these beasts, even roped together, will take quite a bit of handling, and Mr Routledge's hardly in the best of health.'

'I'm every bit as light as my father,' Victoria said pointedly. 'What's more, I'm perfectly capable of leading those beasts all the way to Khartoum and back if necessary. I did it often enough at Hamira.'

'No,' Coffey's voice was sharp and abrupt. Glimpsing the others' eyes upon him, he cursed himself for over-reacting, but he could not bear the thought of Victoria going out alone. 'It's too dangerous,' he added lamely.

'I'm not afraid,' Victoria insisted, 'I can do anything you men can, and as far as the camels are concerned, a damn sight more effectively too. I've had lots of experience.'

'The lady makes sense,' MacAngus told Coffey in his slow drawling way, 'I reckon she'll be safe enough as long as she doesn't dawdle.'

Victoria smiled as she rose to her feet. Her manner seemed light, almost jaunty, as if she had scored some indefinable point. Unhappy and struggling not to show it, Coffey rose with her. He could still recall with vivid clarity the softness of her flesh, the uncontrollable urges which had assailed him in the prison block. Just biology, he thought. Nothing to get in a sweat about. But there was something else, a strange inexpressible yearning he had not experienced for many years. Now a sour pall of dread had gathered in his belly. It wasn't right letting her go like this, but he could think of no way of changing the others' minds. 'Be careful,' he warned.

'I'm always careful,' she promised lightly.

They gobbled down a hasty meal of army iron rations and set out fifteen minutes later, Victoria riding eastward across the *reg*, trailing the camels behind her. Coffey watched her go, the muscles tightening in his throat. Something was happening to him he couldn't quite fathom. Always in the past he had been aware of his feelings, understanding them as he under-

179

stood everything else in life, simply and straightforwardly. Now for the first time he was experiencing something new, a strange wretchedness, an elusive melancholy. Watching Victoria ride off into the distance, he swallowed uncertainly then flung his water *guerba* over one shoulder and set off after the others, his sandalled feet padding softly on the coarse crumbling earth. He was not a complex man. His vision of life was remarkably simple. If that breathless encounter in the prison block at Hamira had been an instinctive reaction to the urgency of the moment, why then did it bother him so much?

He shook his head as he strode resolutely on. No man understood himself completely, he thought. With the world at his fingertips, there was still the unexpected, the inexplicable. Life could unsaddle him with a single throw.

Victoria, for her part, riding eastward with the camels, was going through the same emotional crisis. What had possessed her, she wondered, to demand that Coffey, a perfect stranger, should make love to her? That moment in Hamira had been little short of madness.

And yet, she could still recall the tautness of his body, the hard resilience of muscle and sinew. The memory caused a weakness to rise from her loins, a gnawing longing that threatened to consume her completely.

He was handsome, it was true. He had risked his life to come to her rescue. But was that all it took to shake everything she believed in?

Victoria jerked hard on the rope, forcing the camels to quicken their pace. She could see the Dervish dustcloud far to her left. It would take several hours to circle around in front of them. She would put the thought of Coffey from her mind for the present. With the diamonds in their possession, she would have all the time in the world to think of him then.

It took Coffey and his party four hours to reach the first rambling ramparts of the foothills. Here, high cliffs rose to a central plateau drifting off to the east, the cliffs forming a natural amphitheatre, ten or fifteen miles across, broken in places by a series of narrow gullies which split the wall into a honeycombed network of twisting passageways barely wide enough for a man to ride through.

Sergeant MacAngus surveyed the labyrinth of channels with an appraising eye. He eased himself into the first of the openings, clambering upwards over the loose rolling scree to peer at the rocky cliffs above. 'We'll cut down camel scrub,' he declared. 'Build cradles at the top of the draw. Then we'll fill them up with rocks and shale. Anyone comes riding up this track, we'll give them a hailstorm they'll never forget.'

'Only a maniac would enter this gully unprotected,' Coffey told him flatly. 'Those Dervishes will smell an ambush a mile off.'

MacAngus grinned. 'That's just what I'm counting on, sir,' he said.

Coffey was baffled, but he shrugged resignedly and, under the sergeant's directions, they set to work cutting down the thick clumps of thorny scrub, hacking away at the vegetation and using the pliant saplings to build rough-hewn cradles at the gully's rim. The work was arduous and time-consuming, and as the sun's heat mounted, Coffey felt the sweat flowing freely down his body. He swung his sword, slicing at the tenacious scrub-roots, cursing when the stubborn plants refused to budge, tearing and heaving with his fists until he had dragged them from the soil by sheer muscular force. MacAngus strapped the saplings together with the leather thongs from their *gandouras* and when at last he had finished, he looked at the cradles approvingly.

'What happens now?' Coffey asked.

'We fill them up,' MacAngus ordered, scooping out a heavy rock and dropping it into the first cradle's bottom.

Coffey shook his head in bewilderment, but they followed MacAngus's example, gradually stacking the flimsy frameworks until they were piled high with jagged stones. Then they stood around gasping, their bodies drenched with sweat.

'Even if we manage to lure those bastards in here, which I doubt,' Coffey murmured, 'there's no guarantee the rocks will fall in the right direction when we cut these cradles loose.'

'Who said they were meant to fall any place at all?' MacAngus asked him cryptically.

181

'What the hell are you talking about? We just spent two hours building the bloody things up.'

The sergeant's face looked inscrutable as a cat's. 'It's like ye said, sir, those Dervishes are going to need a little coaxing to do what we want them to.'

Coffey studied him in puzzlement. He was about to speak again when suddenly Driscoll whistled from the top of the draw. 'Somebody's coming,' he shouted. 'Looks like the girl.'

A sense of relief flooded through Coffey. Thank God she's safe, he thought.

'Get down where she can see you,' MacAngus ordered. 'Signal her to steer the camels over here.'

Coffey scrambled down the rocks, his heart fluttering rapidly. He reached the *reg* and saw the cluster of riderless camels moving toward them through the shimmering heathaze. Mounted on the foremost beast, Victoria looked little more than a blur.

He waited until she was almost within hailing distance then waved his arms frenziedly until she turned the camels in his direction. Coffey watched them drawing closer, and pointed toward the mouth of the draw. She nodded to show she understood.

The long ride had covered Victoria with a thin layer of dust. Her hair had scattered in the wind, and now hung in loose ragged tresses across her face and throat.

Coffey grinned at her as she entered the draw below him, dragging the camels with her on the rope. He scrambled down the rocks to meet her, helping her to dismount. 'How'd it go?' he asked.

'Like clockwork,' she told him, but he knew she was lying. He could see the strain in her face.

'Are they coming?'

'I think so. They switched direction as soon as they crossed my trail. I watched their dust cloud.'

'Good,' Coffey declared, smiling with satisfaction. 'At least we'll have fresh camels to take us to Fort Malawa.'

They heard a rattle of stones as Sergeant MacAngus came sliding down toward them, his narrow face oily with sweat. 'Everything all right?' he asked.

182

She nodded silently and MacAngus turned, studying the rocky cliffs above. A new thought had entered his mind, startling in its simplicity. 'If we can move our animals up to the plateau rim,' he said, 'those Dervishes will have to find a way around the cliff bottom before they can follow us. When we've got the diamonds, it could give us a two, maybe three hour lead.'

Coffey stared in amazement at the rocky wall. 'You're not serious,' he whispered.

'Why not?'

'You'll never get camels up there, you idiot.'

'What about the scree-slope?'

Coffey peered at the giant bridal veil of moraine falling in an almost perpendicular line from the topmost precipice to the valley below.

'A man might do it, or a dog maybe, but a camel, never.'

MacAngus spat on the ground. There was a look of determination on his face Coffey had never seen before. Without a word, MacAngus took the rope from Victoria's hand and untied the animals one by one. He removed the ropes from each of the saddlehorns and knotted their ends firmly together. When he was satisfied the knots would hold, he moved to the scree-slope and began to climb, playing out the line behind him. The loose stones rolled and rattled beneath his feet. MacAngus gasped as he scrambled steadily upward, his sandals slipping on the unstable surface.

When he reached the top he leaned forward, gasping at the air, his cheeks flushed with exertion. Painfully, he straightened and peered around. Behind, the plateau roof meandered steadily eastward, vanishing into the distant heat haze. A good escape route, he thought approvingly. The ground looked solid underfoot, hard, pebbly, flat as a billiard table.

Just behind the cliff-edge, a large smooth boulder sat bleaching in the sun. MacAngus curled the rope around it and began the descent, trailing the line behind him. When he reached the bottom he had two separate rope-lengths, the middle looped around the boulder above.

The others watched mystified as MacAngus tied one end to the first of the camels, the other to three of the remaining beasts bunched tightly together.

'Think ye can drive these beggars in the opposite direction?' he asked Driscoll.

Driscoll grinned, realising for the first time what the sergeant was up to. Clucking softly in his throat, he seized the three beasts by their halters and began to lead them away from the cliff. Roaring in protest, they strained against the rope. The line rose in the air, tightened, became taut as a bowstring around the boulder above. Breathlessly, they waited to see if it would take the strain. Driscoll hauled on the halters, pulling the camels forward, and slowly, relentlessly, the rope began to move.

As the first camel was dragged unwillingly toward the scree-slope by the insistent pressure of its three companions, MacAngus gripped the animal's bridle, adding his own strength to the implacable force pulling from above. The camel reached the slope and began to scramble upwards. When it felt its feet sliding on the loose shifting rubble, it shrieked loudly and tried to jerk back but MacAngus held on to its halter, and with the pressure slowly intensifying above, the camel, spitting and protesting, was dragged pendulum-fashion up the steep ragged incline. Its progress was agonisingly slow, but with Driscoll's animals supplying the traction from below, MacAngus forced the unwilling beast gradually up to the summit.

The second camel followed in a similar manner, and when he had two animals on the clifftop, MacAngus switched tactics – instead of the boulder, he fastened the free end of the rope to the camels on the mesa and used the direct upward pull from above to bring up the other beasts one by one.

The line snapped at one point, and the camel in transit slid helplessly downhill, fighting to regain its balance, but MacAngus, without even pausing to curse, re-tied the two broken ends together and continued the same inexorable process.

In the space of barely three hours, the entire party, camels and humans alike, stood safely on the clifftop, the plateau reaching away before them.

Coffey shook his head in wonder. 'Sergeant, you're a marvel,' he breathed.

MacAngus shrugged. He was in no mood for compliments. Only one thing mattered in MacAngus's mind. The diamonds. He turned to examine Lieutenant Benson's camel. Dangling from the saddle was a bulky leather-skinned carrier. 'What have you got in that gripsack, lieutenant?' MacAngus demanded.

'Just a few odds and ends,' Benson said.

'Empty it,' MacAngus ordered curtly. 'Bring it along and come with me.'

Benson hesitated, clearly resentful of the sergeant's tone. He contemplated asserting his own authority, glancing at Coffey and Driscoll for support, but they stared stonily back. In the end, Benson conceded defeat.

'Where are we going?' he asked sullenly.

MacAngus's sunbaked features creased into a network of wrinkles caked with dust. 'On an old-fashioned Pathan snake hunt,' he grinned.

It was almost dusk when the Dervishes reached the foot of the great mesa. The rock cast shadows across the orange sand. The Emir reined in his mount, looking suspiciously at the point where the camel tracks meandered into the mouth of the narrow draw. As Coffey had predicted, his instincts were instantly alerted. He sat in the saddle, staring balefully from left to right as around him his warriors waited in silence, the same thought in each of their minds. The gully was narrow and precipitous. There was one way in and one way out. There could be no logical reason for the escapees to enter it at all except for the purpose of ambush.

The Emir barked out a command and two of the tribesmen dismounted, scrambling up the incline toward the gully's mouth. Silently, the great army of men sat and waited on their camels as the two scouts gingerly edged their way over the ragged jumble of rocks. When they reached the gully opening, it took them barely a moment to spot the wooden cradles MacAngus had built so meticulously high on the upper edge. Drawing back the way they had come, they related their findings to the waiting Emir, who nodded grimly. His assumption had been correct. The runaways were waiting to attack them inside the gully walls.

185

He studied the cliff face intently, shading his eyes against the setting sun. A second gully, even narrower than the first, cut into the rock at an adjacent angle, climbing steadily to a point overlooking the rim of its companion. A small party of men might be able to scale the narrow twisting bed and surprise the ambushers waiting above.

The Emir grunted an order and the nearmost warriors fell into line beside him as he steered his camel toward the mouth of the second draw. Inside its opening, MacAngus crouched among the rocks chuckling under his breath. It had worked. His strategy had worked. The Dervishes, glimpsing the cradles, had decided to use the parallel gully to launch an ambush of their own. Now they were riding toward him barely two abreast, the Emir up front, the leather saddlebag bobbing tantalisingly against his podgy thigh.

The spot in which MacAngus was lying was a far from enviable one, however. The rocky cliff rose perpendicularly above it, and his little cluster of rocks offered only a fractional amount of concealment. But he had instructed the others to leave the rope dangling on the scree-slope so that when the moment came he could use it for escaping to the summit above.

Everything now depended upon Coffey and the others on the clifftop. It was all a question of timing, he had impressed that upon them again and again.

He watched the riders drawing closer, their savage faces tense and alert as their eyes scoured the twisting track ahead. Behind them on the broad expanse of the desert floor, the great army of men waited silently.

MacAngus eased back the hammer of his Colt with his thumb. A few more seconds and it would be time to move.

The riders drew abreast until MacAngus could see the Emir plainly, his saddlebag, with its precious cargo, slapping against his animal's flank.

Something whistled through the air. MacAngus smiled crookedly, squinting upwards. Framed against the sky, a coiled shape twisted obscenely, falling in an almost perfect arc to land among the riders grouped below.

MacAngus saw the Emir's mount start in panic as it

glimpsed the snake wriggling viciously beneath its hooves. Another shape fell, then another. Then the air was alive with twisting, wriggling snakes streaming like raindrops from the rocky heights above.

The Dervishes were caught in a welter of panic and confusion. Their mounts, half-crazed with fear, plunged frenziedly around the narrow twisting defile. The riders dipped and lunged, struggling to retain their balance. A snake fell on a man's neck, wrapping itself instinctively around his throat, and MacAngus heard him cry out loud as its fangs sank deep into his jugular.

MacAngus came out from his crouching place and ran in an uneven line toward the Emir, his feet dancing across the rocks, dodging the twisting tendrils of snakes wriggling and darting between the camel thorn. A rider reared into his path, battling to hold his camel in check. MacAngus loosed off a shot which caught the man high in the chest, and heard him grunt with pain as his body toppled backwards from the saddle.

MacAngus switched the revolver to his free hand and reached downwards at the run, drawing his long curved sword. He ducked and weaved through the milling throng, turning his mind from the twisting reptiles hissing menacingly on his route, moving almost by impulse as if his limbs had taken on a life of their own. He drew level with the Emir and, trusting the Colt inside his robe, snatched at the flesh on the man's mountainous thigh. The Emir lashed down at MacAngus with his riding whip, and MacAngus pushed upwards with all his strength, tipping the man inelegantly from his perch. The Emir hit the ground in a cloud of dust and lay there gasping, his lips spluttering furiously. A snake darted over his ankle, vanishing under his robes, and with a shriek of panic, the Emir scrambled to his feet, twisting and dancing insanely in a vain attempt to dislodge the intruder. He yelled out as the snake bit deep into his ample flesh, then he hit the ground again, rolling over and over in a frenzy of terror and pain.

MacAngus cut the saddlebag strap with his sword. Clutching it firmly in his free hand, he turned and ducked back the way he had come. Snakes coiled in his path and he dodged them, dancing nimbly from side to side, his chest contracting, bursting, his heartbeats growing fiercer, thumping wildly against the confines of his ribcage. He reached the foot of the precipitous scree and grabbed at the dangling rope. Frantically, he drew the knotted loop over his shoulders and jerked hard on the line. At once, he felt the pressure from above as the others began to draw him upward. He scrambled up the steep sliding surface, gripping the rope with his free hand. The blood pounded in his head until his vision dimmed and blurred but above and beyond the urgency of its beat, a wild elation filled him. He had the diamonds firmly in his grasp.

A shot rang out and a bullet ricocheted against the rock beside him. The Dervishes had seen him running. Even amidst the confusion below, there were cool heads intent on bringing him down.

MacAngus stumbled. His ankle caught against a boulder and he felt himself pitch forward, the saddlebag falling from his fingers, tipping open among the shale. He tried to snatch it back but the rope dragged blindly at his waist, hauling him on.

In a fury, MacAngus tore the noose over his head and scurried back the way he had come. Dimly he heard Coffey's voice calling a warning. Two tribesmen had dismounted and were working their way up the incline toward him.

MacAngus reached the saddlebag and began to rake through the rubble, scooping out the spilled diamonds and stuffing them frantically into their leather container. He heard Coffey's voice again – 'Mac!' – and peering up, saw the nearmost tribesman almost upon him. Trembling visibly, he snatched out the Navy Colt and crouched in his tracks, steadying his wrist with his free hand. The gun jerked as he fired, and the man's left eye vanished in a spurt of blood. He fired again, seeing the second man fall back, clutching his side. Then a fusillade of shots rang out from below and MacAngus saw men swarming up the scree-slope toward him, their features twisted in fury.

Clutching the saddlebag against his chest, he scrambled furiously up the precipitous incline. At the top he found the others mounted and waiting, Lieutenant Benson holding the spare camel by its bridle. MacAngus mounted at the run, waving the saddlebag triumphantly at his companions, and before the first of the Dervishes could breast the rocky rim, they had turned their animals eastward and were galloping out of the setting sun.

THIRTEEN

The fort stood in a flat saucer of land, flanked on one side by a stunted palmerie. Its walls were largely intact, though in places Coffey noticed the outer palisades had crumbled away. He shifted wearily in his saddle and tugged the field glasses from their leather case.

All through the night they had ridden hard, Coffey plotting the route from a battered ship's compass strapped to his saddlehorn, and when morning had come, diffusing the sky with a soft rosy hue, they had struck diagonally across the pancake flatness of the open *reg*. Even when one of the camels collapsed and had to be abandoned, Coffey had refused to be downhearted, but now, staring down at their first glimpse of Fort Malawa in the flush of early evening, he felt a spasm of uneasiness as he spotted a handful of birds fluttering above the edge of the parapet, wheeling and dipping lazily in the sunlight. There was no other sign of life.

'Vultures,' Coffey whispered.

Driscoll whistled softly at his side. 'Place looks deserted, squire.'

Coffey pushed the binoculars into their case, his optimism replaced by a feeling of sudden alarm. 'Sergeant?' he said in a cracked voice.

MacAngus straightened.

'Give the diamonds to Lieutenant Driscoll. You and I will ride down and investigate.'

'Aye, sir.'

MacAngus unstrapped the leather bag from his saddlehorn. Now that the diamonds had been recovered, he had reverted to his customary role of NCO, and kicking his camel obediently forward, he followed Coffey down the steep crumbling hillside.

Coffey watched the fort undulating eerily in the evening haze. The battered walls took on new definition as they swayed steadily closer. MacAngus lit a cheroot and the acrid smoke stung Coffey's nostrils, increasing the feeling of tension within him. A new odour filled the air, sharp and pungent, blotting out even the stench of the sergeant's tobacco. It was the same odour, Coffey realised, which hung above the slaughterhouse at Wadi Halfa. 'Smell that?' he whispered.

'Aye, sir. I smell it.'

Coffey's first intimation of what was to come was the sight of a severed head impaled on the crumbling gatepost. The eyes were open, the lips drawn back to reveal a set of gleaming teeth. Dried blood caked the rotting woodwork below, baked by the sun to the texture of burnt gravy.

Coffey braced himself as he rode into the fort compound, but nothing prepared him for the horror of what they found there. Bodies sprawled on the ground, hung staked to the walls, dangled from the parapets. They were not bodies in the true sense, the complete sense, since most of them had been dismembered, the various portions of their anatomies spread around the compound in macabre disarray. Purple entrails spilled from bellies split open from navel to crotch. Severed genitals sprouted between the lips of decapitated heads. Coffey reined in his camel and sat in silence, surveying the scene of carnage with the air of a general on a battlefield, but inside, his stomach was lurching as he peered at the desecrated corpses of Guthrie's Sudanese cavalry, looking for all the world like carcasses in a butcher's shop.

'What kind of animals would do a thing like this?' he breathed.

'Dervishes would,' MacAngus said. 'It's the Dervish way.'

It was all Coffey could do to keep from throwing up. But above and beyond his horror rose the realisation that the reinforcements they had been counting on were no longer here. Desperately, he tried to force himself to think. They were worn to a frazzle, animals and men alike. They were still eighty

191

miles from the railhead, a distance which, in their present exhausted state, might as well be eighty thousand. They had nothing left to fall back on, no hidden resources of energy or strength, no last vestiges of endurance. It was all they could do to keep themselves awake.

'We'd better scout around,' he sighed. 'See if the Dervishes left anything worth salvaging.'

He had no great hope of finding fresh supplies, but it seemed absurd to leave without even a cursory check, and for the next fifteen minutes he and MacAngus moved around the compound looking for water *guerbas*, ammunition, anything at all which might alleviate their desperate situation. The task was distasteful in the extreme. He averted his eyes, but with maddening insistence the horror intruded – a human heart, its arteries still attached, dried like a sponge by the savage sun – a hand and arm severed at the elbow, the fingers still clutching the torn strap of a battered pith helmet.

When he had finished his search, Coffey met MacAngus at the compound's centre. 'Tried the well?' he asked.

'Och, it's been saline for years, sir. That's why they abandoned the fort in the first place.'

'Then we'd better get back to the others.'

They retraced their tracks and the little group of riders sat watching their approach from the hilltop. Driscoll waited until Coffey had reined in his mount, then lifted his eyebrows inquiringly.

'Dervishes beat us to it,' Coffey told him.

'Massacre?'

'Every damned soul.'

Driscoll was silent for a moment, staring at the fort. The scar on his face looked red in the dying sunlight. Coffey glanced at Victoria. Her cheeks were pale as buttermilk and he could see the faint gleam of fear in her eyes.

'Those bastards leave anything we can use?' Driscoll asked. 'Water?'

'Not a drop.'

'That puts us in rather a difficult position. There are no water holes between here and the railhead, and what's left will barely last the night.'

192

'We're not making for the railhead,' Coffey told him curtly. 'We're heading for the Nile.'

Driscoll frowned. 'But, squire, we're too far south. There'll be Dervish patrols all along those riverbanks.'

'We've got to have water, Driscoll. I'd rather take my chances with the river than the desert. Who knows, maybe we'll run into one of Kitchener's gunboats. They say they've been carrying out sorties all the way to Omdurman.'

Driscoll thought for a moment, then nodded. 'Whatever you say, old boy. However, we ought to rest awhile. We'll not get far, the state we're in. Take a look at the animals. They're just about dead on their feet.'

'We all are,' Coffey said. 'Rest is exactly what I had in mind. How much of a lead do you think we've got?'

'Quite a bit, I should say. It would take those Dervishes hours to find a way around that mesa and pick up our tracks again. We can thank the sergeant for that.'

'Then we'll remain here until morning. We'll take turns at sentry duty, four hours per man, Benson first. When dawn breaks, we'll saddle up and head for the river.'

It was a poor camping place, Coffey realised, the ground littered with stones, the air filled with the smell of rotting flesh and the squawking of vultures squabbling over their prey, but their bodies were too spent to move any further. Even with morning, their chances would be pitifully slim. Rested, the camels might stand up to the rigours of the journey, but they were still one animal short and well behind the enemy lines.

Coffey made his mind go blank. He was too tired, too drained to ponder on the dangers ahead. He watched Victoria remove the blanket from under her camel saddle and spread it over the sharp jagged stones. Her robe looked dirty, her tangled hair coated with dust. He moved toward her, kneeling down, helping to arrange her bedding. 'You musn't be frightened,' he told her. 'We're not finished yet.'

She turned her eyes away, smoothing out wrinkles in the blanket's surface. Her slender hands dusted sand from the dark coarse material. 'We'll never make the river, not in the state we're in.'

'We've got to.'

'And then what? We'll still be fifty miles or more in front of the British advance positions.'

'At least we'll have water. And the British are moving southward every day. The longer we wait, the better the odds in our favour.'

She sighed softly, stretching out on her side. 'You're such an optimist,' she whispered.

He squatted down beside her, hooking his arms over his folded knees. He felt glad of a woman's presence, as if in some strange way it alleviated the burden of his own position. Around them, the others were making themselves comfortable for the night.

'I've been hoping for a chance to talk to you,' Victoria said gently.

'Why's that?'

'There's something I'd like to get straight between us. I realise this is an unlikely moment, but I might not get the chance again. What happened back there in the prison block . . .' She hesitated. 'Well, I don't know what you must think of me. It was madness of course. I'd gone a little crazy, that's all. It must have been the excitement. There I was talking about being accepted into civilised society, and all the time behaving like an animal on heat.'

Coffey stared at her, puzzled. 'You think civilised people don't act like that?'

'Civilised people cloak their emotions, hold them in check. They take time to get to know each other. As far as you were concerned, it might have been anyone back there.'

'You're wrong. Besides, even if such a thing had entered my mind, which it didn't, nothing happened in Hamira, remember? We were interrupted.'

Victoria smiled, settling back her head. 'I just wanted it understood between us, that's all.'

Coffey shook his head in wonder as he took the blanket from his own camel and spread it on the ground. Who would understand the ways of women? he thought. The memory of their encounter had unsettled his entire senses, but all Victoria could think about was whether or not he held her cheaply. As if he could. She was the best thing that had happened to him. The best thing in his life.

194

He lay down exhausted, shutting his eyes against the starlight, and within a minute, he was fast asleep.

Coffey woke to find Driscoll shaking him. The sky was dark, and Benson was crouching at Driscoll's side. Something in their eyes made Coffey's senses quicken. 'What is it?' he hissed.

'You were sleeping like a corpse, old son. Better pull yourself together. We've got an emergency here.'

'Dervishes?' Coffey groped for his pistol.

'Nothing so mundane, I'm afraid. It's our sergeant, MacAngus. He's buggered off.'

Coffey rubbed his face with his fingertips. 'What are you talking about?'

'He's taken his camel and one of the water *guerbas*. He's taken something else as well.'

'The diamonds,' Benson hissed. 'He's taken the diamonds.'

Coffey felt his stomach contract. It was like a fever he couldn't control, a half-paralysing thing which swept through his body in a blinding wave. He shook his head, his mind reeling. MacAngus? he thought. Impossible.

'Who was on sentry duty?'

'I was,' Driscoll said.

'Didn't you see him leave?'

'See MacAngus? That man moves like a cat.'

Coffey was conscious of a bitter sense of betrayal. It couldn't be true, surely. MacAngus was more than his sergeant, he was his friend. Coffey could recall a thousand times when he had gambled everything on the sergeant's shrewdness and judgement. How could a man, any man, be capable of such treachery? Coffey felt the fury inside him transmute suddenly into cold and resolute hatred. You seldom despised any enemy so much as the friend who turned against you, he thought. He took a deep breath. 'Which direction did he take?'

'North-east. He's heading for the Nile all right but he clearly intends to cross it higher up where the Dervish patrols will be less concentrated.'

Coffey nodded. That was MacAngus all right. With damn

near all his water gone, he was striking out for the farthest point. An audacious move, but if he pulled it off he could be clear of the Dervishes by sunrise. Then he'd have only the British to worry about.

'We've got to go after him.'

Driscoll looked doubtful. 'We're one camel short, squire.'

'If Miss Routledge and her father rode double, do you think you could get them to the river?'

'What about you?'

'I'll take Lieutenant Benson and see if we can run the sergeant down. Once we've recovered the diamonds we'll move south to join you.'

'And then?'

Coffey sighed. His brain wouldn't think that far. His body felt drained, his limbs filled with a soul-searing emptiness. 'God knows,' he admitted honestly. 'We pray, I suppose.'

Victoria rode through the cool of the pre-dawn morning, adjusting her body to the monotonous rhythm of her camel. She had come to terms with it during the long hours of flight, but when this nightmare was over she hoped she would never have to ride such an animal again.

Behind her in the saddle she could feel her father holding gently to her waist. Driscoll trotted ahead, his soiled robes fluttering in the wind as he picked his way with remarkable precision. There was no uncertainty in his movements, nor did he hesitate or pause to consult the compass in his saddle pouch. He steered by the stars, his shrewd eyes picking out the flickering pinpoints of light in the sky.

Victoria's body felt stunned. The few hours' rest had scarely revived her. Her limbs ached drearily and her brain seemed thick and congested.

It mattered little to Victoria if MacAngus had stolen the diamonds or not. Twelve hours ago they had seemed the most important thing in the world. Now she thought only of survival. What was wealth without life? she asked herself. Thirteen years she had spent in captivity. Her few blessed hours of freedom had made her realise one overpowering truth – she wanted to live, she wanted it more than anything.

But she wanted Coffey too, she realised with a small tremor of shock, recalling the way his eyes crinkled each time he smiled, the way the dust coated the hollows beneath his cheekbones. Coffey, she thought, moulding her lips around the sound of the name. It was a nice name. She could grow attached to a name like that. And he was a nice man, hard and decisive when he had to be, gentle and kind when he didn't.

Victoria felt her spirits racing as she rode determinedly onwards. Pray God they came out of this all right. It would be a dreadful irony if she lost him now, after the empty years of loneliness and waiting.

Dawn came slowly, starting in the east, a pale sheen spreading rapidly across the faultless sky. Soon the land took on new dimensions and she felt the warmth of the lifting sun striking down on her face and chest. The countryside changed subtly as the morning lengthened, the stony *reg* giving way to lusher scrub and sporadic clusters of stunted palms. The vegetation thickened, its greenery contrasting sharply with the dryness of the desert floor. 'How much further?' she asked Driscoll.

'Can't be far. See how the animals are hurrying. They smell water already.'

'Shouldn't we slow down a bit? If we're approaching the Nile, there could be Dervish patrols about.'

'Better to get there before the sun climbs high,' Driscoll said reasonably. 'Then we can hide ourselves in the scrub along the bank. Here we stick out like cherries on a Dundee cake.'

Victoria could hear her father snoring softly behind her. His strength was drained, poor thing; he had ridden himself to a standstill.

'You think Lieutenant Coffey will catch up with the sergeant?'

Driscoll grinned at her. 'Coffey will if anybody can.'

'Then what?'

'That's up to the sergeant. Speaking personally, I wouldn't care to take on either of them single-handed.'

Victoria was thoughtful for a moment, then she said: 'I hope MacAngus gets clean away.'

Driscoll glanced at her with surprise. 'You do? Why?'

'Those diamonds have come between us and our wits. Here we are charging around the countryside chasing phantoms when the only thing that really matters is life itself.'

Driscoll chuckled softly. 'I enjoy life as much as the next man,' he said, 'but I'd enjoy it a damned sight better with a few million pounds in my bank balance.'

His voice broke off, fading into a grunt of surprise and she saw him lean back in the saddle, hauling on his reins. Peering ahead, Victoria froze. So intent had they been on their discussion they had ridden unsuspecting into a little hollow in the desert *reg*. It was scarcely deep enough to be termed a *wadi*, but so bland were its contours, it had been impossible to discern on the flat shimmering floor. In the bed of this shallow defile, a group of Dervish tribesmen, their eyes still misty with sleep, were busy saddling their camels. The early morning sunlight illuminated the vivid patches on their ragged jibbahs, and fell in slanting rays across the carved ivory stocks of their ancient flintlock rifles.

The tribesmen themselves were just as startled as Victoria and Driscoll, and for a moment they also froze into a silent tableau, warriors and riders alike. Then Driscoll pulled himself together. 'Back,' he shouted, 'get back. Head for the scrub.'

Victoria jerked hard on the camel's reins. She heard her father's startled exclamation of surprise as he came suddenly awake. Then they turned in one fluid motion, and with Driscoll flanking her, she whipped her mount furiously into a desperate stumbling sprint. She could see the thicket ahead, green and prickly on the arid *reg*. It would offer them cover of sorts, though for how long, she scarcely knew.

Shots rang out as the Dervishes recomposed themselves. She felt her father stiffen and knew at once that he had been hit. Something moist and warm splashed across her neck and she felt his fingers slacken at her waist.

'Father,' she gasped.

The saddle creaked, and the weight behind her suddenly lightened as he tumbled helplessly into the dust. A scream lodged in her throat and she dragged the camel to a halt, skidding wildly.

Her father was sprawled among the rocks, his face pressed against the ground, the upper portion of his features completely obliterated where the bullet had entered his cranium and emerged through the front of his skull. Horror engulfed her. She felt her brain beginning to swoon as waves of nausea came rippling upwards through her chest. She swayed dangerously, and started to yell. There was no sense or reason in her voice, just an aimless protest against the awfulness of the moment.

'For God's sake, don't stop,' Driscoll bellowed. 'Can't you see the poor beggar's dead?'

He turned back toward her, seizing her bridle, and with Victoria clinging sobbing to the saddlehorn, he pounded furiously on toward the cluster of prickly scrub.

More shots. Dimly, she heard the bullets streaking the air above her head. She felt no sense of danger. She was caught in a paroxysm of shock and disbelief, her father's face, shattered beyond recognition, imprinted relentlessly in her mind.

Suddenly Driscoll jerked upright, blood spurting between his lips. She saw his eyes bulge, and his hand left her bridle, clawing futilely in the area of his lower spine. He rolled sideways, hitting the ground shoulder first, scattering the sand in a grotesque shower which sprayed across her lower legs.

She felt the shock drain from her body, repelled by the urgency of the moment. Driscoll was wounded. She had to get him under cover.

Victoria turned back her camel and slid to the ground. Driscoll was lying on his side, blood spreading thickly across the front of his *gandoura*. The bullet had emerged through his stomach, ripping a hole through which Victoria could see the blue-veined entrails clearly protruding. His skin had gone deathly grey, and spittle traced a spidery web across the wiry bristles of his beard.

Sobbing helplessly, Victoria seized him by the armpits and began to drag him backwards across the empty sand. She was only dimly conscious of the Dervishes mounting and turning in her direction. She reached the thicket and let Driscoll drop, tears streaming down her cheeks.

'The rifle,' Driscoll croaked. 'Fetch the rifle, hurry.'

He spoke almost without moving his lips, his features curiously slack and heavy.

Victoria stared across the desert flat. She could see Driscoll's camel, motionless now, chewing contentedly at a clump of thorn. The stock of Driscoll's Martini protruded from the saddle scabbard. Victoria sprinted back as hard as she could run. She could see the Dervishes drawing closer, the elongated barrels of their ancient rifles etched against the sky. She reached the camel and fumbled desperately with the leather buckles, drawing the Martini free. It seemed incredibly heavy in her grasp. She glimpsed the first of the riders framed against the sunlight, and bringing the rifle to her shoulder, sqeezed the trigger with her finger. Nothing happened. A sob of anguish choked in her throat as she realised she had never fired a rifle before. She did not know how.

'Bring it over here,' Driscoll croaked, grimacing with pain. 'The ammunition pouch too.'

Still weeping hysterically, Victoria scurried back the way she had come, clutching the rifle and saddlepouch in her trembling fingers. Driscoll propped himself against a boulder. He took the Martini from her hands and levered a cartridge into the chamber. He released the safety catch and, almost without aiming, snapped off a shot which brought the lead rider down in a flurry of whirling arms and legs. Driscoll cleared the chamber rapidly, switching his aim with the barest economy of movement. He fired again, grunting with savage satisfaction as a second rider tumbled from his saddle, his foot catching in his horse's stirrup, dragging him along as the animal bolted in panic. The other riders turned back, sliding from their mounts and scurrying into the hollow, looking for cover.

Driscoll lowered the rifle and propped his head against the rock. Sweat streamed down his face, mingling with the blood and saliva oozing relentlessly into his beard.

'That'll hold them for a bit,' he muttered weakly. 'They'll probably get us next time, when they get their nerve back. That's if the sun and thirst haven't finished us first.'

MacAngus saw the river through the thin haze of the early morning. He'd known he was close, could smell it even in that strange way he had, a knack he had learned as a boy which had remained with him ever since. He was glad though when he glimpsed the sunlight on the muddy current and realised his frantic dash across the desert was over. He didn't know how much longer his animal could keep going, the way he was pushing it. Damned camels, they were the craziest creatures ever devised, always so full of contrariness and deep-throated protestations they made a man hate them by the time his journey was done. This one though had done better than most. Strong as an ox, it had been. Still, you could push a camel only so hard and then damned if the thing wouldn't drop right down and die, that was how crazy and stupid they were.

The long drive across the empty sands had drained MacAngus' strength and at times he'd had to hold himself tight to keep from falling asleep in the saddle. But it wasn't the tiredness which worried him so much as the other feeling that had settled stubbornly in his gut. He knew what it was all right, had sensed it, identified it, and was trying now to turn his mind from it. But no matter how he shied, his brain returned with nagging persistence to the little bag of stones joggling at his thigh. He was ashamed, that was the size of it, ashamed of what he had done to Coffey.

Guilt was not a natural part of MacAngus' nature. He had never felt guilty before, not that he could recollect. But then, he had never turned his back on a friend before either. He was sorry for the others, of course. Sorry for the way he had used them. But the diamonds had been too important to ignore. The diamonds could buy him a new identity, a new life. He could spirit himself away, far from the influence of the law. They offered more than a future. They offered survival.

Of course, he was still in a tricky position, and a man could die with paradise at his fingertips, but he put that thought from his mind as he let his mount drink. He found a little spot where the water seeped through sand and pebbles into a natural crystal-clear pool with just a fly or two cluttering its surface, and lying down, he lowered his face and gulped the precious life-giving strength-imbibing liquid into his body.

The banks looked empty, cluttered with thick patches of scrub and mimosa, but he knew there would be villages higher up, Dervish villages, and Dervish patrols riding between them. Following the river would be dangerous and foolhardy unless he moved inland apiece. A mile or two should do it. That way he would always know the river was on his right, and the Dervish strongholds would begin to dwindle as he approached the British front.

MacAngus replenished his water *guerba* and slung it from the saddlehorn. His hand instinctively ran down the bulky bag where the diamonds lay, feeling the hard little stones pressing against his fingers. He knew he had taken the right decision. Wealth and affluence, they made a sorry peg for a man to hang his life on. But wealth and affluence could buy him freedom, and nothing in the world was too high a price to pay for that.

He remounted and followed the riverbank, planning to veer off when the notion pleased him, enjoying the calm unhurried flow of the water, the scrub-cluttered banks, the sun shining clear and bright on the lazy current. He liked rivers, he thought, for a river pleased a man's eye, gave him a notion of coming and going, of moving on to places yet untouched and undiscovered, unlike the desert which chilled a man's blood, for all the heat it absorbed and radiated.

The river bent like the sweep of a longbow, its water tumbling into the raging torrent of a distant cataract, and MacAngus, following it, frowned suddenly as he spotted above the crumbling red bank, vultures dipping and wheeling in clumsy confusion. MacAngus reached beneath his robe and took out a thin cheroot, lighting it carefully. There was something dead up front. He could smell it already, the same chilling odour that had settled in his nostrils at Fort Malawa. Could be a camel, he thought, or some miserable donkey abandoned by its owner. But he unslung his Martini rifle as he nudged his animal forward, and rested it ready-cocked across the front of his saddle.

At a point where the river bent, with the water running dark over cold flat stones, the shattered wreckage of an Arab *dahabeeyah* lay keeled over on its side. There was something strangely familiar about the craft, its splintered hull smoke-blackened and shimmering in the sun. MacAngus could see its crew sprawled about the deck, their bones gleaming white through flesh picked clean by desert scavengers. Then he remembered. This was the wreck they had seen the night the gunboat put them ashore. Unwittingly he had come upon the very spot from which they had started.

MacAngus dismounted and led his camel down to the water's edge, leaving it to drink there while he moved toward the battered shell, examining it critically. He counted eight corpses in all, and a ninth still bobbing in the shallows. In the stern lay the ancient metal cannon with its scarred muzzle and ornate casing, and the tiny gunpowder barrel caulked with tar. MacAngus shook his head in wonder. The Dervish crew, using a weapon centuries old, with gunpowder made among the villages of the Meidob and Tabago, had taken on a British patrol boat armed to the teeth with modern artillery. It was an unequal struggle when you came right down to it. Even the Khalifa must realise the inevitable outcome of the war he was fighting.

MacAngus was thinking this when he heard, quite distinctly, the rasping snort of a camel. Scrambling up the riverbank, he threw himself flat between two clumps of mimosa. The land shimmered in the morning heat, cluttered with great patches of sandy foliage which shut off his line of vision. Squinting, he was able to discern through the rippling waves two riders coming hard towards him, clad in the dark blue robes and headress of the Hoggar Tuareg. The man leading he recognised instantly. Coffey. MacAngus would have known Coffey from five miles off on a foggy night. The way he sat in that saddle was unmistakable. The other one would be either Lieutenant Benson or Driscoll.

Damn fools. Instead of running for the river to the south, they had followed his tracks, the tracks MacAngus hadn't even bothered to conceal, calculating no one would be crazy enough to come after him, the condition they were in.

Coffey, that lunatic son-of-a-bitch, was after the diamonds, MacAngus' diamonds, his present and future. There was only one answer MacAngus could see.

He slipped a bullet into the Martini chamber and licking one finger, carefully moistened the front sight to give him aim.

Then using the earth as a steadier, he settled his cheek to the stock and levelled the barrel at Coffey's chest. He did not want to kill Coffey. He liked him better than any other officer he had served under. But he did not want to lose the diamonds either. The diamonds could bring him security and MacAngus was prepared to kill anyone for that.

Coffey had slowed his pace, seeing the river ahead, and now his outline offered a target MacAngus just couldn't miss. One light squeeze, gentle as a desert wind, and Coffey would go tumbling lifeless out of his saddle. MacAngus's finger tightened on the trigger.

Nothing happened. He waited like a man caught in a seizure, unable to move, unable to do a thing except lie there. Swearing softly, he lowered the weapon. He couldn't kill Coffey, no matter what, he should have realised that from the beginning. If he wanted to hold on to those diamonds, his only hope was to find some way of staying ahead, of crossing the river maybe and heading up north on the opposite side.

A sudden commotion caught MacAngus's ear, and craning his head he glimpsed eight mounted horsemen riding across the skyline. MacAngus's mouth gaped open in astonishment. Clad in chainmail and heavy armour, the horsemen looked like medieval Crusaders, the sunlight glinting fiercely on their metal shields and helmets. He watched as they reined in their mounts, their eyes sweeping the scrub-cluttered riverbank. They spotted Coffey and his companion, and turned swiftly in their direction.

Victoria crouched among the camel scrub and listened to the monotonous rhythm of the Dervish rifle fire. For more than an hour they had kept up a steady barrage of shots, most of them drifting far wide of their target, thank God, for their weapons were ancient and notoriously unstable. Once or twice, a tribesman more daring than the rest had left the safety of the hollow, wriggling his way toward them in the hope of securing a clearer range of fire, but each time, Driscoll, operating the Martini with admirable dexterity, had sent the man scurrying backwards searching for cover.

Driscoll was dying, Victoria knew that. She had struggled

desperately to staunch the blood pouring in bucketfuls from the vicious hole in his stomach, but death was inevitable, Victoria could tell. Driscoll knew it too. His strength was fading with each passing minute, and soon he would be too weak even to raise the Martini to his shoulder. She shivered violently as she watched his futile battle to cling to the last vestiges of existence. Poor Driscoll. Though she scarcely knew the man, she liked him, trusted him, felt secure in his company. He had risked his life to rescue her, and by that single act of deliverance had lost his own. It was all she could do to keep herself from crying.

Her shock and horror at her father's death had been replaced by a feeling of despair at the hopelessness of their position. She shuddered when she thought of the ordeal ahead. She had already made up her mind what she would do. When Driscoll faded, she would take the rifle and blow out her brains. She had watched him operate it, knew now how to load and fire. She would place the barrel in her mouth and squeeze the trigger with her toe. One fractional movement and – pouf – the Dervishes would never be able to harm her again.

Driscoll coughed painfully as blood choked in his throat. She leaned forward, wiping the crimson flecks from his lips. His eyes looked dazed as they focused with difficulty on her face.

'You've got to get out of here,' he croaked.

'Don't talk. It'll sap your strength.'

'Listen to me. You've got to make a run for the river.'

'And leave you behind? What do you take me for?'

Sweat streamed down his face and she used the sleeve of her robe to gently mop his brow. His skin had the yellowish texture of melted wax.

'Take my camel,' he choked. 'It's still grazing at the back of the thicket. Steer due east into the sun. The Nile can't be far. Another few miles, possibly less. At least you'll have water.'

'You must have a poor opinion of me, if you think I'd leave you in a state like this.'

'I'm gutshot, Miss Routledge. For me, it's only a matter of time. Take the camel. I'll hold the bastards off until you get clear.'

'Lieutenant Driscoll, I am not going anywhere without you.'

Suddenly his features tightened and his muscles contracted, forcing his body into a rigid arc. His eyes closed in pain and he groped at her wrist.

'Grab my hand,' he gasped.

She felt his fingers clutch hers.

'Now squeeze very hard. Hard as you can.'

Victoria tightened her grip, feeling his strength shuddering along her forearm. For almost a full minute he lay squeezing and grinding his teeth, then his body abruptly relaxed and his head fell back against the rock, exhausted.

'Does it hurt badly?' she asked.

'Like the whole of my abdomen's blown away. How long do you think I've got? An hour?'

'Don't talk like that.'

'I'm finding it difficult to talk at all. That's why you must go without delay. I don't know how much longer I can keep this up.'

'You think I'd let you die like a dog at the roadside, after all we've gone through?'

'God knows I don't want to die,' he breathed, 'I hate the thought of dying, always have. I want to live Miss Routledge, and go back to England a rich man. But if I've got to go, I'd like at least to think there's some purpose behind it.'

'You've already done more than enough,' she told him. 'You've saved me from a life of slavery, isn't that worth something?'

His lips drew back in a painful grin. 'My God, I hope you enjoyed your few hours of freedom, Miss Routledge. You paid a hell of a price for them.'

'It's been worth every minute. I couldn't have gone on living in that hellhole.'

Driscoll's frame shuddered as he coughed, and the ravaged contours of his face twisted into a grimace of anguish and pain. Fresh blood spurted into his beard, and leaning forward, Victoria gently began to wipe his mouth.

'I want you . . . I want you to listen to a dying man's wish,' he whispered hoarsely. 'You mustn't deny me the chance of becoming a martyr. It rather appeals to my dramatic instincts.'

'I'm not leaving you, do you hear me?'

'Please. I want to go out in a blaze of glory, Miss Routledge. It'll make the perfect curtain call, don't you see?'

Driscoll was trying to smile but in his agony his lips had twisted into a grotesque grimace.

Unable to help herself any longer, Victoria felt the tears springing to her eyes. Her shoulders shook as sobs racked her body.

'I hope you're not crying for me,' Driscoll said. 'I never could stand to see a woman's tears.'

Victoria shook her head, chewing hard at her lip.

'Take what's left of the water,' he muttered, 'I won't need it. Leave the rifle and ammunition and I'll do what I can. But for God's sake, hurry.'

Victoria controlled herself with an effort. Driscoll was right. There was no sense in both of them dying. Her chances were slim, but they were worth a try.

Leaning forward, she kissed him lightly on the forehead. His skin felt clammy against her lips.

'Go now,' he whispered. 'You've wasted too much time already. Keep riding toward the sun. Sooner or later you'll reach the river.'

Gently Victoria eased backwards through the thicket. She heard Driscoll coughing as a fresh bout of haemorrhaging burst in his throat.

'Miss Routledge?' he croaked.

She glanced back. He was watching her intently, blood smeared in a bizarre pattern across the front of his *gandoura*.

'Make sure everyone knows what a hero I've been, won't you? I'd hate to think I'm doing this for nothing.'

She waved in assent and wriggled forward to where Driscoll's camel squatted in the scrub, its rubbery lips chewing contentedly at the twisted tendrils of vegetation. Victoria slid into the saddle and slapped the animal to its feet. The boom-boom of Driscoll's rifle split the air as, with the tears still streaming down her cheeks, Victoria kicked the camel's flanks and rode vigorously into the sun.

FOURTEEN

Coffey stared in amazement at the line of iron-clad riders galloping toward him, their polished helmets and breastplates glittering in the pale glow of the early morning. A sense of unreality shook him, a feeling that the world had somehow come askew. 'My God,' he whispered. 'Will you look at that.'

'They're . . . they're knights in armour,' Lieutenant Benson breathed.

'Dervishes. Can't be anything else.'

Coffey glanced swiftly around. Scrub cluttered the land in all directions. Ahead, the Nile curved through the morning sunlight, its waters gleaming brightly.

'The river's our best chance,' he said. 'If they follow us into the water wearing that lot, they'll sink like stones.'

He kicked his camel into a run, holding fiercely to the saddlehorn, watching the ground dip and undulate ahead, conscious of Lieutenant Benson following, conscious of the river shimmering ahead, deep and green and cool. He galloped across the last few yards, dismounted at the run and stumbled headlong into the swirling current, feeling the water soothe his fevered skin. The riverbed seemed treacly, tugging at his sandals as he waded forward as hard as he could go, pushing against the current's pull until his toes had left the bottom. His robes bunched up, lifted high by the bobbing tide. The heavy fabric clung to his thrashing limbs, dragging him back.

Benson overtook him, swimming hard, his pale face glistening through the spray. At eye level, Coffey could see flies dancing across the rippling surface. Ahead, so far away it seemed little more than a hazy ghostline, lay the opposite shore.

North, the river narrowed, the water tumbling into the frothy tumult of a raging cataract. Coffey glimpsed the dark hummocks of rocky islands rearing out of the white-capped spray.

Behind them, the armoured warriors had come to a halt along the riverbank, making no attempt to follow. Instead, they were watching and – Coffey froze when he realised this – laughing, actually laughing.

He felt a chill sweep through his body as, just ahead, swaying toward them out of a narrow inlet, he spotted a boat, its brown triangular sail billowing in the wind. A nuggar.

It looked almost graceful as it sped across the rippling water, its prow bobbing and dipping in the swell. Gathered along the vessel's hull dark-skinned Dervishes smirked savagely as they waited with poised spears for Benson and Coffey to come within range.

Benson saw the boat at almost the same moment. 'We're trapped,' he choked, kicking wildly as he struggled to change direction.

'No sense going back,' Coffey told him. 'They're waiting for us on the riverbank.'

He could see the Dervishes clearly now, their ragged robes fluttering on their scrawny bodies, their faces twisted into wicked grins as they pranced about on the nuggar's deck, brandishing their spears.

'Duck under,' Benson gasped.

'No point. They'll just wait till we come up for air.'

'Christ.'

The boat drew nearer, and instinctively they struck out for the shoreline, though Coffey knew no sanctuary lay in that direction, for already the mounted warriors were clustering the water's edge, driving in their horses as far as they would go while they waited for the swimmers to approach within slaughtering distance.

Coffey saw spears curving through the air above them. The dark shafts sliced the water as they swam. Something clipped his skull and he felt his mind go blank, his ears ringing with a strange roaring sound. He blinked hard, pain shooting through his brain as blood streamed over his hair into his eyes.

He had been struck a glancing blow by a lance-tip, and he felt dizziness engulf him as the water swirled into his face. The world seemed fragmented and grotesque. He remembered the severed heads and limbs at Fort Malawa, the disemboweled corpses. For God's sake, if he was going to die, let it be quick.

Then something echoed in his ears, a distant thunder vibrating heavily across the glistening water. Blinking, Coffey paused in mid-stroke and glanced back as the prow of the boat suddenly erupted in a great shower of splintered timber. The men who a second before had been dancing and laughing along its hull were scattered across the river's surface, their torn bodies lifting in the swell as entrails and viscera eddied outwards in macabre confusion.

Coffey brushed the moisture from his eyes, struggling to discern the meaning of this new development. Dazedly, he treaded water as the explosion's echoes reverberated in his ears. The nuggar was listing now, the pitiful remnants of its crew running up and down its deck, shouting in panic.

Coffey squinted along the riverbank. He could see something at the water's edge, a boat of sorts, or what was left of one. Crouched in its stern he spotted a tall rawboned man with jagged cheekbones leaning back against the vessel's mast, fumbling with an ancient metal cannon. MacAngus!

The roar came again, accompanied this time by a vivid flash. Coffey heard the rush of grapeshot as it swept across the river's surface. For a moment there was silence, and then, as Coffey watched, the nuggar seemed to disintegrate before his eyes, its hull bursting outwards, showering pieces of ruptured timber everywhere. He saw a man ripped to shreds, the lower part of his torso still kicking furiously as it hit the water and sank in a crimson cascade. Squirming bodies splashed in the current, spewing out blood and pieces of ragged flesh.

Benson stared at the scene in bewilderment, his hair plastered damply over his forehead. 'What the hell is happening?' he gasped.

'It's MacAngus,' Coffey shouted jubilantly. 'He's blown the bastards out of the water with their own bloody cannon.'

He glanced swiftly around. Blood was streaming from his forehead, eddying into the fast-moving current. His vision blurred, turning the river into a confused flurry of distorted images. He spat to clear the water from his mouth. 'Come on,' he snapped, 'no sense drowning. Let's swim for the opposite bank.'

MacAngus watched the remains of the nuggar sinking slowly beneath the surface. The bodies of the Arab tribesmen bobbed obscenely around the last fragments of wreckage. He could see Coffey and Lieutenant Benson swimming determinedly away, and grunted as he took the half-smoked cheroot from his lips and threw it into the water. It had been a chance in a million, he realised. The old cannon had been so clapped out, he'd half expected the damned thing to blow up in his face. But the gunpowder had done the trick. That grapeshot had cut down everything in its path, and he was glad Coffey and Benson hadn't been a few yards closer or it would have torn them both to bits.

MacAngus let his gaze sweep along the shoreline. The armoured warriors were staring at him dumbfounded. The unexpectedness of his appearance had momentarily confused them. For several seconds they studied him in silence, frozen to their saddles in amazement. Then, gripping their lances, they turned in his direction, kicking their horses into a gallop. MacAngus watched them spread out in a ragged line, the glint of their armour strangely muted with the sun now behind them. He levered a fresh cartridge into the Martini and fired once, not counting on a hit, feeling gratified when one of the riders tumbled into the dust, his breastplate breaking loose with the impact.

MacAngus raced for his camel, mounting at a run. He knew the animal was on the brink of exhaustion, but the Dervish mounts were weighed down with the chainmail they were carrying. He still had a chance.

He loosed off another shot that missed by a mile, then kicked his camel into a run, steering it furiously through the thorny mimosa to the brightness of the empty *reg*.

Yelling insanely, the Dervishes thundered relentlessly in his wake.

*   *   *

Victoria scarcely knew how long she had been riding. Her camel was stumbling ominously and on the verge of collapse. In every direction the desert stretched away interminably and she thought of Lieutenant Driscoll, feeling a wave of gratitude as she recalled how he had covered her escape. But her first flush of elation at finding herself still alive faded rapidly. She was alone in a savage country. Before her lay the Nile. To the north, fifty or sixty miles away, the British army and safety. But between them was the desert, flat and malevolent, filled with roaming bands of barbaric tribesmen.

Victoria's spirits drooped as she considered the hopelessness of her position. Never in her life had she felt so terribly alone. Her father was gone, Driscoll was probably dead by now, and Coffey was off on a wild goosechase of his own, chasing fantasies of wealth and riches.

She rode almost without thinking, the dullness in her brain making her head feel thick and woolly. Fear alone kept her from drifting into sleep as slowly the land began to flatten, the contours and hollows levelling out. Mimosa bushes cluttered her path, and she watched the ground rise in a gentle incline to a parapet of harsh red earth framed against the sky. She followed a spine of rock, crossed a narrow wadi and entered a twisting tangle of vegetation. The river couldn't be far, she reasoned. A few hours, Driscoll had said. Surely she must be within striking distance by now. She felt as if she'd been riding for days.

Suddenly a fusillade of sharp cracking noises broke on the bright morning air, and Victoria straightened in the saddle, sucking in her breath. Shots. The sound was unmistakable. They came again, rattling confusedly in her eardrums, and behind them she heard the sonorous boom-boom of deeper explosions. Artillery. Victoria's heart began to pound.

She left her camel grazing in the scrub and scrambled up the sandy incline, lifting her head above its rim. Her breath caught in her throat as the broad sweep of the river swung into view, its water sleek and slow-running as it looped beneath her in a massive arc. The Nile!

On the opposite bank Dervish warriors in white robes crouched among the mimosa firing their rifles at a white-painted sternwheeler chugging sedately through the central current. Victoria felt her excitement mount as she stared fascinated at the gunboat, its funnel belching smoke into the clear blue sky. The vessel was three-tiered with metal palisades built along its decks, and from its mast the Union Jack fluttered merrily alongside the Egyptian white star and crescent.

She could see men moving to and fro like tiny ants, and as she watched, a flash of flame emerged from the gunboat's stern. Almost simultaneously, the deep satisfying boom of artillery came resounding toward her, and on the opposite bank a column of earth mushroomed into the sky, tossing men and animals contemptuously aside like clumsy confetti.

Victoria's mouth went dry. She watched the Dervishes milling about in helpless confusion as *keeeeruuuumph*, another shell exploded and a tree was hurled in the air like a piece of matchwood. *Vrooomph vrooomph*, a clump of palms disintegrated in a spreading pumpkin of flame, scattering splintered timber across the open river. Screams of pain and terror rang in Victoria's ears. A man staggered into the water, his robe ablaze. He spun wildly as a piece of twisted shrapnel caught him in the spine, ripping his body almost in two. Then the Maxim opened up again, and this time the warriors left their positions and began to scramble panic-stricken through the thick thorny scrub. She heard the faint echo of a cheer drifting from the gunboat's deck.

Desperately, Victoria tried to pull herself together. She was within a hair's breadth of safety, except for one thing. In her Dervish robes, she looked identical to the savage tribesmen engaging the gunboat from the other side of the river. If she rose from her position, the artillerymen would simply swing the lethal Maxim in her direction, and she felt a surge of panic as she watched the great craft drift majestically around, heading back the way it had come. Anger started up inside her. She had gone through too much to lie here in stupefied dismay and watch her last hope fade into the sunlight. Her brain worked furiously. An idea came to her but she summarily dismissed it. She couldn't, she thought, she simply couldn't.

Yet the boat was leaving. Its wheel was thrashing the muddy water, sending ripples in every direction as it swung into the central current. Soon it would disappear for ever.

Victoria made her decision fearfully. She slid back, moving below the parapet, and began to fumble with her robes, drawing them feverishly over her head, feeling the touch of the cool morning air bathing her naked skin. Her face and arms had been tanned by the sun, but the rest of her was pale as alabaster as, naked, she rose and stepped up to the riverbluff, standing outlined against the sky.

Staring across the water, she willed the gunboat to stop, willed the crew to peer in her direction. A startled cry echoed inarticulately across the current and Victoria felt triumph in her breast. They had seen her. Along the gunboat's decks, miniscule heads were turning rapidly.

For a moment she remained perfectly still, her white body gleaming, the sunlight bathing her shoulders and breasts. There must be no mistake. The men on board must realise beyond any question it was a woman – and a white woman at that – they were gazing at.

When she was satisfied the attention of the entire crew was fixed upon her, Victoria walked slowly down to the river's edge and entered the water. It was many years since she had tried to swim, but she moved her arms persistently and was gratified to see, when she paused for breath, that the gunboat was some distance nearer.

A knotted rope was lowered from its gunwale, and with her hair hanging in sodden strands around her naked shoulders, she was hauled up to the vessel's deck. A young subaltern helped her over the rail, his eyes bulging at the sight of a nude white woman, dripping wet, clambering out of the river fifty miles behind the Dervish positions.

Three minutes later, wearing the subaltern's Royal Navy tunic, Victoria stood on the bridge and gabbled out her story to the astonished gunboat commander.

The movement of the river distorted Coffey's senses. The insistent pull of the current washed furiously over his face each time he swung his body into another stroke. He had swallowed so much water he calculated he must be practically awash inside, and his brain was spinning as blood from his head wound trickled relentlessly into the tumbling stream.

He felt the pressure building up around him until he was swimming in a daze, his movements no longer smooth and co-ordinated but rhythmless, disjointed, hopelessly despairing. I can't keep this up much longer, he thought.

There was no distinct point at which his strength gave out, but slowly, gradually, painfully, the realisation settled in his brain that he would never make it to the opposite shore. A draining lightness swept through his skull and he felt his body losing density, becoming light as air, a bubble tossed on the dancing current. 'Benson,' he choked, 'Benson.'

Benson looked back, his pale face bobbing above the spray. The scar on his cheek glistened fiercely in the morning sunlight. 'What's wrong?'

'I can't make it.'

'You've got to make it, damn you. You've got to.'

'I can't. I'm clapped.'

Coffey felt lifeless, part of the river itself. Closing his eyes, his body filled with a strange lethargy, he felt the undertow grab at his legs, pulling him along. He sensed the strength of it and let himself relax, turning over and over in the rushing flow. There was no longer any need to fight or hope or pray; it was better by far to accept the blessed peace of oblivion.

Suddenly he realised why the current was moving faster. They were being sucked into the boiling waters of the cataract. Ahead, jagged outcrops rose above the ferment, their surfaces glistening as they churned the white waves into a swirling cauldron. The roar of the cataract hammered at Coffey's ears as he was swept relentlessly toward it. No sense of alarm responded in his brain for he was already beyond all that, blinded and buffeted by the surging flow which held him.

Benson spotted the maelstrom ahead and his glistening face turned visibly paler. 'Kick,' he bellowed. 'Kick, for God's sake.'

But Coffey was spinning along at a dizzy rate, caught in a strange separation of mind and body. The water took him. turning him gently, almost tenderly. His body felt cold and numb, the pain in his head accentuated by each beat of his heart, but he turned his mind from that, forgetting the danger, aware only of the wonderful release from fear, the glorious freedom from caring he had never before experienced.

His sight blurred as he went under and he glimpsed the dark wall of mud dredged from the river floor. He was hurtling along like a bullet, conscious of the bottom dipping and undulating beneath his chest. Then his head broke the surface and he spotted Benson splashing toward him. Benson was shouting above the wave crests, but the sounds were lost in the thunder of the cataract.

A hand gripped Coffey's shoulder, dragging his head higher. He heard Benson bellowing: 'Kick, damn your eyes. Do you want to get us both killed?'

Coffey lashed out with his feet, thinking in that fractional moment how strange it was that Benson of all people, his old enemy and sparring partner, should be helping him now.

And then the torrent was all around them, seething and boiling, blotting out sight and sound and reason, battering their bodies from every direction. Above the ferment Coffey glimpsed the jagged columns of rock rearing in their path and his stomach plunged. The glistening buttresses rose out of the water swathed by delicate ribbons of spray, their dark slabs intensifying the current's roar until Coffey felt he was being sucked into a frenzied vortex of noise. The river was like a living force intent on their destruction. Fear pumped through his body and once again he felt Benson's hand gripping his shoulder, Benson's voice yelling into his ear: 'Harder, harder. We've got to make that rock.'

Coffey struggled. Dimly, at one point, he caught a glimpse of the opposite bank; it was whipping by in a dizzy blur, but before Coffey could get a grip on his senses, the river came leaping in again and his brain froze as he spotted the nearmost rock almost upon them. It reared above the spray, sharp and angular, riddled with cracks and fissures and narrow ledges. Benson had one hand gripping the outcrop's corner, the other holding on to Coffey's robe. Coffey heard the robe tearing, he heard Benson shouting, heard the river roaring and clenched his teeth as the torrent thundered against his skull, lashing his cheeks, pounding his throat and spine, plunging his body and mind alike into a pit of helpless oblivion.

*   *   *

216

MacAngus knew his camel was finished. He had felt it staggering for more than a mile now and its neck had lowered as if the wiry column could barely support the weight of the head above it. MacAngus drew the animal to a halt. It was cruel to punish the poor beast further. Better to choose a place to die in.

The horsemen spread out behind him, their mounts kicking up dust, as they pounded triumphantly in for the kill.

MacAngus didn't bother to take cover. He spat on the ground, stuck a cheroot in his mouth and lit it carefully. Then he loaded the Martini, laying the rest of the cartridges in the sand where he could get at them if he needed to. All the while, his eyes, slitted against the sun, watched the horsemen's approach with steely absorption.

He let them get within thirty yards, then, moving with no sign of haste, he brought the Martini to his shoulder, took aim and gently squeezed the trigger. Metal hit metal, and MacAngus saw the lead rider throw up his arms and tumble from the saddle, hitting the earth in a great jumble of thrashing legs and eddying dust.

Biting hard on the cheroot, MacAngus cleared the chamber and slipped in a fresh round, switching aim with the barest expenditure of effort. He watched his next target swing into frame then – ca-rack – the man's helmet buckled inward as he went into a backward somersault, writhing and kicking in the frenzied convulsions of encroaching death.

MacAngus was ejecting the cartridge case when suddenly, for no clear reason he could think of, he was lying flat on his back, staring at the sky. He frowned, puzzled at this strange phenomenon, then the echo of a rifle crack reverberated in his ears and he realised he had been shot. The fact surprised him. He had been unaware the Dervishes were carrying rifles.

He felt no pain, that was the strangest part, only a curious numbness which crept through his abdomen to his lower chest. His Martini was lying several feet away, resting in the dust. He could roll toward it, he reasoned, but not quickly enough. Instead he groped beneath his robe, his fingers locating the ribbed handle of his Navy Colt. He dragged it out, drawing back the hammer in one fluid motion. The foremost warrior

217

was almost upon him and MacAngus saw the man's face quite clearly beneath his shiny steel visor. MacAngus fired directly upwards, holding the pistol at arm's length, gripping his right wrist with his left hand to keep it steady as he aimed for the warrior's open mouth.

He missed.

Instead the bullet caught the front of the Dervish's breastplate and ricocheted upwards, entering the man's skull beneath his chin and emerging through the top of his helmet in a gory halo of metal, blood and bone fragments.

The man almost landed on MacAngus' chest as he hit the ground and rolled over to lie twitching in the swirling dust. MacAngus switched his aim, firing twice at the next rider, seeing only his outline framed against the sun as he reared in the saddle and wheeled away, clutching his side.

MacAngus waited, watching the sky and his outstretched arms. Three shots left, he thought. Only three. There would be no freedom now. No fresh start, no new identity. He had thought the diamonds the answer to everything – now he realised they had been the answer to nothing. He had betrayed his friends, turned his back on everything he believed in, and for what? A dream so distorted he must have been mad to imagine he could ever make it real. He understood that now, at the moment it was too late. But he was glad he understood it, just the same. It gave some purpose to his dying. God knew there had been precious little purpose to his life.

So MacAngus waited, with his finger on the trigger, for the warriors to come. Minutes stretched and nothing happened. Cautiously he lowered his pistol and lifted his head, squinting through the glare. The desert *reg* lay flat as a pancake all the way to the skyline. There was not a soul in sight. Puzzled, he let his head drop back, feeling dizzy and nauseous. Too hard to think, he told himself. Too hard to figure things out. Besides, the desert was fading. He was back again in the hills above Kilbirnie, watching the sun set over the ruins of Glengarnoch Castle, turning the sombre stones into a blaze of purple and pink. Someone was bending over him, his mother, her beautiful face creased in sympathy and concern as gently she touched his wound.

So absorbed was MacAngus in this vision that he did not hear the soft rattle of accoutrements, nor did he see the brown jerseys and sand-coloured trousers of an Egyptian patrol riding slowly toward him through the blistering sunlight.

For more than an hour, Coffey and Benson lay sprawled on the rock with the river roaring around them. It was, Coffey realised, a far from enviable position, for their desperate struggle to escape the cataract had destroyed their last vestiges of energy and now they were marooned in the centre of the current with no hope on earth of reaching either bank alive. They felt no discomfort, for their bodies were too spent and exhausted, but a dangerous lassitude had invaded their limbs taking away initiative, awareness. The sun drove little spirals of steam out of their saturated clothing and spittle trickled aimlessly over their ravaged features.

'How's the head?' Benson croaked, his voice strained and distorted.

'Throbbing.'

'Bound to. Nasty cut you've got.'

Coffey was silent for a moment. It had not yet fully sunk in that it had been Benson, of all people, who had dragged him like a drowning kitten from the fury of the rapids. Nothing in life was quite the way it seemed, he thought. All men possessed within them a depth and complexity that far outweighed the frameworks of reason.

'I was finished back there,' he whispered. 'If you hadn't hauled me out I'd have gone straight to the bottom. You saved my life.'

'Well, don't rub it in.'

'Why didn't you let me drown?'

'I don't know,' Benson admitted frankly. 'Just couldn't resist the temptation to play the bloody hero, I suppose.'

Coffey's lips twitched painfully. 'Benson, I'm beginning to suspect that underneath that cold exterior you're really a decent human being.'

He closed his eyes, water running from his robes down the steep incline of the rocky shelf on which they lay. Spray from the thundering cataract swept their faces, depositing little globules of moisture on his haggard cheeks. Though it was very hot Coffey could barely detect the warmth of his own body. The world seemed shapeless and unreal. He let his thoughts flow in a sluggish drift, trying to assess his physical condition, concentrating on the different sections of his body limb by limb, organ by organ. At length he gave up. There was no sensation he could atune to. He was like an empty shell, caught in a vacuum of fatigue. They would never survive the day, he realised. The sun would get them. Or the river. Or both.

He wondered about Victoria. His mind was fanciful, recalling the calm symmetry of her features, the hint of promise in her beautiful eyes. Was she still alive? he wondered. Would she make it through to the British lines? He wished sadly that he had known her better, had known some of the secret, intimate things about her; now he supposed he never would.

A series of shudders ran through Lieutenant Benson's frame. For a moment Coffey thought he was caught in the grip of some strange unnatural fever, then he realised Benson was laughing. No sound emerged from Benson's lips but his mouth stretched back and his teeth glinted fiercely in the sunlight. For no reason he could clearly explain Coffey joined in, the guffaws issuing from his chest, dry and rasping. They laughed hysterically for several minutes before their merriment subsided and they lay gasping in the sun.

'Christ knows what we're laughing at,' Coffey said, 'we can't stay here.'

'No, we'll burn to a frazzle on this rock.'

'We could take our chances in the water.'

'We'd never make it, sport.'

Coffey grunted. Benson was right. They may have escaped the river, but their craggy refuge offered only a temporary respite from death, nothing more.

An hour passed.

'Think Driscoll got through?' Benson asked.

'Maybe.'

'It's MacAngus I'm envious of. He's still got the diamonds.'

'Bastard.'

'He saved our lives, remember?'

'Doesn't alter the fact he's a bastard.'

Soon it grew too hot to talk and they passed into silence, their bodies draped across the rock. The morning lengthened and Coffey closed his eyes, listening to the roaring of the current. How strange life had been, he thought. What experiences he had endured. And now this. An ending so incongruous he wanted to laugh at the irony of it.

Soon his brain gave up altogether and he lapsed into long stretches of mindless torpor. There was nothing to think about any more, only the simple hope, envisaged but not expressed, that death when it came would be unoppressive, a peaceful drift into an endless sleep with no sense of termination when the breathing stopped. Death, like everything else, he told himself, was merely an illusion, and he waited patiently for oblivion as a man might wait for an imminent moment of fulfilment.

It was Benson's voice which brought him back to consciousness.

'Coffey,' Benson hissed. 'Look up the river.'

Coffey blinked, screwing up his eyes against the glare of the sun. Something danced in his vision, blurring weirdly. As he watched, it gradually came into focus. He spotted a Union Jack fluttering in the wind. White-painted decks gleaming in the sunlight. Smoke curling from a blackened funnel.

A British gunboat.

'Is it a mirage?' Benson choked.

A wave of elation swept through Coffey's battered body. He had thought death inevitable, had come to terms with it, embracing the prospect with the resignation lack of choice engenders, but now suddenly, like a vision from some scarcely believable reverie, deliverance was here at hand.

'It's no mirage,' he croaked excitedly. 'That's Miss Routledge on the deck. Wave your arms, Benson. Wave them hard, for God's sake. We are going to be rescued.'

FIFTEEN

'Remarkable,' Kengle breathed.

The old lady smiled gently. In the lamplight her face looked almost young again, as if recounting the past had rejuvenated her in some strange way. On the table, the dinner dishes stood untouched. Kengle's brandy glass, empty now, rested by his wrist. Through the window he could see stars twinkling in the warm softness of the summer evening. A clock ticked monotonously in the corner of the room.

'The story was suppressed, of course,' the old lady told him. 'My mother was adamant that no one should know she had been a Dervish slave. Though accounts of the diamonds were heavily publicised, it was agreed by everyone concerned that the details of their discovery should be kept a closely guarded secret.'

Kengle smiled. 'And you thought I'd be disillusioned by the knowledge that your father, Sir Stephen Coffey, had tried to steal them?'

'No,' Lady Catherine said, 'I didn't think that at all.'

'Then what . . .?'

'I haven't finished yet, Mr Kengle.'

He glanced at his watch. 'It's after midnight,' he protested, 'I must get back to London.'

'Be patient. I am coming to the most important part.'

Rising from her chair, the old lady moved to the cocktail cabinet and poured a large glass of Scotch. Without a word she placed it on the table beside Kengle's wrist. He looked up at her in surprise. 'What's this?' he grunted.

'Take it, Mr Kengle,' she said, staring at him beadily. 'I

have a feeling that when you hear what I have to say, you are going to need a good stiff drink.'

Victoria picked up the teapot and refilled Coffey's cup. She was dressed in the uniform of a Seaforth Highlander, complete with kilt and tunic. The jacket was at least two sizes too big for her but it did little to tone down the lines of her splendid body.

They were sitting in the empty mess-tent, the sounds of life and movement drifting in from the camp and railhead outside. Several hours had passed since Coffey's rescue from the cataract and he was beginning at last to absorb the realisation, shattering in its impact, that he was not after all on the threshold of death, but back amid the safety of his own people. His wound had been dressed, he had delivered his report to Colonel Guthrie, and, apart from a desperate weariness which seemed to pervade every limb, he felt, in the circumstances, surprisingly chipper.

'I'm sorry about your father,' he said.

'My father died a free man,' Victoria answered gently, 'and in his mind at least . . . a rich one. He felt no pain. That's something to be thankful for.'

'I wish things could have been different, that's all. A man who's suffered so much ought to be allowed to live out his life in comfort and peace.'

'Well, he's at peace now. Lieutenant Driscoll too.'

Coffey was silent as he stirred his tea. He felt a flash of anguish as he thought of Lieutenant Driscoll, recalling his wild eyes, the jagged scar, the twisted indelible grin. He had liked Driscoll, and the news of the man's death had saddened him greatly. 'There'll be a decoration,' he murmured, 'posthumous, of course.'

'He was a very brave man.'

Coffey nodded. Leaning back in the deckchair, he ran his fingertips over the padded dressing on the back of his skull. His head was still tender, but the wound was clean, the doctor said, and would soon heal.

'What about you?' he asked. 'Feeling better?'

'I'm recovering,' she smiled. 'A cup of tea does wonders.'

They were strangely uneasy in each other's company as if the knowledge that the past was over, that there would, in spite of everything, be a future after all, unnerved them. It wasn't easy to accept the future, Coffey thought, when you had stopped believing in it.

Victoria glanced at her cup. 'You know, I never really got to thank you for what you did for us, my father and me.'

'It was damn all we did.'

'You risked your life. Lieutenant Driscoll sacrificed his.'

'That was our duty,' Coffey said.

How smug he sounded. Well, he felt smug. Smug and satisfied and glad to be alive. Tonight he would sleep for a week, and when the sleeping was over, he would start again. A new beginning.

He looked at Victoria. 'What will happen to you now?'

'That's up to the mission people, I suppose. They'll have to accept some responsibility for me, with my father dead. They'll send me to Cairo, I imagine, then back to England as soon as arrangements can be made. I've been away so long it'll seem like another world.'

He felt strangely morose at the thought of her leaving. It was as if, once she had gone, the past would be severed for ever.

She leaned forward to place her cup on the table and the tunic fell open, giving him a tantalising glimpse of her breasts. He flushed as he recalled the warm softness of her flesh in the prison block at Hamira, the close intimacy of that breathless unreal moment.

'What about you?' she asked.

He shrugged. 'I go where the army sends me.'

'Khartoum?'

'God willing.'

'And afterwards?'

'Who knows? There's talk of a new war in South Africa.'

She stared at the ground. 'I'd hate to think I'd never see you again.'

Something caught in Coffey's throat. He studied her face, her eyes, her mouth, aware of a sensation he had never experienced before, startling in its intensity. It was like waking after

224

a long and forced hibernation. He heard himself mutter: 'Let me know where you are in England. I'll visit you when I'm home on leave.'

'Promise?'

'I promise.'

His voice seemed to falter as he recognised the emptiness of his words. What if he lost her completely? The realisation jolted him. He had to make a decision. It could be the last chance he would ever get.

'For God's sake,' he snapped, 'why are we talking like this? You know damned well I can't bear the thought of you going away.'

A faint smile touched the corners of her mouth. 'But we scarcely know each other.'

'Does it matter?'

'I'm a savage, remember? A slave.'

'Stop talking rubbish. I want you to stay here. With me.'

She was smiling openly now. 'Wouldn't that be rather irregular?'

'You can tell the mission people you've changed your mind. You're not going back to England after all.'

'They might not like it.'

'Then to hell with them.'

'You're a very persuasive man, lieutenant.'

'Give me your answer. Yes or no?'

Without a word, she rose from her chair, moved toward him, and bending over, kissed him hard on the mouth. He felt her body soft against his chest. She leaned back looking at him through the filtered sunlight. 'Satisfied?' she whispered.

Never in his life had he experienced such happiness, such certainty for the future. He was about to answer when suddenly the tentflap was thrust rudely aside and Lieutenant Benson entered. Benson was dressed in his khaki uniform, his sprucely scrubbed face still displaying the rigours of his desert ordeal, his cheeks and throat scorched red by the blazing sun. He hesitated, taken aback at the sight of Victoria caught in Coffey's embrace, and Coffey could tell by the look in his eyes that something was wrong.

'What's up?' he demanded.

'They've just brought MacAngus in,' Benson said.

Coffey's body stiffened. His new-found happiness faded abruptly. He had forgotten MacAngus in the excitement of being rescued. Now a savage resentment settled in his breast. It mattered little to Coffey that MacAngus had saved their lives at the river. All he could think of was the overwhelming bitterness of betrayal. Coffey's lips twisted into a grimace of hate.

He rose to his feet, kissing Victoria lightly on the forehead. 'Wait here,' he ordered.

She looked at him anxiously. 'What are you going to do?'

'I'm going to have a little chat with that sergeant of ours.'

'Stephen,' she said earnestly, 'it's over now, can't you see that?'

'No,' he answered in a clipped voice, 'it's only just beginning.'

There was no question of forgiveness in Coffey's mind. Only a burning desire to bring things into the open. His brain was filled with images of dark deeds and darker thoughts, of friends lost and enemies found, of confrontation and denunciation. With Benson at his heels he strode swiftly through the crowded campsite, elbowing aside the troops milling in his way. The hospital tent was practically empty when they got there; there had been no casualties in the last few days, apart from two cases of jaundice and a man whose leg had become swollen and infected after stepping on a piece of camel thorn.

Sergeant MacAngus lay on the farthermost bunk, his cheeks pale beneath their surface tan. When he heard them coming his eyes opened and he looked at them. No expression crossed his face but a hint of colour seemed to deepen above the jagged frontal bones.

'Well,' Coffey said, drawing to a halt at the foot of the bed, 'I'm glad to see that you at least have the grace to look ashamed.'

MacAngus didn't answer. He lay back against the pillow and gently closed his eyes.

'I suppose you think you're a bloody hero, blowing that boat out of the water the way you did?'

MacAngus considered this for a moment, then modestly he nodded.

226

'I want those diamonds, sergeant,' Coffey said quietly.

Silence.

'Hand them over, damn you.'

Lieutenant Benson coughed uncomfortably. 'Be reasonable, sergeant,' he said in a soothing tone. 'Those diamonds belong to all of us, not just you.'

Still no answer.

Benson tried again. 'I know what you did for us, and we're grateful, believe me. If you hadn't fired that grapeshot we'd have been cut to pieces at the river back there. But that doesn't alter the fact that the diamonds are our communal property.'

'I didna fire any grapeshot,' MacAngus snapped.

'What's that?'

'I didna have any grapeshot. I used the only damned thing I had.'

Watching, Coffey saw a shock run through Benson's body. Benson turned to look at him, his cheeks ghastly, and a cold chill gathered in Coffey's stomach as the terrible truth settled in his mind. 'You fired the diamonds?' he whispered.

MacAngus nodded.

Coffey felt his legs turn rubbery. Stunned, he struggled to adjust his senses. He recalled the moment at the river when he had heard the swish of grapeshot on the hot morning air, and a flash of outrage filled him. It couldn't be true, not after all they had gone through. He had thought his problems over. He had thought his life beginning afresh. Now his dream was being shattered in a manner so ludicrous, so unutterably grotesque, he could barely believe it.

Benson was staring at him with an air of blank dismay. Then, to Coffey's astonishment, Benson started to laugh. It was like the breaking of a dam, a spontaneous and unreserved release. Benson doubled over, choking helplessly.

Coffey turned to MacAngus with an expression of bewilderment. Even MacAngus was laughing, he realised, cackling dryly from his bandaged chest. Unable to help himself, Coffey felt his own laughter starting, bubbling up in his stomach, bursting from his throat. It was the only response he was capable of. Caught in a spasm of hysteria the three men roared in unison, their voices rising, swelling, strengthening, drifting through the walls of the little hospital tent to mingle with the creaking of leather, the clattering of wagons, the hissing of locomotive valves and the gently lapping waters of the River Nile.

Kengle looked at the old lady, thunderstruck. 'I . . . I don't understand,' he whispered weakly.

She chuckled. 'It's perfectly simple. The diamonds are lying in the mud and silt on the riverbottom.'

'Then what on earth . . .?'

'The Churchill collection? Strontium titanate. Superb imitations, but strictly synthetic. Crystals cut and polished to look like diamonds, but lacking the hardness and lustre of the real thing.'

Kengle took a deep breath, his head swimming dizzily. 'Are you telling me the stones stolen this morning were nothing but fakes?'

'Mr Kengle, I am telling you that the diamond collection upon which this entire Foundation has been based were nothing but fakes.'

Kengle felt suddenly weak and shivery. Coldness filled him, and instinctively he groped for the whisky glass. Raising it to his lips, he swallowed the fiery liquid in one desperate gulp and mopped at his mouth with his handkerchief.

'It's insane,' he breathed.

The old lady smiled, her eyes glittering as she savoured the effect her words had created. Her manner had changed in a way he was not perceptive enough to recognise, but mingled with the relief of unburdening he sensed a faint glimmer of triumph. 'Only a single stone survived from the original hoard,' she explained. 'The one Churchill found lodged in MacAngus's belt. He turned it in to the military authorities and it now forms part of the British Crown Jewels. The army of course had been well aware of the diamonds' existence, and it wasn't difficult for my father to convince them he had the others still in his possession. When they ordered him to hand them over, he refused adamantly. In the end, a compromise was reached. MacAngus' stone would remain the property of the Crown, and Coffey could hold on to the rest providing he undertook never to sell them outside the British Isles.'

'And then he had fakes made?' Kengle muttered.

'Excellent fakes, Mr Kengle. Perfect replicas in every detail. Only a professional *diamantaire* would have been able to detect the difference. Happily, the only *diamantaires* ever to examine them closely were men in my father's employ, members of the Driscoll Dozen.'

'The committee set up within the Foundation.'

'Precisely. Their job was to administer all details concerning the diamonds' safety and welfare. They included lawyers, insurance brokers, diamond experts, businessmen, all carefully screened and vetted. Only the most trusted associates were invited to join that elite little assembly. They were paid handsomely to ensure that my father's secret would never be disclosed. You see, Mr Kengle, when Lieutenant Coffey returned from the Sudan, he found himself a national celebrity. Stories about his newly acquired wealth appeared in every newspaper in the country. On the strength of those fabulous diamonds he was able to borrow vast sums of money and use that money to lay the foundations for his future business empire.'

'But surely the financiers would have wanted to examine his collateral?'

The old lady smiled. 'My father was fast on his feet,' she explained. 'The experts who did the examining were invariably members of his own committee. The diamonds, don't forget, had become a British legend, and because of that they provided a financial bulwark that sustained my father through the lean early years. Because of the privations of his youth, he was filled with a burning need to succeed. He took risks, extraordinary risks, and he took them with other people's money. But the fact remains it was his own flair, his own extraordinary talent that allowed his business ventures to grow and flourish. Of course, he never had to worry about financial backing. Whatever he wanted to borrow, people were only too happy to give. After all, was he not the owner of the most extravagant jewellery collection in the world?'

Kengle shook his head. 'It's unbelievable,' he hissed.

'Yes, my father was always conscious of the delicate game

he was playing. Even the people who insured the diamonds were part of the bewildering array of front companies set up by the Driscoll Dozen.'

'And it was the Driscoll Dozen which ordered this morning's robbery?'

'They had no choice. The British government was about to put pressure on the Foundation to return the collection to the Sudanese. You can imagine the effect that would have had? However, no one will be the loser. The insurance companies belong to the Foundation anyhow. And as time goes by, the Churchill Diamonds will simply become one of the world's great unsolved mysteries.'

Kengle realised he was trembling. He glanced down at his hand and noticed the fingers would not keep still. It was too much for his stunned brain to assimilate. He felt like a man who had driven into a cul-de-sac and was desperately seeking a means of escape. When he spoke, his voice sounded hoarse and unreal. 'What about Ben Crowley's file? The links with organised crime?'

The old lady snorted. 'There never were any links. My father used his money to help his two fellow conspirators. He backed Lieutenant Benson's political career, and Benson eventually became part of Churchill's wartime Cabinet in 1941.'

'And Sergeant MacAngus?'

'MacAngus was wanted by the British police. My father bought him a new identity.'

'So the sergeant didn't die in the desert after all?'

'Of course not. The man was as strong as an ox. He went off to the United States as Garry Ulterfeld Kurtzman. Unfortunately, he got himself into bad company and became a notorious figure in the American underworld. But that didn't stop him and my father remaining firm friends. Those so-called word codes Ben Crowley discovered were innocent letters and cablegrams. Both my parents visited MacAngus frequently throughout his lifetime, but there were never any business dealings between them.'

Gently, Kengle rubbed his temples with his fingertips. His senses felt ragged and uneven.

'Mr Kengle,' the old lady said quietly, 'have you ever heard of the celebrated confidence trick in which a man sold the Eiffel Tower to a demolition company for scrap metal? If my father was guilty of anything, he was guilty of that – a confidence trick, probably the most audacious confidence trick of the century.'

The clock striking three made Kengle jump. He peered miserably around the darkened room as he struggled to assemble his senses. 'I have to go,' he croaked.

'You wanted the truth, Mr Kengle.'

'I must . . . leave. Immediately. I have an important meeting in the morning.'

'What will you say there?' she whispered.

'Say?' He blinked at her. 'I don't know,' he admitted honestly.

It was true. For the monent he couldn't even think straight. The old lady's story had destroyed his reasoning faculties, leaving him battered and numb.

He pushed back his chair and rose unsteadily to his feet. Like a man who had just spent a long sojourn in hospital, his knees trembled under the strain. 'It's too early to take all this in,' he said. 'I'll call from the office when I've sorted out things in my mind.'

The old lady was silent for a moment, then she said: 'Mr Kengle, my father lied in order to borrow money. He was wrong to do that, and I can't deny it. But the things he achieved were achieved by his own ability. He created a fortune, and rather than keep that fortune to himself, he used it to help others. He started with the unfortunates in his own society, the poor, the helpless, the underprivileged, then he extended his activities to Africa and the Far East. He was a good man, humane and compassionate. You have in your possession enough knowledge to destroy his reputation for ever.'

Kengle frowned at her. 'You misjudge me, ma'am,' he said. 'It is my own future I need to consider. If you knew me better you would understand I could never do anything to harm the Foundation. Ben Crowley's file will be destroyed at once. Your father's reputation will be safe with me.'

For the first time that evening the old lady's expression

231

visibly softened. She looked up at Kengle, her eyes smiling in the lamplight. From where he was standing, the lines and wrinkles seemed erased from her features and he realised with a small sense of shock that she had once been a beautiful woman.

'I was wrong,' she admitted softly.

'Wrong?' he echoed.

'When they wanted to make you Foundation president, I voted against the proposal. I thought you were too young, too green, too headstrong. Now I realise I made a dreadful mistake. You *are* the Foundation, Mr Kengle. I hope you will remain and continue to run it as brilliantly as you have for the past six years. We need you. We all need you.'

Kengle nodded silently. He felt hollowed out, conscious of a bitter remorse that his old naivety could never be the same again. For the past few hours he had been transported to a world beyond his wildest imagination. It was a world that had gone now for ever. The people in it – Coffey, Driscoll, Victoria Routledge – had become as real as his most intimate acquaintances. He had lived with them, fought with them, sweated, struggled, suffered. And at the end of it all, he had been forced to accept that the most cherished precepts of his life had been nothing more than illusory.

He walked to the door, pausing with his hand on the knob as he glanced back. The old lady was sitting at the table, her hair braided, gathered into a coil at the back of her head. Her eyes were glistening.

'You know, one way and another,' he said, 'your parents played a damned good joke on us all. The funny thing is, I can't help feeling that if I listen in a certain way, I can hear them laughing still.'

She smiled, the tears issuing from her eyes, rolling down the hollow craters of her cheeks. Kengle smiled back. Then he went out, closing the door gently behind him.

A light rain was falling as he drove back to London in the cool softness of the early morning.